THE GIRLFLESH INSTITUTE

The food arrived: a plate for Zara and a bowl for Vanessa.

'Eat up like a good pet,' Zara commanded.

Vanessa buried her face in it, trying not to think about the strange unsettling people around her.

After a few minutes she felt Zara's hand slide over her upraised haunches. Her fingers circled the crinkles of her anus and then dipped into the soft cleft-pouch beneath.

Nearly choking, Vanessa glanced up. Zara was not even looking at her. She was casually eating with a fork in one hand while idly fondling her with the other. And nobody else appeared to be taking the slightest bit of notice. And why should they, Vanessa thought wretchedly? Here such behaviour was normal. She was the one with her instincts and sensibilities out of place.

She tried to ignore Zara's touch and focus on eating, but it was no good. Before a restaurant full of people she was being fingered and responding by getting wet. It was insane. What had they done to her?

THE GIRLFLESH INSTITUTE

Adriana Arden

This book is a work of fiction.
In real life, make sure you practise safe, sane and
consensual sex.

First published in 2007 by
Nexus
Thames Wharf Studios
Rainville Rd
London W6 9HA

Copyright © Adriana Arden 2007

The right of Adriana Arden to be identified as the Author
of the Work has been asserted by her in accordance with
the Copyright, Designs and Patents Act 1988.

www.nexus-books.com

Typeset by TW Typesetting, Plymouth, Devon

Printed and bound by Clays Ltd, St Ives PLC

ISBN 978 0 352 34101 3

One

The young woman struggled wildly as the two security guards stripped the clothes off her. But her outraged shrieks echoed unanswered round the cell-like room, while the guards grinned approvingly at what was revealed.

The intruder's wide fearful eyes were of a clear hazel. A mass of dark fluffy hair, released from the pins that had secured it under her cap, spilled over bare shoulders. Her straining, well-toned muscles stood out tautly. Freed of their confining bra, her milk-pale breasts, with their contrasting sharply defined nipple-crowns, heaved as she squirmed. The soft swell of her stomach rose and fell tremulously as the thick matt of pubic hair framing her deep in-rolling cleft was finally exposed.

When she was totally naked, one of the guards pinned her arms behind her back, while the other produced a phone-sized device fitted with a loop antenna, which he ran across their prisoner's discarded clothing and then every curve and hollow of her squirming body. The loop was even thrust between her pink vulval lips, causing the girl's eyes to roll and bringing a scarlet flush of shame to her cheeks.

'No bugs or tracers, Director,' the guard reported at last.

'The Director' was a slender, mature woman, perhaps in her mid-fifties, with a strong straight nose and smooth unlined face. With her short, well-groomed hair and immaculate dark-blue business suit, she seemed somehow apart from the strange scene being played out before her. But her bright-blue eyes missed nothing and intense interest shaped her narrow, intelligent face. When she spoke, her words shaded by a slight but unidentifiable accent, her calm self-assurance contrasted starkly with the younger woman's high emotion.

'My name is F. G. Shiller. I apologise for inflicting this minor indignity on you, but I would like to know why you broke into my building.'

Trying to steady her ragged breathing, the captive gasped: 'Right . . . you've had your fun . . . now give me back my clothes! If . . . if you're accusing me of burglary then call the police!'

'Don't insult my intelligence, young woman,' Shiller said. 'You are no common burglar and you know I will not call the police.'

The girl writhed in the grasp of the strong hands that held her, clenching her thighs together in an unconscious effort to preserve one slight scrap of dignity. 'Then let me go!'

'Perhaps, once you tell me your name and who sent you.' She motioned to the intruder's possessions, which had been laid out on a bench in one corner. 'A sophisticated electronic toolkit, a hidden camera, a set of keys, some cash, a cell phone with an empty memory, but no form of identification. Nothing to give you away if any item was lost. I'm sure we can trace their origins, given time, but it would be quicker if you co-operate.'

The girl chewed her lip for a moment in evident indecision, then took a deep breath and said: 'My name's Vanessa Buckingham ... I'm a reporter for the *Daily Globe*. My paper knows I'm here ... so if you don't let me go right now all hell'll break loose!'

The Director had stiffened slightly as Vanessa spoke, and there was a new edge to her voice as she asked: 'Exactly who at the *Globe* sent you and how did you get into my building?'

'What does that matter?' Vanessa retorted, anger briefly overcoming her fear and embarrassment. 'It's over! You're finished, the whole putrid lot of you!'

'Will you answer my question?' the Director persisted. 'I understand you might be confused, but I can assure you that everything you've seen here is entirely consensual.'

'You expect me to believe that?' Vanessa spat back.

'At least let me explain the facts.'

'I won't listen to any of your lies,' Vanessa retorted contemptuously. 'You're a bunch of filthy sex-traffickers!'

'I see you have closed your mind,' Shiller said. 'And as we cannot spare more time to convince you by reason, we must use other means ...' She considered Vanessa intently for a moment, then turned to a figure who had so far played no active role in the proceedings. 'Well, Miss Kyle? Do you think she's a suitable subject for ... special handling?'

Miss Kyle was a dark-eyed brunette, perhaps a little older than Vanessa's twenty-two years, and coolly beautiful. Her sensuous lips were very red and her flawless skin pale. She wore, as though it were an outrageous uniform, thigh-length black leather boots and a dark body stocking. Her full breasts strained at the translucent fabric that covered them like a shadow, her nipples forming swelling points of darker flesh. The gauze moulded itself into the deep cleft of her shaven pubic lips. From a broad belt encircling her narrow waist hung a bamboo cane and a coiled whip.

She walked round Vanessa's trembling body, looking her up and down with unashamed approval. She trailed her fingers across Vanessa's breasts, toying with her nipples and watching the expression of dismay spread across her face. Suddenly she cupped Vanessa's deep-cleft pubic delta in one hand, caught a fistful of her hair in the other and looked her square in the eye.

'Tell me, girl,' she asked. 'Has anything you've seen down here excited you?'

'What?' Vanessa sounded genuinely aghast. 'You . . . you twisted bitch! How could I possibly be excited by anything in this perverted place? I saw what you did to that girl next door, you sadist!'

Miss Kyle released her grasp and turned to the Director with a smile of satisfaction.

'She's suitable, Director. Full of righteous anger and fear, of course, but the state of her nipples and pussy says she's lying about not being aroused . . .' She lifted the hand that had cupped Vanessa's pubes to her nose and inhaled. 'And she smells as good as she looks.'

'It's agreed, then.' The Director motioned to the guards: 'Put her on the rack . . .'

Vanessa struggled frantically, her slender, shapely legs flailing about as the guards dragged her across to a device that stood in one corner of the cell-like room.

It was an 'X'-shaped rack mounted at an angle on a pivoting stand. Jointed tubular metal arms extended from the corners of a padded rectangular centre section, while various other attachments were folded underneath. A short bracket with a shallow metal cup on the end rose up to form a headrest.

Vanessa's arms were pulled over her head and parted until solid clamps of rubber and metal could be closed around her wrists. Her legs were wrenched wide and similar clamps locked about her ankles. Vanessa fluttered feebly like a pale, pinned butterfly. Her buttocks clenched as she jerked her hips and arched her back in a vain attempt to pull free.

Miss Kyle drew out a broad leather belt from under the rack and buckled it across Vanessa's stomach, causing the flesh to swell on either side as she tightened it. A second shorter strap went around Vanessa's neck, forcing her head back into its rest. Miss Kyle bent over the foot of the rack and there came a clicking of ratchets. The lower struts of the cross hinged both where they joined the central block and beneath Vanessa's knees. As her hip joints were bent upwards and apart, her knees were bent downwards, splaying her legs and opening her wide as though for a gynaecological examination. Miss Kyle tightened straps just above Vanessa's knees, holding her limbs firmly against the struts.

This enforced posture revealed the soft inner flesh of Vanessa's thighs and the strong tendons of her groin. Her pubic mound was starkly exposed, its pink lips pouting from amid the thick forest of surrounding hair. Even that most secret dark pucker of her anus was tautly displayed for all to see.

The fight drained out of Vanessa and a cold sweat beaded her body as her stomach knotted. Chest heaving and eyes wide, she hung trembling and silent in her bonds. She was absolutely helpless and frighteningly vulnerable.

A brief smile played about the Director's pursed lips. 'Thank you,' she said to the guards. 'Please return to your duties. Miss Kyle, attend to our guest as necessary . . .'

As the security guards filed out, closing the heavy door behind them, Miss Kyle took up position beside Vanessa's stretched and helpless body and smiled masterfully down at her. Vanessa gave a little shudder.

The Director drew over a chair from the corner of the room and seated herself in front of the rack, almost between Vanessa's doubled back and splayed legs. Her eyes travelled over the body so blatantly exhibited before her.

Vanessa's thighs twitched as she tried instinctively to close them, but it was quite futile. In desperation she gasped: 'If you don't let me go right now the shit'll hit the fan and – aghh!'

Miss Kyle's cane had hissed across Vanessa's exposed buttocks and the pouting pubic mound between them. A livid red line blossomed on her pale flesh.

'Don't be coarse when you speak to the Director!' she warned.

Vanessa gulped, shocked at the suddenness of the blow, but somehow maintained her defiance. 'It's over, understand? You . . . you can do what you like with me but you're finished! I've seen what you are! You and the rest of your sick friends can go to hell, you fucking bastard – awww!'

This time Miss Kyle had brought her cane downwards across the upper slopes of Vanessa's breasts, causing them to bounce and shiver. The unexpected location and sharpness of the blow made Vanessa's face contort in pain even as tears misted her eyes.

Shiller wagged an admonishing finger.

'You may defy me, Vanessa, but you will refrain from employing further mindless expletives and crudities. Do you think withholding the information gives you some sort of bargaining counter, or is it just out of stubbornness? I simply want to know who put you up to this and how you got in here. You must realise we'll get the information one way or another. It's no hardship to induce an attractive girl in your position to co-operate . . .' Shiller paused, looking Vanessa's naked, bound and helpless body up and down once more, then added with a smile: 'In fact some people might think it a privilege and a pleasure . . .'

Vanessa gulped at the words, feeling her courage ebbing away. 'You . . . you can't treat me like this!'

Shiller sighed. 'Quite evidently, we can treat you exactly like this. Considering the low opinion you have already formed of us, why should you be surprised? Now, for the very last time, will you answer my question?'

Biting her lip, Vanessa gave no reply.

'Very well,' Shiller said gravely. 'You've had your chance, now we are done with reason. Miss Kyle, I want you to break Vanessa's will to resist. Use whatever means you think best . . .'

Miss Kyle's eyes flashed in delight. She reached behind the bracket supporting Vanessa's head and drew out a red ball-gag threaded through with a loop of thick rubber cord. Even as Vanessa gasped in dismay, Miss Kyle forced the ball into her mouth. The cords cut into her cheeks, pulling her lips back and leaving her exposed white teeth clamping on the ball itself.

From under each side of the padded board Miss Kyle drew out what looked like two halves of a front-fastening bra. The cups were metal bands capped by open-topped domes of springy wire and the straps black elastic cords. She slid the cups over Vanessa's breasts, ignoring her gurgles and groans of protest as her nipples squeezed out of the open tops. A turnscrew tightened the base bands until soft flesh bulged out through the wire lattice. Miss Kyle clipped

7

the two cups together and Vanessa's breasts were transformed into twin pale mushrooms of flesh topped by dark inflamed nipples. To Vanessa they felt both caged and horribly exposed.

From the wall behind the rack, which bore an array of strange devices on hooks and shelves, Miss Kyle collected something resembling a garden-hose spray gun. A transparent plastic cup was fitted about the barrel, which extended into a long flexible rubber nozzle; behind it trailed a bundle of three coloured hoses connected to a tap in the wall.

Briskly Miss Kyle inserted the tube into Vanessa's anus, slid it up to its full length so that the cup pressed firmly against her skin, and pressed the trigger.

Vanessa gasped as warm water flooded through her rectal passage. She was being given an enema, but why? No, surely not . . .

She moaned and shook her head desperately. Yet perversely she felt a tingle of anticipation in her loins and the first sensation of warm wetness flow through the fleshy folds of her vulva. Her body was preparing for what her mind still fought against.

Air hissed, sucking the waste water out of the plastic cup as it spurted out of Vanessa's bottom. When she was clean, Miss Kyle pumped a plunger with her thumb and Vanessa felt lubricating jelly spurt into her and begin to melt away.

Miss Kyle pulled the enema gun free and inspected Vanessa's vagina with an experienced finger, smiling when it came away already glistening with natural lubrication. She hooked the gun on to the side of the rack and unfolded another device from the centre section, which she locked into place between Vanessa's thighs. Fighting the pressure of her neck strap and the springs that held her bit in place,

Vanessa looked down between her distorted breasts and gave a choking gasp.

Twin dildos projected from a metal box, mounted one above the other so that they were only a few centimetres apart. The upper dildo was longer and thicker, and had a spray of rubber prongs bristling from its base. Miss Kyle positioned the device so that the tip of the upper phallus nuzzled between the lips of Vanessa's trembling cleft in line with her vaginal passage, while the lower centred on her anus.

From the shelves Miss Kyle now selected a short-handled device on which was mounted a small metal wheel, like a rider's spur, bearing a dozen glittering spikes. Holding the spur-wheel in one hand, Miss Kyle smiled down at Vanessa as she threw a switch under the rack.

The motor driving the twin dildos hummed into life and began inexorably propelling them forward and back, at the same time setting them vibrating fiercely. Vanessa's clenched vaginal muscles were forced to open as the larger dildo plunged its full length deep into her secret passage. As it withdrew, its smaller twin drove into her tight bottom hole, spreading its reluctant guardian sphincter and sinking deep into the hot, greased sheath of her rectum.

Vanessa strained and squirmed in her bonds, venting muffled shrieks and groans as her front and back passages were alternately penetrated in a remorseless rhythm. What was even worse, the vibration of the larger dildo set the bristling prongs about its base trembling fiercely as they rode up her moist cleft, parting the folds of flesh and exposing Vanessa's clitoris to their pulsating touch.

Vanessa shuddered helplessly. No man or sex toy inside her had ever previously felt like this.

A pinpoint ring of fire burned into life on the

bulging dome of her right breast, forcing a muffled yelp past her gag. Miss Kyle had rolled the spur-wheel across her flesh in a circle about the edge of its areola. The spikes were too short to do any real harm, not penetrating beyond the fatty tissue that sheathed Vanessa's breasts and gave them their graceful contours, but they stung unbearably.

Before she could recover, Miss Kyle drew another circle in the pliant mound of Vanessa's left breast.

Vanessa yelped again, drooling round her gag, even as she felt the blood pulsing through her caged breasts to her nipples, swelling them into erection. And all the while the dildos pumped away inside her. She was being totally humiliated and abused, yet incredibly she was also becoming deeply aroused. Her whole body was coming alive. She was aware of every exposed square centimetre of her flesh. Crudely applied pain alone she could have fought, but this was something else and she felt her will crumbling.

Soon a dozen pinprick trails crossed Vanessa's breasts. Helplessly she responded to the stinging pain and pulses of raw pleasure that coursed through her body in the only way left to her.

Through misted eyes, Vanessa saw the Director leaning forwards slightly in her chair as the dildos reamed into her, watching her clitoris rise into hard erection and her bottom bulge as it was filled. The sight sent a fresh thrill of shameful excitement coursing through Vanessa. She was being tortured and masturbated in front of a sadistic pervert. From her pincushion breasts to her dripping vagina, Shiller could see every intimate detail of her ordeal as it led to its inevitable climax.

And Vanessa was going to come, more quickly than she could have imagined. The pressure was building inside her. She couldn't fight it any longer . . .

She screamed behind her gag as her body went into orgasm, straining with wonderful futility against the straps and clamps that held her so securely. The muscles of her vagina clamped on to the plunging upper phallus and for a moment its driving motor growled in protest. Discharge sprayed from her tightly plugged orifice and trickled down the impaling shafts. Then she went limp as she descended into the warm dark pit of release . . .

Vanessa was dimly aware of the dildos being extracted. Her gag was removed and a beaker of water was pressed against her lips. Automatically she drank. Her groin ached with its exertions and her breasts burned. Sweat was drying on her body. Blinking her eyes open, she saw Miss Kyle and the Director examining her with obvious satisfaction, and knew with despairing certainty that they had made their point. They controlled whatever pain or pleasure she experienced. Her pinpricked breasts throbbed in their wire cages. The stinging had diminished to a tolerable level, but it was a continuing reminder of what could be done again.

'Now,' Shiller said briskly, 'perhaps you will tell us what we want to know?'

Too shocked to resist any further, Vanessa choked out: 'All right . . . just . . . please . . . don't do that again . . .'

'Address the Director properly,' Miss Kyle said, giving a warning pinch and twist to Vanessa's engorged left nipple.

To her intense shame, Vanessa found the humble, subservient words bubbling from her lips. 'I'll tell you everything . . . Director. About a month ago, Mr Enwright . . . my editor . . . said he wanted to speak to me . . .'

Two

Enwright was alone in the boardroom when Vanessa entered, but displayed on the big video-conference screen was the head and shoulders of a thickset man in his late fifties. He had grizzled hair and a heavy jaw, and in one hand held a cigar that he was jabbing at Enwright.

Vanessa gave a start at the sight of the famous features. It was Sir Harvey J. Rochester, owner of the *Globe*, half a dozen regional newspapers and numerous other international business interests.

Enwright motioned for Vanessa to take a seat. Sir Harvey's eyes flickered as he looked her up and down through the camera mounted over the screen.

'So you're Buckingham,' the magnate said in his familiar gravelly tones. 'Enwright tells me you show a lot of promise. Bright, enthusiastic, go-getting.' Sir Harvey took a puff on his cigar and waved it at Vanessa with a chuckle. 'Reminds me a little of myself when I started out.'

'That's very kind of him . . . and you, Sir Harvey,' Vanessa said meekly.

'Enwright wasn't being kind and neither am I,' Sir Harvey replied bluntly. 'I can recognise talent when I see it. This may be your chance to show us what you're really made of. Think you're up to handling a big story, Vanessa, one that'll put your name on the front page?'

'I'd like the chance, of course, Sir Harvey. But if it's as big as you say, wouldn't it be better to use someone more experienced?'

Sir Harvey shook his head. 'I have a hunch this'll need a different approach, a fresh angle. Maybe by somebody who doesn't look like a reporter. It might mean undercover work and may be risky. Well?'

Thrilled and excited, Vanessa took a deep breath. 'I'll do my best, Sir Harvey.'

Sir Harvey favoured her with a craggy smile. 'Good for you. Now, tell me what you know about the F. G. Shiller Company?'

'Uh . . . well, Shiller Co. is based in London. It's a successful medium-sized general management company with a range of service, technical and medical subsidiaries. That's about it.'

'That'll do for a start,' Sir Harvey said. 'Your job is to find out all about them. I mean everything. Find out how they earn their last penny! I have my suspicions about what's going at Shillers, something so shocking you'd hardly believe it possible . . .' He frowned. 'But I won't say any more. You must go in absolutely unprejudiced, find out the truth for yourself and get cast-iron evidence to prove it! Start with their London office. You can have any resources you need to get the job done. Report directly to Enwright. Nobody else must know what you're working on. Understand?'

'Yes, Sir Harvey.'

'Then get started, Vanessa. And good luck.'

The conference screen went blank.

The next week was spent on intensive research. Vanessa obtained copies of Shillers' financial statements, business reports, corporate structure and even architectural plans of its London offices.

The company appeared perfectly legitimate. Service sector interests were its most profitable division, and obviously provided the capital for additional investment in its other areas. It was efficiently run and was well thought of in the City, who regarded it as a safe investment. However, her enquiries did unearth a couple of curious facts.

First, Shillers was very selective about hiring its staff, never using temping agencies or advertising in the usual papers. In fact it had an unusually low turnover of personnel for a company of its size. What induced such loyalty?

Then there was the matter of the construction of its London offices, which occupied a modern tower block overlooking the Thames. Vanessa noticed that the entrance foyer, reception rooms and a few general office spaces on the landward side were separated from the bulk of the building by a comprehensive system of security doors, with key-card locks specified on the plans. It was well beyond what Vanessa would have considered normal for such a building. That section also had separate lift access to the tower's two levels of underground car parking. Entry to the lowest of these levels was further restricted by a set of internal security gates.

It was curious, but to find out more would mean somehow penetrating Shillers' apparently loyal and close-knit structure from the outside. That would be risky, and such questioning might only alert the company. Winning an employee's confidence by contriving an acquaintance could also take months.

The next option was to get a job at Shillers and work from the inside. Considering its highly selective employment policy, that might come to nothing, but it was worth trying. With her paper's help Vanessa created a glowing if semi-fictitious CV, and sent it off. While she was waiting for the response she surreptitiously reconnoitred Shiller Tower.

For two weeks she photographed the building and anyone entering or leaving from every angle. Her attention was soon drawn to the traffic using the car-park entrance at the side of the building. Some vehicles were obviously employees' cars while others were from office supply and service companies, which appeared about as often as might be expected. But there were also cars with tinted windows, small unmarked vans, 7.5 tonne lorries, even a horse transporter.

Vanessa rented an empty office in a building almost opposite the Tower and extended her watch late into the night and the early hours. She recorded the types of these anomalous vehicles, their usual routes and the times they came and went. It soon became evident that there was far too much traffic for a typical building of that size. Something strange was going on, but what?

Then Shillers returned her CV with a polite letter saying they were not hiring staff at present. That left only one option. Somehow she would have to risk entering the building covertly. After careful thought and calling on some of the *Globe*'s more specialised contacts, Vanessa made her plans . . .

Braydon Road was a narrow, featureless street formed by the backs of small industrial units and high service-yard walls, often used as a rat-run by goods vehicles. Before six in the morning, with the grey light of dawn flushing the sky, there was normally little private traffic. But as the box-sided lorry turned into the street, a car was revealed angled across the road with its bonnet raised. The driver, bent over the engine, signalled that he would only be a moment longer.

The lorry pulled up while the motorist fiddled with the engine, got back into his car, started it successfully, jumped out again to close the bonnet, returned to his seat with a quick wave of thanks and drove off. The lorry continued on its way and turned towards Shiller Tower. In a couple of minutes it halted at the security gate guarding the entrance to the car park.

Clinging on tightly to the lorry's underframe, secured by snaplink cords attached to a climbing harness, Vanessa's heart thudded. She heard a few casual words exchanged between the driver and the gate guard, then the barrier lifted and the lorry moved forwards into a world of echoing concrete and the harsh light of fluorescent tubes. The vehicle slowed again and there came the rattle of a mesh gate rolling aside to let it through. That was the inner gate dividing the car park. Her gamble had paid off. She was entering the Tower's mysterious high-security zone. The lorry swung down a ramp to the lower level, came to a brief halt, backed a little way, then stopped.

The engine cut and Vanessa heard the driver jump down from his cab. Footsteps sounded on the concrete, the rear doors of the lorry opened and a ramp was lowered.

'All OK?' the driver asked.

'No problem,' came a woman's voice from within. 'They slept most of the way.'

'What was that hold-up about?' a second male voice asked.

Vanessa's heart skipped a beat. Two people had been travelling in the back of the lorry.

'Just a stalled car,' the driver explained.

Vanessa breathed again. It was sheer luck that they hadn't heard her stowing away beneath them.

'Right, let's get them down below,' the woman said.

'Down below?' Vanessa wondered. But they were already on the lowest level.

'Want them to take the gear down with them?' her companion asked.

'No,' the woman said. 'Send up another chain for it later. This lot deserve a rest. They've had a busy night.'

'Another chain?' Again Vanessa wondered at the odd phrase.

The other man chuckled. 'Fair enough.'

Vanessa heard a soft scuffing whisper of movement from within the lorry, accompanied by a metallic clinking. This odd procession of sound passed slowly down the ramp and off across the concrete floor. Then came the swish and whirr of lift doors opening.

'I'll go up and have a bite to eat,' said the driver. 'See you later . . .'

As the echo of his footsteps receded, the shuffling and rattling sounds inside the lorry ceased. There was a soft clunk of closing doors, then the fading sound of the lift in motion.

For the moment at least, Vanessa was alone.

Taking a deep breath, she unclipped her securing lines and dropped into a crouch under the lorry. Still doubled over, she stripped off her harness and packed it away into the toolbox slung beside her, removing from it a blue peaked cap bearing the Shiller logo. This matched the overalls she was wearing, based upon photos she had previously taken of Shiller maintenance staff at work.

Vanessa slipped out from under the lorry and cautiously peered round its bulk.

17

Except for half a dozen cars and two plain vans, the level was empty.

She glanced into the still open rear of the lorry. Down each side ran tall mesh frames, which she took to be tool racks. There were also several large chests on wheels, of the sort stage crews used to transport concert props and equipment. She would like to have investigated their contents but she had no time to waste.

Opposite the open back of the lorry were the recessed doors of a large lift with a stairwell door to one side. Mounted on the wall beside the call buttons, just as the building plans had shown, was a keycard reader. A similar device was incorporated in the lock of the stairwell door.

Vanessa crossed quickly to the lift. Opening her toolkit, she took out a slim wafer of metal and plastic and slid it into the jaws of the reader, with which it merged almost invisibly. Then she pressed a miniature camera, concealed within a grey cornice-like shell, into the shadowy inner angle of the lift-door recess, to which it adhered. Finally she went round to the back of the stairwell block and waited.

A few minutes later she heard the lift ascend. So there was another level below this one. The doors opened. The voice of the man who had ridden in the back of the lorry said: 'Right, get that lot unloaded . . .'

Again came the odd shuffling and clinking, followed by what she took to be the sounds of the wheeled crates being rolled down the ramp and across to the lift. After a minute or so the doors shut again and the lift departed.

Vanessa let out her breath. They had not noticed her spying devices, but she needed somebody to open the doors from the outside.

An agonising half-hour passed before a car came down the ramp into the park. Vanessa heard a couple of chattering women get out and make for the lift. They keyed their way in and set off upwards.

As soon as the doors closed, Vanessa darted round to the door recess, recovered her pirate reader and camera and returned to the back of the stairs.

The reader plugged into a specialised gadget in her toolkit. When this flashed a green light she withdrew from its slot a new keycard. If everything had functioned correctly, this was a clone of the one last used to access the lift.

The camera downloaded on to a small screen where it showed the lift-door keypad. She magnified the image and played it over until she could read the pass-code number the last user had entered.

Vanessa closed her toolkit and walked round to the door side. Heart pounding, she swiped her pirated card through the reader and punched in the code. The lift door opened smoothly.

She stepped inside the roomy car and studied the controls. Level B2 was illuminated and the panel did not show anything lower. But there had to be something. What was the trick to get down to the secret level? She noticed the B2 button looked far more worn than the B1. Just how much traffic could there be from a half-empty car park? Perhaps . . . she pressed the B2 three times.

The doors closed and the lift started downwards.

Vanessa opened her toolbox and switched on the video camera concealed within it. On impulse she also took out a torch, then contrived to put a slightly bored expression on her face. I'm just one of maintenance crew checking for burnt-out light bulbs, she thought.

The lift halted, the doors opened, and Vanessa took a step forwards . . .

Only the reassuring solidity of the torch in her hand and the mental preparation she had already made enabled her to continue putting one foot in front of the other. She moved unhurriedly to one side and played its beam over an electrical conduit that fed the ceiling light above the lift doors. The expression of virtuous concentration on her face gave no hint that she had just seen anything out of the ordinary. Inwardly, however, her mind whirled in disbelief.

Waiting to enter the lift were a dozen naked women, chained by the neck in four rows of three across. Their hands were cuffed behind their backs, their mouths were filled with bright-red ball-gags and their ankles were confined by hobble chains. A large blond man dressed in black singlet, shorts and trainers stood behind the huddled group. As Vanessa stepped clear of the doorway he gave her the briefest of nods, then said: 'Forward!' and the girls obeyed.

As the captives filed into the lift they made the same curious shuffling clink Vanessa had heard twice before on the level above, both leaving and then unloading the lorry. Out of her tumbling thoughts came the realisation that they had the same cause. The 'chains' the lorry crew had spoken of were literally chains of girls.

Then the lift door closed leaving her alone and Vanessa sagged weakly against the wall.

What had she got herself into? Girls being treated like slaves under an office block in the middle of London. Not just singly but dozens at a time. They had even been in the lorry she had hidden under. The true scale of the thing suddenly struck her. This was what Sir Harvey had suspected: Shillers were slavers . . . people traffickers . . . sex traders.

She took a deep breath, trying to keep her nerve. First, she must get her bearings . . .

Level B3 seemed to be at least as large as the car park above, but it was far less utilitarian.

The sky-blue painted ceiling, formed from a series of arching vaults rather than flat slabs, was illuminated not by fluorescent tubes but by artfully placed uplighters, making it seem loftier than it was. Long broad corridors stretched away from the lift block to the left, right and straight ahead, bounded by rectangular structures with concrete-block walls painted in different colours. They were lower than the vaulted roof and might have been open-topped. Large potted shrubs lined the corridors, each bathed in light from racks of mini-spots, adding their scents to the warm fresh air. Around the lift the floor was woodblocked, but the corridors were carpeted with thick, dark-blue rubber matting. A distant murmur hinted at activity, but for the moment nobody was in sight.

Cautiously, Vanessa circled the stairwell. In a row on each side of it – quite incongruously – were three compact single-storey wooden chalets, complete with small verandas and roofs almost brushing the painted ceiling. All the windows Vanessa could see were curtained.

At the back of the chalets behind the lifts, a shorter and very worn and wheel-marked woodblock corridor ran between more colourfully painted partition walls to a junction at the far end of the chamber, where it was crossed by a strip of green. Halfway down on the left-hand side, a large double doorway stood wide open. Indistinct sounds were coming from within.

Steeling herself for whatever she might find, Vanessa walked towards the doorway, torch and toolbox at the ready.

Through the door was a stable yard, open to the false blue sky. There was a row of wooden stalls,

21

polished harness hanging on the walls and a pile of hay bales in one corner. But peering over the low stall doors were beasts with the torsos of naked women and the heads of horses.

Suddenly Vanessa realised that they were actually women, their heads enclosed in elaborate equine masks moulded out of translucent plastic. Collars reaching from chin to sternum, with rings embedded in the plastic, confined the women's necks. Horse-like snouts complete with flared nostrils extended the line of their jaws, while long fluted ears, facing forwards, rose from the sides of their heads.

Bridles encased their masked heads, and bits, extending back up their false snouts, filled their mouths. Blinkers drawn together and fastened by pop-studs hid their eyes. Their hair had been pulled out through slots in the top and back of the masks, so that it hung down over their shoulders like a long mane.

Pairs of tethers clipped to their collar rings were hooked to the doorposts, keeping the women in place and on display. Their arms were obviously bound tightly behind them. Although they could not see, their attention seemed to be focused on the centre of the small yard. Here a large black man, dressed in black leather knee-high boots and matching thong, was harnessing four more horse-girls to a small two-wheeled carriage.

The man glanced round as Vanessa appeared, and she immediately feigned a deep interest in the sound-ness of the conduit that supplied the light above the stable door. The man returned to his task and she continued to watch him out of the corner of her eye. She felt a sense of sick fascination as he meticulously checked each helpless woman's harness, stroking and patting the bare flesh under his hands as he did so.

These four naked human ponies were bound tightly shoulder to shoulder, arranged not in pairs but in a single row. Their wrists were confined in front by cuffs fastened to broad belts buckled about their slender waists. A tapering strap ran from each belt down over their lower bellies, to be swallowed by the glistening clefts of their naked pudenda, emerging once more from between their full, firm buttocks. Ponytails matching the colour of their own manes jutted from the small of their backs.

Their crooked arms were drawn sharply backwards, thrusting out their pert bare breasts, and were held in place by a horizontal pole which had been threaded through the gap between the small of their backs and the inner angle of their elbows. Straps bound about the pole and their elbows prevented them slipping free of its constraint. From a pivoting mount in the centre of this cross-pole, a single curving shaft ran back to connect with the carriage.

Through the slightly misty plastic of their masks, Vanessa could see their white teeth clamped about black rubber bits. Streaks of saliva dribbled from the corners of their wide-stretched mouths. Clipped to the snaffle-rings on their cheeks, reins passed over their shoulders. Their blinkers were open, extending well forwards and allowing them to see only what was directly ahead of them.

Completing his check, their master climbed into the low seat of the carriage and gathered up the reins in one hand. In the other he picked up a carriage whip, which he flicked over the backs of his ponies.

'Walk on!' he commanded, and the wretched girls obeyed.

He hardly glanced at Vanessa as he wheeled his team out through the stable doors, turning them left and down the corridor.

Vanessa saw the jiggle and bounce of their glossy breasts and the bob of their tails across firmly rounded buttocks. Then they were past her, leaving a whiff of feminine perfume in their wake. As the carriage reached the T-junction with the green-floored corridor, the driver turned left again, cracking his whip across the row of rolling buttocks before him to urge them into a trot. Then they were gone.

Numbly, Vanessa walked along to the junction and peered after the carriage. A strip of green-painted board flooring extended in each direction until it banked and curved away out of sight, like an indoor running track without marked lanes. Presumably it encircled the whole level.

She stood there so long in a daze, struggling to accept what she had seen, that she was only roused by the sound of the carriage once more. Suddenly it bowled into view, coming from the other direction, having made a complete circuit.

The girls were leaning forwards now, their legs pumping desperately as they hauled their load at the equivalent of a gallop. Vanessa heard the driver's whip crack across their backs and saw that their straining bodies were already beaded in sweat, their chests heaving and breasts bouncing. He was treating them like animals. She felt inclined to throw her toolbox at him rather than covertly recording his cruelty. Instead she forced herself to give a casual wave as the cart sped past and received a flashing grin in response. The girls' glossy, straining buttocks beneath their flying tails were already mottled with scarlet whip marks.

When the carriage had disappeared again round the curve of the track, Vanessa turned back the way she had come. The whole thing was so incredible, so blatant . . .

Muffled snorts and throaty whinnies were emerging from the open door of the stable, not unlike the sounds made by real horses. Curious, Vanessa peered inside.

The remaining half-dozen pony-girls were tossing their manes and turning their heads and long false ears to one another as they exchanged their odd medley of sounds. Vanessa imagined she could hear slurred words under the animal whines and snuffles. A language of their own forced upon them by their bits and masks, perhaps?

Despite her pity and disgust, Vanessa knew what she had to do. Stepping quietly into the stable, she played her toolbox camera over the pony-girls, recording their blind and helpless condition.

After a minute, one of the women gave what sounded disturbingly like an apologetic neigh, and backed away from the stall door, evidently fighting the resistance of the taut twin tethers clipped to her collar. Vanessa moved closer and peered over the low door. The tethers ran through pulleys to weights suspended on either side of the stall door.

The woman had squatted down over a small, lidless toilet bowl built into the corner of the stall. With her legs splayed wide to brace against the pull of her tethers, she voided her bladder, the stream of urine hissing from between bare pink depilated pubic lips.

When she was done, a jet of water spouted from the bowl in the manner of a bidet, washing her groin clean. She stood up, wiggling her hips to shake the droplets from her pubes, then allowed the tethers to pull her back to her former position, announcing her return to her companions' strange conversation with a snort.

Vanessa hastily stepped back, lowering her camera, feeling guilty at the intimate scene she had recorded.

25

A vague idea of rescuing the women, or at least reassuring them that help was close at hand, passed through her mind. No, she could not risk giving herself away. Yet it was so hard to do nothing.

Suddenly she felt she could not breathe. She stumbled out of the stable and back towards the lift block. It was too much to take in. She had to get out of here.

Then she took hold of herself. No, she had to explore a little further, to get as much damning evidence as she could about the people exploiting these helpless women. Taking a deep breath, she continued on.

In front of the lift once more, she wondered where to go next.

The long, wide central corridor seemed somehow too daunting, so she took the right-hand path past the chalets. Who lived in them, she wondered? The carriage driver, perhaps, and the blond man she had seen herding the girl chain into the lift? And how many others like them? Whoever they were they would surely be made to suffer.

The green track also crossed the end of this corridor. As she heard the carriage approaching again she turned quickly left into a slightly narrower path.

It looked disconcertingly like a quiet mews fronted by a double row of small shops, each having identical large low windows, sheltered by a striped awning, with a single recessed door set beside it. Most of the windows were dark, a few had internal curtains drawn across and three further along were illuminated. Each window, she now saw, had a pair of loudspeakers mounted in its upper corners, with a switch mounted on the lintel between them. Presumably this was so that onlookers could both see and hear what went on inside the rooms if they chose. She could make out nothing inside the darkened 'shops', as the glass seemed slightly misty. Cautiously she made her way along to the nearest illuminated window and peered inside.

The room was bare except for a single low bed, its foot almost touching the inside of the window. A naked blonde woman was lying spread-eagled upon it, her outstretched arms and legs bound with ropes, so that Vanessa found herself looking up between her parted legs into the open wet gash of her vulva. The woman's head was raised on a pillow, so that Vanessa saw her pretty face almost full-on. A gag strap covered her mouth, but she was not blindfolded and her bright eyes were wide and expectant as she looked down the valley of her proud breasts, which were capped by bright-red nipples, seemingly gazing directly at Vanessa.

Vanessa flinched back guiltily, ashamed to be caught staring at somebody in such a wretched and humiliating position, and gave an apologetic shrug. But the girl showed no sign she had seen her, and after a moment turned her head to one side and stared at the wall.

Suddenly Vanessa understood the purpose of the bright lights and shading awnings. The poor girl couldn't see her because the window was made of one-way glass. From the other side it probably looked like a mirror. All she could see was herself, spread out, exposed, waiting helplessly for anybody to come in and make use of her as they wished . . .

Vanessa shuddered. Who could possibly contrive such degradation?

In the window of the next illuminated room, Vanessa was presented with a well-rounded pair of blushing-red buttocks, criss-crossed with purple weals and strap marks. A woman had been bent over a sturdy trestle and her wrists and ankles tied to the base of its frame. Her spread legs exposed plump dark-haired pudenda which swelled ripely beneath the deep cleft of her abused bottom. To add to her misery, a plumb-line weight had been clipped to her inner labia, stretching them into thin taut pink tongues as it hung between her thighs. Beside her was a rack of hooks on which was suspended a selection of crops, whips and tawses.

Even as Vanessa's stomach churned at the thought of the suffering she must have undergone, she glimpsed out of the corner of her eye a figure approaching from the other end of the alley. Immediately she began examining the stanchion that supported the window awning, taking out an adjustable spanner from her toolkit and checking the tightness of its mounting bolts. Risking a sideways glance, she saw a voluptuous woman, dressed in black thigh boots and a body stocking, carrying an oddly shaped rod or stick. As Vanessa watched, she entered the last illuminated room in the row.

Continuing her show of checking the awnings, Vanessa edged along as quickly as she dared to the window of the room and looked in. A girl with coffee-dark skin was doubled up and suspended from a heavy bar, which dangled from a large ring set in the middle of the ceiling.

From hooks set close to each end of the bar hung chains which connected to heavy rubber and metal cuffs locked about the captive's ankles, splaying her legs painfully wide so that the tendons behind her slightly bent knees stood out sharply. Her wrists were cuffed to the bar directly above her shoulders, drawing her arms straight upwards either side of her head. Another of the red ball-gags plugged her mouth. The weight of her upper body tipped her bottom up and forwards until she was in balance, as though offering up her exposed private parts. Her plump pudenda pouted through a crown of tight, glossy black curls. Under the tension of her spread legs her lips gaped wide, exposing the intimate folds of her inner labia and the mouth of her vagina. Below the fleshy fullness of her vulva was the sooty wellhead of her anus.

The body-stockinged woman was walking round her, stroking and petting her captive, talking as she did so. The girl's large, soft brown eyes rolled appealingly in their sockets as she strove to follow her. Vanessa pressed the button and the speakers came to life: '. . . so I think we'll work on making your anus a little more accommodating,' the woman was saying. 'You don't want to disappoint the clients, do you?'

The girl shook her head.

The woman unhooked the chains suspending the girl's ankles, letting out some slack and allowing her to lower her legs until they were level with the ground. Then she hooked the chains back over hooks at the very ends of the bar. This drew the girl's legs straight out sideways along the line of the bar, leaving her suspended as though she was performing the splits in mid-air. The big tendons of her groin stood out like cables.

The woman then knelt down and placed the rod-like device she had been carrying beneath the captive girl's open groin. Vanessa now saw the device had a dinner-plate-sized rubber pad on its base. A glistening black dildo with silver studs running down its sides was mounted on its upper end, while a black box with control buttons and an LED display clamped to its middle section.

The dildo slid up into the girl's distended anus, driving a squeak of pain from behind her gag. The pad was settled firmly on the floor so that the device was upright and the girl could not possibly dislodge it. The woman worked the buttons on the control box, saying: 'One jolt every ten seconds should be right . . .'

A red light flashed on the control box. At the same moment the girl's eyes bulged, she gave a tiny gasp of pain, her arms tightened and she briefly lifted herself so that a few centimetres of the electric dildo slid out of her anus, before her strength failed and she sank back on to the shaft that was so cruelly impaling her. After a few seconds the light flashed again and she repeated her helpless response.

The woman got to her feet smiling and stroking the girl's gaping vulva which, Vanessa was horrified to see, was now glistening wetly. 'Good girl. I expect to see you've come at least once by the time I get back . . .'

Dizzy and confused, overwhelmed by all she had seen, Vanessa suddenly felt her nerve going.

She dared not intervene, yet she could not stay and watch any more. She had enough for her story, enough to show the police and get the place raided. She had to get out now.

Turning away from the degrading spectacle, she made her way back to the lift. She would take no further risks. Her phone wouldn't work down here, but as soon as she was back above ground she would call Enwright and tell him what she'd found. She would wait here until the police came. She wanted to see the look on those perverts' faces when they realised it was all over.

Vanessa was actually reaching for the lift call button when its door unexpectedly opened and two large security guards stepped out.

Their automatic smiles and nods turned to mild frowns as they saw a strange face. Vanessa lowered her eyes and tried to slide past them, but one grabbed her shoulder. She swung her toolbox at his head but he blocked the blow and twisted her arm behind her back.

Vanessa kicked and screamed: 'Let go of me, you bastard!' But he was too strong for her.

His companion lifted his radio mike to his lips and said urgently: 'We've caught an intruder in level B3. You'd better tell the Director . . .'

Three

'So Harvey Rochester put you up to this,' Shiller said, when Vanessa had finished her account. 'But he's taking no active part in your investigations, is that correct?'

'Yes, Director,' Vanessa agreed meekly.

'I think I understand . . .' the Director smiled thinly to herself. Though obviously deep in thought, she appeared perfectly calm.

Vanessa had hoped Shiller would look fearful by now, knowing that somebody as powerful as Sir Harvey was supporting her investigations. Telling her story had allowed her to regain some composure. Although still desperately frightened and revolted by what they had done to her, she was once again contemplating Shillers' utter destruction. But the shameful ache in her ravaged loins and the stinging of her breasts kept her outwardly servile. Sickening as it was, she had no choice but to co-operate . . . for the moment.

'And what about your editor, Enwright?' Shiller asked.

'Waiting in a car a couple of streets away, Director. We agreed I'd try simply to walk out through the front gate when I was done here. Otherwise, if I had to get out the same way I got in, he'd follow me until he could pick me up.'

'What will he do if he doesn't hear from you?'

'If I don't call him in by midday, he'll tell the police what I'm doing and then come looking for me, Director.'

'I see.' Shiller consulted her watch. 'A little over three hours from now. Well, a lot can happen in that time.' Shiller rose and gathered up Vanessa's keys and phone. 'We shall talk again later, Vanessa. Meanwhile, I leave you in Miss Kyle's capable hands. Miss Kyle, I want her malleable and obedient, you understand?'

'Perfectly, Director,' Miss Kyle replied.

Shiller turned to go, then paused, eyes suddenly narrowing in thought. 'By the way, do you live alone, Vanessa?'

Vanessa answered the seemingly innocent question automatically: 'Yes, Director.'

'Do you have a regular boy or girlfriend at the moment?'

'No, Director.'

'Good,' she said, and walked briskly out.

Miss Kyle looked down at Vanessa, her eyes flashing with passion and anger. Vanessa shivered.

'So, you're a reporter who loses her nerve and runs away with only half a story,' Miss Kyle said. 'And you can't see the big picture even now. Stupid girl! You think we're monsters. Then why did we loosen your tongue by giving you the best orgasm you've had in years? Don't deny it! Now you're going to learn the truth the hard way. The Director thinks you've got potential, and she's always right about people. She wants you "malleable and obedient", so I've got to work on you some more. By the time I'm through you'll be begging to serve!'

She refilled the mug she had used to revive Vanessa after her forced orgasm and pushed it against

Vanessa's lips. 'Drink!' she commanded, and Vanessa gulped down the water until the mug was empty.

'Open!' she commanded, and Vanessa opened her mouth so that the ball-gag could be reinserted.

'I'm going to start by putting you on show ...' Miss Kyle swung the rack round on its large castors, pushed it up against the curtains that covered one wall of the cell, and pulled a hanging cord. Vanessa gurgled behind her gag, shaking her head and squirming helplessly in her bonds as the curtains drew back to reveal a reflection of herself.

Her vulva was still engorged, her inner labia glossy, pouting and flushed, her nipples crimson and erect, standing out on her hot, caged breasts. But far worse, just visible behind her image was the ghostly outline of the "mews" with its windows displaying helpless slaves. Now she had joined their shameful ranks. It seemed to Vanessa the ultimate degree of exposure. But then Miss Kyle added a further devilish refinement.

Bending over Vanessa's spread thighs she drew out four lengths of elastic cord fastened to the underside of the rack frame. On their free ends were small, spring-toothed metal clamps. Teasing out Vanessa's inner labia from where they lay between her thicker love-lips, she pinched them between the spring jaws. Vanessa whimpered as, one by one, four sets of metal teeth bit into her tender flesh-lips.

Miss Kyle stepped aside so that Vanessa could admire her handiwork in the mirror. Vanessa choked and whimpered in utter dismay. The upper pair of cords crossed over her hips and ran along the fold between the mound of her delta and her thighs. The lower pair came up over the curves of her taut buttocks. Between them the tension of the cords stretched the delicate flesh petals so that her vulva was spread wide open like an orchid in bloom, exposing the naked hood of her clitoris, the tiny pit of her urethra and the dark crinkled mouth of her vaginal passage. Anybody could look in on her and see every last intimate detail, as though she was laid out for some perverted gynaecological examination.

Vanessa felt hot tears of shame and despair pricking her eyes. How could they do this to her?

'Feeling sorry for yourself, are you, girl?' Miss Kyle asked. 'Well it's your own fault. The Director offered to explain but you wouldn't listen. Now you live with the consequences . . .'

And she walked out, voluptuous buttocks rolling beneath her sheer body-stocking, locking the door behind her and leaving Vanessa alone.

For a while Vanessa gave in to fear and self-pity and cried softly, all the time stomach-churningly aware of the shadowy figures peering in at her from behind her reflection. Never in her wildest dreams had she ever imagined she could feel so completely humiliated, exposed and helpless. All that sustained her was the promise of rescue. She prayed that Enwright would not wait a minute longer than agreed in alerting the police when she did not call, though the thought of being discovered as she was right now was almost too much to contemplate.

But what if rescue never came? Suppose Shiller simply denied all knowledge of her? Could Enwright prove she even entered the building? And even if a search were made would they find this secret dungeon? Shiller was bound to take extra precautions after her break-in. And who would dream anybody could be concealing an entire basement level? They might keep her down here for months.

She shrank away from that terrifying possibility. No, surely they would not want the unwelcome attention her disappearance would cause. On the other hand, they dare not release her. Obviously they would wipe her camera so that no hard evidence remained, but she still knew too much. Was that why they had not been more brutal with her? The pinpricks and cane stripes on her breasts would quickly fade, and the padded cuffs and straps would leave no lasting marks. Perhaps this outrageous humiliation was meant to confuse her, to break her will, even make her seem a little crazy. Without hard proof her story would seem too incredible to be believed. Yes, it made sense.

She had to resist the throbbing ache in her cruelly stretched tendons that were fast becoming ropes of fire. They dare not keep her here too long. She screwed up her eyes and tried to pretend there was nobody on the other side of the mirror. All she had to do was keep a clear head and wait . . .

In less than half an hour Vanessa was sweating and squirming in torment.

It was not due to the pain of her bondage or the shame of her exposure, but something utterly mundane yet also insidiously uncomfortable.

She desperately needed to pee.

The two mugs of water she'd been given had joined the half thermos of coffee she'd nervously downed in the early hours while waiting for the target lorry. Bound as she was, she could not even clench her thighs together to help hold it in. But if she relieved herself now it would be in full view of whoever was watching. Except for the intervening glass, it would literally be in their faces.

As the minutes passed, her misery plumbed hitherto unimagined depths. The tension from her splayed thighs and clamped labia working against the internal pressure from her bladder was teasing her clitoris. Being on display in such a blatantly inviting posture, she was becoming acutely aware of that sensitive and now totally exposed organ.

Helplessly, perversely, she could feel her clit rising and hardening in sympathy with her already engorged and erect nipples.

She sobbed in despair, her cheeks burning with renewed shame. Miss Kyle had planned this torment. Who needed a cane when you had a full bladder working for you? But how could she react like this, unless there had been some sort of aphrodisiac in the water? Had they drugged her, or was she deceiving herself? Her body might simply be instinctively responding to stimulation. It didn't mean she was really enjoying it. That was not possible.

Whatever the cause, she could not stand such torment much longer. Anything was better than this.

Did she really mean that? Could she swallow her pride and accept the shame of begging to serve, just as Miss Kyle had promised she would? Perhaps she could pretend to co-operate, to be broken, to have gone a little crazy. Perhaps . . .

It was too late.

With a muffled groan of despair, a stream of pee hissed from her peeled-back pudenda and splashed over the mirror.

A wave of wonderful, degrading, joyous relief flooded through her as she disgraced herself so completely; knowing people were watching every drop issue from her and that there was absolutely nothing she could do about it. For a few dizzy seconds, almost like a miniature orgasm, she was filled with the wild paradoxical freedom of total surrender to the inevitable, of not needing to care, only having to respond as instinct dictated.

As the last spurts became a trickle that ran down into the tunnel of her gaping vagina and the crack of her anus, the strangely thrilling glow faded. Vanessa burst into tears as humiliation once more took hold and wrapped her in misery.

When Vanessa opened her bleary eyes again, Miss Kyle was in the cell looking down at her.

'When I remove your gag you'd better have something worthwhile to tell me,' she said. 'Insults will be punished and pleas for release will be ignored, understand?'

Vanessa nodded as far as the strap across her neck allowed. She understood only too well.

Miss Kyle pulled the ball-gag out from between Vanessa's aching jaws, gave her a sip of water and then waited expectantly.

'Please don't make me do that again, Miss Kyle,' Vanessa said in a rush, hating the servile tremble in her voice. 'I'll do anything you want, I ...' she gulped, but could not help adding: '... I beg you.'

Miss Kyle smiled coolly. 'Haven't you enjoyed being on display?'

'No, Miss Kyle.'

'Why not?'

How could she ask, Vanessa wondered dimly? But aloud she said: 'It's ... frightening ... humiliating. Knowing all those people are looking at me.'

'A little humiliation won't kill you. Is it so hard to take?'

'For me it is, Miss Kyle.'

'Not because being on the rack for an hour and a half hurts if you aren't used to it?'

Why hadn't she mentioned the physical pain first, Vanessa wondered? The shock of her unwilling arousal had put it out of her mind. 'That as well,

Miss Kyle,' she said quickly. But it's being so ... so open that's worse.'

'Didn't any of it excite you, even for a few seconds?'

She knows, Vanessa thought with horror. That shameful moment when she lost all control in public and it had felt so disgustingly good. That was what had really scared her the most. And the fear that it might happen again ...

'No, Miss Kyle. Please ... put me somewhere else.'

Miss Kyle looked thoughtful. 'I suppose I could chain you up in the corner over there. You understand we've got to keep you secure until we decide what to do with you, and this is the best place. You're the uninvited guest. We can't make exceptions.'

'Use as many chains as you want, Miss Kyle,' Vanessa said, amazed and revolted by her own words. 'I won't give you any trouble. But please ... close the curtains.'

'The problem is, the rules say the only time the curtains are closed is when a girl is entertaining. Of course, when she's fulfilled her quota, she might be taken off display and given a nice soft mat to rest on while she recovers.'

'What ... quota, Miss Kyle?'

'How many screws a girl gives, or whatever other pleasure her user requires. That's what they're here for, after all. As you're new to this I'll let you off the rack for just three: me and Josh and Harry. They're the guards whose shins you gave a good kicking.'

Vanessa gaped at her incredulously. 'You ... you can't mean that! No way! You perverted bitch, you ... ahhh ... awww ... nnugh!

Miss Kyle had swung her cane three times across Vanessa's constrained and exposed breasts in quick succession, their springy wire cups making them wobble and bounce wildly. The first blow struck their soft bulging undercurves while the second, slicing downwards, smacked into their concave upper slopes. The last dipping swish clipped both her erect nipples with agonising precision. Scarlet welts blazed on her captive globes.

The caning had reduced Vanessa's tirade to sobs and moans. Before she could recover, Miss Kyle grasped her hair and twisted her head round so that they were eye to eye.

'What did I say about insults, you stupid girl?'

'Tha . . . that they'd be punished, M . . . Miss Kyle,' Vanessa choked out wretchedly, blinking back her tears.

'Will I ever have to remind you again?'

'N . . . No, Miss Kyle. Sorry, Miss Kyle.'

'Who's in charge here?'

'You are, Miss Kyle,' Vanessa gasped. For the first time she felt the truth of this simple statement deep inside her. Miss Kyle was in charge and she was her helpless prisoner.

'That's better,' said Miss Kyle. 'Now pay attention, girl. You might even learn something useful. I could have you right now if I wanted and you could do nothing to stop me, true?'

'Y . . . yes, Miss Kyle.'

'I could give you to half the men in this building to play with, true?'

Vanessa shivered at the thought of it. 'Yes, Miss Kyle.'

'But instead I'm giving you a choice. You either go back on display as you were . . . or you beg to serve Josh, Harry and me.'

Vanessa cringed. 'Please, Miss Kyle . . . I couldn't do that!'

Miss Kyle shrugged. 'You'd be surprised what you can do if you really want, girl, but it's your decision. Stay like you are until the Director decides what to do with you. After another three or four hours maybe you'll be ready to co-operate. Of course, your editor might come storming in here with the police and rescue you before then ... but I wouldn't bet on it.'

Miss Kyle pulled the ball-gag back over Vanessa's head. 'Open!'

'No ... please don't,' Vanessa protested.

'Well?' Miss Kyle asked.

Vanessa felt detached, her heart thudding, everything fading into the background except Miss Kyle's expectant, or was it contemptuous, face? Didn't she think Vanessa had the courage to make the choice? She expected her just to lie there and be humiliated. Well she'd show her ...

'I ... I beg to serve.'

There, it was said. She had crossed some great divide and a strange new land lay before her.

'Let me hear it properly, girl.'

'I beg to serve you, Miss Kyle ...'

'Just me?'

'And ... Josh and Harry –'

'That's Mr Willfield and Mr Parks to you, girl.'

'– and Mr Willfield and Mr Parks.'

'How will you serve us?'

The words came more easily now she was committed. 'By giving you pleasure ... with my body.'

'Do you promise to do your best to please us?'

Why not? She could do anything. 'I promise, Miss Kyle.'

Miss Kyle smiled. 'Then as you're going to have visitors we'd better clean this place up.' She opened the cell-room door, briefly reached outside, and drew back her hand. It held a chain leash fastened to the plain white collar of a slave-girl.

She was a neat slip of a thing who could barely have been eighteen, with small, high breasts, slim hips and a shaven pubis. In hands manacled by a short length of chain, she was carrying a mop, bucket and cloth. A slightly longer chain ran between her ankle cuffs, hobbling her feet. Her head was completely enclosed in a tight-fitting black rubber hood, with only a small triangle cut out for her nostrils at the front and a slot at the back through which a ponytail of blonde hair bobbed jauntily.

'Sandra will clean up your mess, then she'll attend while you're serving,' Miss Kyle explained.

The girl must have been waiting all the time, Vanessa realised. Had Miss Kyle been so sure what choice she'd make?

Miss Kyle rolled the rack back a little way from the window and Sandra set to work mopping Vanessa's pee off the rubber floor tiles. Somehow she knew exactly where to clean. How many times had she done this before, Vanessa wondered?

While she worked, Miss Kyle took out the enema gun, detached its nozzle and used the water jets to flush Vanessa out and wash the urine from her pubes. A blast of warm air dried her curls. Miss Kyle ran her fingers through them.

'You've got a nice thick fluffy bush, girl.'

Automatically Vanessa found herself saying: 'Thank you, Miss Kyle.'

Sandra finished wiping down the window. 'Put your things in the corner and fetch a mat,' Miss Kyle ordered.

The slave-girl placed the mop and bucket neatly in a corner and, by touch from the equipment shelves, selected a small foam rubber mat, which she placed on the floor by the rack. Miss Kyle clipped the free end of her leash to the rack frame.

'Sit,' she commanded, and Sandra gracefully settled herself cross-legged on the mat, resting her chained hands neatly in her lap and looking the model of perfect subservience.

Miss Kyle ignored her, turning her full attention to Vanessa. Her sensuous mouth shaped into a hungry smile and her eyes grew large with lust.

She took off her belt, unzipped her boots and peeled down her body stocking. Vanessa had never seen anybody look so at ease with their own body. Even naked she radiated masterful self-assurance.

Miss Kyle tilted the rack flat and lowered it until Vanessa's head was level with her bare, pouting pubic mound and the deep fold that clove it. Unfastening the wire cups that confined Vanessa's breasts, Miss Kyle kissed the burning welts that crossed them and then sucked her sore, hard nipples. Vanessa groaned and squirmed in her bonds.

'Have you ever had sex with another girl before?' Miss Kyle asked huskily.

'Once, Miss . . . at college,' she added, feeling compelled to be truthful. 'It . . . wasn't very good.'

'This will be better,' Miss Kyle promised.

She moved to the head of the rack, bent over and kissed Vanessa on the lips, grasping her hair to hold her still. Vanessa's lips parted under the force of her kiss and the insistence of the older woman's mobile, questing tongue. Miss Kyle tasted sweet and her breath was fresh and hot. Reaching out with her other hand, she cupped Vanessa's pubic delta and her fingers began to probe her furrow.

To Vanessa's shame she felt aroused. The pulse grew stronger in her loins, her lubrication flowed and her clitoris rose under the skilful teasing of Miss Kyle's fingers. She couldn't help herself. Despite knowing what Miss Kyle was, she was responding to her like a lover.

Miss Kyle mounted Vanessa's face, lifting one leg to straddle her head and then, her toes still lightly resting on the floor, lying across her body so that she could bestow a kiss on her pubic bush. Soft strong thighs closed about Vanessa's cheeks as the woman's weight bore down, pressing her naked scented pudenda into her face. Her slit gaped wide as though to swallow Vanessa whole, sucking her in to share its secrets. Miss Kyle's tongue teased Vanessa's clit, demanding she respond in kind. Helplessly, Vanessa did so.

The hot slippery sex-pouch ground across her nose and mouth as Miss Kyle rode her face, with Vanessa kissing and licking every fleshy fold. With utter abandon her tongue delved into the tunnel of Miss Kyle's vagina and furled around the hard bud of her clitoris. In a corner of her mind, pushed aside by the instinct that seemed to be ruling her body, she cursed Miss Kyle for being right. This was better sex than she'd had before, far better. How could that be?

With a sigh and shudder and clenching of her thighs, Miss Kyle came, drenching Vanessa with her fragrant discharge. For a few moments she lay limp across Vanessa, then she climbed off her reluctant lover.

Vanessa's face was glistening and sticky, blushing with desire, her cuffed and strapped body trembling with unfulfilled need. 'Please, Miss . . . I beg you,' she gasped, knowing how pitiful she sounded but unable to stop herself, 'I haven't come yet . . . finish me off!'

Miss Kyle smiled, her own cheeks happily flushed. 'But this hasn't been about your pleasure. You've been serving me, remember? Maybe you'll come while the men are using you. Think of it as motivation . . .'

As Vanessa watched in an agony of frustration, Miss Kyle used the hose gun to wash and dry her own pubes, then dressed once again in her outrageous costume.

'Sandra will freshen you up for Josh and Harry. I'm sure you'll do your best to please them. But then, you've really no other choice.' She kissed Vanessa affectionately on the forehead and ruffled her hair as one might a pet. 'That's what makes it so exciting . . .' And she left.

Sandra, who had been perfectly still all this time, now moved. Working blindly but surely, she produced a moist, lightly scented cloth from a store under the rack and wiped Miss Kyle's drying juices from Vanessa's face. Then she unhooked the hose gun, slid her hands over Vanessa's taut splayed body until she found her pouting, sticky cleft, parted the puffy, flushed lips and inserted the rubber nozzle. Warm water flushed Vanessa's passage clean, followed by cold to cool her flesh and tighten up her internal muscles. Finally a squirt of lubrication was deposited in her vagina and anus to ensure she would be easy to enter.

It was so intimately but deftly done that Vanessa automatically murmured, 'Thank you.'

Sandra bobbed her head in acknowledgement, replaced the hose gun and resumed her position on her mat, leaving Vanessa to her thoughts.

They were trying to break her down with pain, pleasure and shame. She must not forget that, however good some bits might seem. It was all meant to confuse and discredit her when the time came to let her go. She had to stick to her principles and stay focused.

But it was so hard!

A large man entered the cell room. Immediately a broad grin spread across his face as he saw Vanessa displayed on the rack. He was the taller of the two security guards who had caught her . . . how long ago? A couple of hours, or a lifetime?

He loomed over Vanessa, standing between her spread legs and closely looking her naked and bound body up and down. A fresh shiver of arousal coursed through her as she saw a bulge growing in the front of his trousers. It was really happening. He was going to fuck her and there was nothing she could do to stop it. A wet trickle ran out of her cleft and down to the dark tight pucker of her anus. She could smell her own excitement.

'Not so much fight in you now, girl, is there?' he said.

'No, sir,' Vanessa said in a tiny voice.

He unzipped his trousers and pulled out a thick, purple-tipped erection, which he cupped in his hand for her to see.

'Think you can take this up you?'

'I'll . . . have to, sir.'

'Too right you will. But which hole's going to be the more fun?'

'Either, sir. I'll . . . try my best to please you, sir. You'll enjoy both. Just fuck me, sir, please fuck me!'

She was appalled by her own words, which seemed to flow from her without conscious thought. Was she desperate to get the ordeal over, or eager to get it started?

There was no foreplay. He simply braced himself against her waist with one hand and fed the head of his hard cock into the gaping tunnel of her vagina with the other. Then, taking firm hold of her hips, he rammed into her.

Vanessa gave a choking cry as he filled her passage to the hilt, withdrew a little way and then plunged in again. She squirmed and strained at her bonds, even as her internal muscles contracted about the rod of flesh reaming out her insides. There was nothing left for her to do but to respond naturally to her violation. The world had become a wonderfully simple place. She just accepted whatever was done to her. She had been mastered and now she must serve.

The guard was pumping into her faster and faster, thudding into her pubic mound without any thought for her comfort. His thrusts were making the frame of the rack shake and setting her breasts trembling. His eyes were half closed and his face contorted with concentration, focusing entirely on his own pleasure. But that was what she was there for: to give pleasure.

With a groan of dismay, she felt his sperm burst within her. Not again! She still hadn't come. His hips jerked spasmodically, ejecting the last few drops. For a few seconds he stood hunched over her, breathing heavily, a faraway look of perfect satisfaction on his face. Then he slowly withdrew his glistening shaft from her reluctant passage and zipped himself up.

Vanessa ached with doubly unsatisfied need. She'd no idea denial could be such torture. She wanted to beg him to bring her off with his fingers, but knew it would do no good. What she wanted didn't matter.

'Thank you, sir,' she choked out.

He grinned. 'Hope we meet again.' Then he turned and left the cell. It had all taken less than ten minutes.

As Sandra dutifully cleansed her once more, Vanessa wrestled with her disjointed thoughts.

She'd just had sex with a strange man while tied to a rack. Had it been rape? No, she'd begged him like a slut on heat. It had been her choice, in a way. Was this better than hours of public exposure before the perverts outside? Her choice, but look where it had got her. Why had Sir Harvey chosen her of all people to investigate Shiller? Why had she been so clever getting herself inside but not out again? Dare she ever write about how she felt right now?

She twisted her head round to look at Sandra, mute and hooded, placidly seated beside the rack.

How could the girl be so perfectly calm, so ... peaceful? Had the fight been driven out of her? If she was kept here long enough, would that happen to her?

Ten minutes later the stouter of the two guards entered her cell. Was he Josh or Harry? Did it matter?

He closed the door and immediately started undressing. In a minute he was naked, a slight paunch overhanging his swelling, protruding, purple-veined penis.

He circled the rack, examining Vanessa intently from all angles. She twisted her head to follow him with wide, anxious eyes, but she said nothing. The sense of utter helplessness combined with mounting excitement grew within her once more. Her nipples, which had softened slightly with waiting, now hardened again. Her hot, gaping holes ached to be filled. She was nothing but a slut on heat who needed serving.

The man stepped nearer and gently touched her cheek, then her shoulder. He rubbed the soft hollow of her armpit, he squeezed her pectorals, circled her abused breasts with his fingertips, pinched and rolled her nipples, kneaded the trembling flesh of her stomach and ran his palms over her widespread inner thighs. With the satisfaction of a connoisseur he cupped her wet cleft mound, tugged her pubic hair and ground his thumb into the hard bud of her clitoris.

His erection was standing out rock-hard now, and Vanessa saw a drop of natural lubrication glistening on its tip. She knew that rod of flesh would soon be inside her.

His thumb slid down her cleft and into the dripping mouth of her vagina, while his forefinger slipped easily past the sphincter of her greased anus and tickled the soft elastic tunnel within. She was so open, so ready. Vanessa closed her eyes and groaned in ecstasy at his teasing touch. Yes, he would bring her the release she craved. It was wonderful . . .

Thwack!

Vanessa gave a shriek of surprise at the band of fire that exploded across her bottom. She opened her eyes to find the man had taken a cane from the wall rack and lashed it across her taut buttocks and bulging mound of Venus. A second and third blow followed in quick succession. She jerked at her bonds, the tendons of her inner thighs standing out as she tried futilely to close them.

After six cuts, the man threw the cane aside, positioned himself between Vanessa's scarlet buttocks and rammed his cock into the dark pit of her bottom.

Vanessa gasped as the piston of flesh parted her tight orifice. She'd never had proper anal sex. The rubber dildo had not prepared her for the feel of a real penis forcing its way up her most intimate entrance. She felt shamed, disgusted, violated . . . and more excited and aroused than she had ever known.

Desperately she jerked her hips the few centimetres her straps allowed and clenched her anal ring in a forlorn attempt to keep him inside her forever. His sperm pumped into her entrails as her own orgasm erupted, sending her body into a wild spasm.

'Thank you . . .' she screamed aloud.

When Vanessa became aware of her surroundings again through her post-orgasmic haze, the man was gone and Sandra was flushing his sperm out of her rectum.

But this time, before returning to her mat, Sandra gently stroked and patted Vanessa's stinging thighs, her swollen pudenda and tender bottom cheeks.

Vanessa was puzzled by the unexpected gesture. Was it meant as commiseration or encouragement? Perhaps both. Shortly afterwards, Miss Kyle arrived and Sandra was led away. Vanessa wondered whether she would see her again or ever know what she looked like under that mask.

Miss Kyle released the straps and clamps that had held her so firmly to the rack and tilted it upright. Unsupported, Vanessa slithered to the floor with a groan of pain. Her limbs were locked in the position she had been bound in. Miss Kyle chuckled as Vanessa twitched and squirmed painfully. 'Don't worry, girl, you'll get over it.'

She then clamped Vanessa's ankle with a metal cuff from which trailed a length of chain. As life gradually returned to Vanessa's limbs, Miss Kyle made her crawl to a corner of the room where a rubber mat had been laid out, locking the end of the chain to a ring in the wall. Numbed and aching, hugging her sore groin, Vanessa curled up in a ball and fell into an exhausted sleep.

'Wake up, Vanessa . . .'

Vanessa jerked suddenly into shocking alertness. Memory flooded back and her cheeks reddened with shame. It hadn't been a dream. Shiller and Miss Kyle were standing over her. She shrank back into the corner, instinctively trying to cover her breasts and pubes, causing Miss Kyle to smile.

'It's half past eleven,' the Director said briskly. 'Shortly you will contact your editor, assure him you are well and that there is no need to call the police. You will arrange to meet him in person later this afternoon and he will drive you back to your flat.' She saw the expression of hope on Vanessa's face. 'Naturally, we shall take precautions to ensure you do not reveal what you have discovered.' She pointed to the bench on which an odd assortment of items had been laid out. 'Our research department has some experience in producing specialised devices to control the activities of young women. They will ensure you say and do only what we allow . . .'

'On your feet, girl!' Miss Kyle ordered.

Vanessa was made to stand with her legs spread, back straight, breasts thrust out and hands clasped behind her head, lifting her thick mane of hair off her shoulders. The Director looked her over, noting the fading cane marks on her breasts and buttocks. Despite the punishment they had undergone, Vanessa felt her teats swelling and hardening painfully under her gaze. She hung her head in shame at her display, but the Director merely smiled.

'First, we must be able to monitor your actions at a distance and communicate with you in turn . . .'

Miss Kyle pressed a slim, contoured metal plate to the nape of Vanessa's neck just below the hairline. From each end of the box thin transparent arms curved round to her ears, where they divided into an upper loop, which extended over the top of each ear and round into the earholes, and a lower section tipped by a slim metal bar that slipped through her pierced earlobes from underneath. The bars folded over, pointing forwards and locking themselves into place.

'You will receive instructions through the earphones. The bars of the earrings contain optical fibre lenses connected to a camera and transmitter with a range of several kilometres. We shall be able to see what you are doing at all times.'

Next came a thin metal-strap choker band. Contacts on the inside of the band pressed against Vanessa's skin just under her Adam's apple. At the back it locked into the same metal plate as the camera and earphones.

'The band incorporates both external and throat microphones, so that we can hear you even if you whisper or sub-vocalise. It can also control your speech, but we'll come to that in a moment . . .'

Miss Kyle held up what looked like a normal underwired white bra. But inside at the apex of the cups were bare metal rings. As Miss Kyle fitted the bra on to her, Vanessa bit her lip as small sprung points concealed within the rings pricked against the sides of her erect nipples.

'The contacts can deliver various forms of stimulation,' Shiller said, confirming Vanessa's worst fears.

The last item was a white hipster thong to match the bra. But what caused Vanessa to gulp in dismay were the two dildo-like projections that extended from the inside of the crotch. They were moulded of black rubber with metal strips set into their sides. The rear prong was somewhat bulbous with a tapered neck, the forward more lifelike.

'The phalluses contain the system batteries and other control devices,' Shiller explained.

She trembled as Miss Kyle pulled the thong on to her, gasping as the dildos plugged her front and rear. Her anus stretched almost painfully wide until the bulbous anterior dildo slipped inside her and her muscle ring could close over its narrower neck with relief. Despite appearances, the thong was not elasticated, so she could not simply slide it off. It was locked in place by the integral clip in the back strap.

'Apart from other functions, the phalluses will remind you at all times that we control the most intimate and vulnerable parts of your body,' Shiller said. 'It will be easier for you if you remember that.'

Vanessa gulped.

Miss Kyle plugged a flat, segmented metal cable into a socket at the back of the thong. The cable hugged the curve of Vanessa's spine, connecting in turn to the bra, choker and earphone camera plate.

'All the casings are titanium and the fabric itself is reinforced by titanium mesh,' Shiller explained. 'It is a hard metal and cannot be cut by ordinary tools. All the fastenings are electronically activated. You will only be able to remove the devices when we allow.'

Shiller seated herself on the bench, rested a laptop on her knees and plugged in a headset and microphone.

Miss Kyle unfastened the ankle cuff that had secured Vanessa to the wall. For the first time in hours she was free of any obvious physical restraint. But she knew that freedom was an illusion.

'I, or whoever is controlling you remotely through this system, will be referred to as "Monitor", and you will be known as "Puppet",' Shiller said. 'All we require is that you obey your orders without question. Obedience will be rewarded, insubordination will be punished, like so . . .' She touched a control on the laptop.

Vanessa tensed, but felt only a light tingling, first about her nipples, then the soft flesh of her anus, then deep inside her cleft. The sensation moved about her like an intimate caress. It was unexpectedly warming and arousing, and she began to respond, squirming and wriggling helplessly.

'That was a reward. But if you are unco-operative . . .'

It felt as if hot needles were stabbing through her nipples, vagina and rectum. With a shriek she fell to the ground, clawing futilely at the torturing underwear.

Then the pain was gone, leaving behind only a lingering ache. Vanessa sobbed and gasped with relief. She had thought what she had already suffered had been severe, but it had been nothing so intense, so intimate as this.

'Stand up!' the Director commanded.

Vanessa sprang to her feet and stood to attention, shivering with fear.

'That was close to maximum stimulation,' the Director said. 'I trust I will not have to use it again?'

'No, Director,' Vanessa said, hating herself even as she spoke.

'Good. Shortly you will phone Mr Enwright. Despite this demonstration, you might think it worthwhile to give him some sort of warning. This will not be permitted. The choker you wear senses your speech patterns and compares them to whatever words you are being instructed to say. Any significant deviation will be detected and cut short like this . . .'

Vanessa felt a stabbing sensation in her throat that locked her vocal cords and made her gasp.

'. . . followed by whatever disciplinary stimulus is judged appropriate. Do you understand?'

Vanessa nodded.

The Director held up Vanessa's phone, which was now connected to a small black box displaying a glowing green light. 'This relay will enable the phone to operate down here. Now we will rehearse with you repeating my words exactly . . .'

Ten minutes later, Vanessa rang Enwright.

'Mr Enwright? It's Vanessa.'

'Vanessa! Are you all right? It's nearly twelve. I was getting worried . . .'

Vanessa heard Shiller's words in her ear and repeated them obediently. 'I'm fine, but I can't talk for long. I haven't seen anything out of the ordinary yet, but I think I've found a way to do a proper investigation on Shiller from the inside. Be waiting to pick me up about five-thirty and I'll tell you if it worked out. Bye . . .'

She rang off.

Shiller smiled and Vanessa felt a pleasant tingle course through her loins. She had been rewarded. An electronic pat on the head for an obedient dog performing a trick to order. She felt sick.

'Good,' Shiller said. 'We have a few more hours of grace. Next we will check the system functions remotely. Go outside and I'll direct you further . . .'

Miserably, Vanessa crossed to the cell door. Although she was now at least half-dressed, she recoiled at facing the shadowy figures she had sensed earlier peering in on her humiliating exposure. But like any puppet, she had no choice.

Taking a deep breath, she stepped out into the mews.

Four

The mews was full of naked slave-girls.

There were a few older men and women in office shirt-sleeves, standing out amid the display of bare flesh, but quite unconcernedly the slave-girls flowed around them, chattering among themselves and peering into windows like shoppers in any town arcade. They had different-coloured collars round their necks; some were barefoot while others wore sandals or even high-heels. Bracelets and bangles hung round wrists and ankles, while rings sparkled about ears, nipples and labia. They carried purses and ribbons festooned their hair. But they were undeniably slaves.

What they did not have, as far as Vanessa could see, was any other visible means of restraint apart from their collars. No chains, leashes or whips. She could not make sense of it.

'Turn left, Puppet,' Shiller's voice sounded in Vanessa's ear, snapping her out of her confusion.

She received a few curious glances as she walked along the mews in her new underwear. Everybody else was either fully dressed or bare. But nobody said anything or obstructed her.

Some of the cells had raised their one-way mirror windows and put out stands on which papers and magazines, fruits and sweets, perfume and ribbons, footwear and jewellery were on display. They looked almost like any other small shop, except none she had ever seen had a naked slave-girl serving behind the counter. Each illuminated cell had its own helpless captive on show.

Vanessa's mind spun as she tried to take in the contrast. Naked abused flesh next door to newspapers. Or was pretty, bound flesh merely another kind of produce to be bought and sold down here in this perverted underworld?

The cells attracted almost as much attention from the slaves promenading along the mews as the sweets and jewellery. But the girls peering in showed no sign of outrage at what was being done. Instead they pointed and laughed or winced in good-natured sympathy at the suffering of their sisters.

The clothed office workers were also inspecting the captives in their cells. Vanessa saw a pair of slave-girls lower their eyes and move aside deferentially for a balding man in a blue shirt. He entered a cell containing a young woman secured in a set of stocks and pulled the curtains. The pair of girls outside grinned knowingly to each other.

What was going on?

Vanessa reached the far end of the mews, where it was crossed by another alleyway. The junction was decorated with more of the large potted shrubs, some the size of small trees. Among them was a pot with a slave-girl planted in it.

She was buried up to her ankles in the stone chippings that filled the pot. A large, forked dry branch, stripped of its bark and polished smooth, had been sunk into the pot behind her, and it was to this she had been bound with lengths of artificial ivy, her arms outstretched along the spreading limbs. Black rubber straps held circular pads over her eyes and a ball-gag in her mouth. Her skin was pale and freckled and a cap of close-cropped auburn hair covered her head.

'Go over to her, Puppet,' Shiller commanded.

Vanessa realised with a shiver that the Director could see everything she was looking at through her camera earrings. Reluctantly, she stepped up to the grotesquely bound girl.

Her breasts were full, smooth and pale, capped by large brown nipples. A fluffy russet pubic bush blossomed from between her thighs. She wore a pale-purple collar, from which hung a metal tag with the inscription 'Bethany 5 Lavender' stamped on it.

'Touch her,' Shiller commanded. 'Cup and squeeze her breasts.'

'What?' Vanessa said. 'No way – ahhh!' A needle of pain had stabbed through her nipples, making her wince. The red-haired girl raised her head curiously as she heard her gasp.

'Obey me, Puppet!'

Vanessa gritted her teeth. 'Haven't you degraded her enough without making me hurt her any more – eeek!'

Her vagina throbbed with fire.

'You will obey and you will also respond to commands as instructed,' Shiller said ominously.

Blinking back her tears, Vanessa replied miserably: 'I obey ... Monitor.'

She cupped the girl's breasts in her hands and gave them a token squeeze. They were warm, perfectly pliant and heavy.

The girl sighed behind her gag and strained at her bonds, lifting her chest to press her breasts harder into Vanessa's palms.

Shiller said: 'You see, Puppet, Bethany wants to be touched. She knows she is there to be enjoyed, to be stared at, to be stroked and fondled. She is offering herself up for your pleasure . . .'

'I hate doing this, Monitor!' Vanessa hissed.

'Why? Is she unpleasant to touch?'

'No, but . . .'

'Look at her nipples swelling. She's responding to you, asking for more. Do you insult her by denying her gift?'

It took an effort to shape her response in measured words and not the expletives she wanted to use. 'What you're doing to her is wrong, Monitor!'

'How do you know? Have you asked Bethany? Have you yet asked any slave here what she feels about her situation? Did any of the girls you have just passed look unhappy?'

'They . . . they don't have any choice, Monitor. You've forced them to behave that way.'

'Perhaps we've just given them the opportunity to behave as they wish.'

'I'll never believe that, Monitor!'

'We shall see, Puppet. Now kiss Bethany's nipples and thank her for the pleasure she has given you.'

'This hasn't given me any pleasure – owww!' Her anal plug stabbed her rectum with electric fire.

'The monitor system incorporates basic biometric feedback,' Shiller said tersely. 'Your nipples are erect and your vagina is lubricating. Do not lie to me or insult Bethany!'

Blushing with shame and anger, Vanessa took a deep breath, bent forwards and kissed Bethany's tumescent nubs of flesh, each as hard as India rubber.

'Thank you,' she whispered.

Bethany lowered her head and sank back against the branch, looking perfectly relaxed in her bonds once more.

'Continue on your way, Puppet,'

Vanessa walked on. She noticed another of the one-way mirror windows was set in the wall on her left.

'You may look through the observation window if you wish,' Shiller said.

Vanessa went up to the window. On the other side was an enclosed yard, larger than the stables, and laid out with a variety of posts, racks and frames, all of which were hung about with cuffs and chains. But even more disturbing were the dozen dog kennels arrayed along one wall. The entrance to each was large enough to admit a person crawling on all-fours, and was closed by a sturdy barred gate.

'This is the training area for new recruits,' Shiller explained.

Vanessa could not keep the contempt from her voice. 'Is that what you call them, Monitor?'

'That is what they are, Puppet. Perhaps you will have a chance to judge for yourself quite soon. Now continue on . . .'

The alley opened out near the top end of the running track the pony-girl carriage had used.

'Begin jogging,' Shiller commanded. 'I want to check the connections are secure . . .'

Vanessa set off around the track.

More shrub-filled pots and planters lined each side of the track, many curving over her head and virtually hiding the false concrete sky, so that it was almost like jogging through a leafy tunnel. Observation windows and the mouths of other alleys peeped out from between them. Every effort had clearly been made to create a pleasant environment in this secret subterranean slave camp. She realised bitterly that the building plans she had studied had only shown what any normal inspection would reveal. Somehow this whole level had been left off them. How much had it cost? Whatever it was, she reminded herself, it would ultimately be the girls themselves who paid.

It felt good to move, working out the lingering aches from her time on the rack. However, the motion made her even more conscious of the phalluses filling her passages and the contacts ringing her nipples. It was a relentless stimulation centred on the most intimate parts of her body and, despite herself, she was responding to it. But how could she become aroused in such circumstances?

Had Miss Kyle been right? Was she really a slut for such treatment?

Rounding the lower bend, Vanessa noticed that she did not have the track all to herself. A dozen slave-girls, all wearing orange collars, were shuffling along as they carried a heavy timber pole between them. Vanessa's steps faltered as she saw just how they bore the burden.

The pole was divided into three sections linked by sturdy two-way hinge joints to accommodate bends. There were four girls to each section, all straddling the pole so that it hung between the soft curves of their inner thighs. Ring-bolts were screwed into its upper side, one in front and one behind each girl. Chains ran from these to her wrists, which were cuffed behind her, and up between her sweat-beaded breasts to the front ring of her collar. Between the ring-bolts, where the girl's thighs straddled the pole, two close-spaced, thick black rubber dildos jutted up at convergent angles and penetrated her front and rear.

Despite their impalement, the girls walked perfectly in step and somehow appeared graceful, even as they rounded the banked curve of the track. But however carefully they moved, the heavy pole swayed beneath them, transmitting the motion through the dildos. The rubber prongs twisted and churned within their bulging fleshy sheaths. The girls' thighs were wet with lubrication, their swollen pubic lips flushed, the pole beneath stained dark from this steady rain of female juices.

With a start, Vanessa realised she had been running through the trail their arousal left on the track behind them. The scent of it filled her nostrils. Suddenly her own phalluses didn't seem so intrusive after all.

The girls' teeth were clamped about rubber bits. Drool ran from the sides of their mouths and off their chins to trickle and drip on to their swaying breasts. The expressions on their faces appeared both far away and determined. They hardly seemed aware of Vanessa as she jogged past them, lost in some other world of exertion and enforced arousal.

'Why are you punishing them like this, Monitor?' she asked.

'This isn't punishment,' Shiller said. 'This is part of Peach chain's regular training programme.'

'What can this possibly train them for?'

'Apart from the obvious benefits and satisfaction of intense physical exertion, it reinforces their identity as a team sharing in the performance of an arduous, if stimulating, task. Experiencing pleasure and suffering together without inhibition reinforces the bond. They are more sensual, responsive beings for it.'

'You mean they're better slaves, Monitor. They're doing this because you've driven them until their spirit's broken.'

'Really? And exactly who is driving them right now?'

'So you're saying they're doing this because they enjoy it, Monitor? If it's all voluntary, why do they need the collars and chains?'

'Collars and chains can be donned voluntarily also, Puppet. You have so much to learn . . .'

* * *

Shiller made Vanessa jog another half-dozen laps before she was satisfied the control and monitoring devices were functioning perfectly. Then she was recalled to the cell where Shiller and Miss Kyle were waiting.

'Kneel before the Director,' Miss Kyle commanded, pointing to the rubber mat Sandra had used, which had been placed in front of Shiller's chair.

To Vanessa's relief, Shiller put the laptop control unit aside and looked down at her intently. 'Are you an honest reporter?' she asked.

Vanessa was caught off-guard. 'What?'

'It's a simple enough question. Do you do your job fairly and without prejudice or distortion of the truth?'

Eyeing Miss Kyle's cane warily, Vanessa replied: 'I try my best, Director.'

Shiller smiled. 'That is all any of us can do. And I accept that you are both honest and honourable. You notice that I have not attempted to bribe you. I'm very wealthy. I could offer you a large sum of money to forget what you have seen here.'

'I don't take bribes,' Vanessa said flatly.

'Good. I would have nothing further to do with you had it been otherwise. So we are left with honesty and integrity. You are no doubt feeling both upset and confused about what you have experienced so far, true?'

'Yes, Director,' Vanessa admitted.

'And I tell you there is much more to learn, which may shock and surprise you even further. Now, is that an ideal state of mind in which to write an honest and accurate report?'

'Then I'd record my feelings as they occurred to me at the time, Director, and put them into context later,' Vanessa said.

Shiller smiled. ' "Context", yes, that's a good word. Without knowing the proper context for your observations you cannot be certain they are accurate. I know you have already passed what you believe is the only possible judgement on us, but I suggest that it is based upon misunderstanding and incomplete research. As the honest reporter you claim to be, you should put aside this superficial assessment and search for the deeper truth.'

'If you're trying to kid me what I've seen isn't industrial-scale slavery, you're wasting your time, Director,' Vanessa replied coldly.

'Of course it is industrial slavery,' Shiller said, 'but of an ethical and non-coercive nature.'

'With pension schemes and private health care, I suppose?' Vanessa said contemptuously.

'Exactly so,' Shiller agreed. 'Our girls are a most valuable resource, so naturally we take great care of them.'

'You sell them to people for sex, Director!'

'We rent out their services to carefully vetted clients.'

'It's forced prostitution.'

'Not if the girls are willing, and no girl ever puts on a Shiller collar who is not only willing but also eager to serve. Is that so hard to believe? Do you deny there are many women in this country with genuine submissive and masochistic tendencies?'

'Well . . . no. A few, maybe, but you've got dozens . . . hundreds of them down here.'

'Do their numbers alone make any difference? Individuals brought together for a common purpose are still individuals. Or do you deny the reality of their personal needs and desires just because it disconcerts you to see them in a group?'

Vanessa felt confused. Shiller was making everything sound so reasonable. 'But doing it for money means you're exploiting them,' she argued desperately.

'Why should they not be compensated for employing their special talent to give pleasure? People sell themselves as commodities all the time. Look at the behaviour of sports personalities, media celebrities and those merely famous for being famous. What are they selling but their name, face or body? And do they do this for nothing? There is a demand for girls of a slavish nature, so we supply it discreetly and efficiently. We act as their managers, if you like. We are not a charity, though we support many good causes, so of course we charge an appropriate fee for our service.'

Vanessa shook her head. It couldn't be like this. It had to be wrong.

Shiller smiled sympathetically down at her. 'I warned you it wouldn't be easy to comprehend, did I not? Well, listen to what I have to propose. For the moment say nothing about what you have discovered, and in return I will give you the chance to work here for one month, ostensibly as part of your ongoing investigation. During that time you will be free to talk to the girls and see how our operation is run. Test the facts fully and fairly. When that time is up, submit whatever story you like to your editor ... and to Harvey Rochester.'

'You'd risk all this on me changing my mind about you in one month?' Vanessa said incredulously. 'After what you've done to me! Why should I believe a word you say – ahhh!'

Miss Kyle had flicked her cane across Vanessa's stomach.

'The Director never breaks her word,' she said angrily. 'Don't ever accuse her of lying again!'

'Thank you, Miss Kyle,' Shiller said, as Vanessa rubbed her stinging midriff. 'But she must learn that for herself.' She turned back to Vanessa. 'Whatever I have done to you, I have not lied. However, it's quite natural that, with your mind full of suspicion at this moment, you do not believe I will honour the terms of my offer. Equally, I cannot be sure you would keep any promise not to reveal what you know the moment you get the chance, so I will not ask you to give one. Therefore, to enforce your side of the agreement, you will be subject to control and monitoring at all times outside these walls.'

'I'd wear this . . . this "spywear" get-up for a whole month?' Vanessa asked doubtfully.

'Only in public, or when in any position to give us away, and with your co-operation that time can be kept to a minimum. Consider, I'm not asking you to betray your employers, merely to have a little patience. What is true today will still be so a month from now . . . unless you're frightened you might change your mind.'

'Nothing's going to do that!' Vanessa assured her.

'Then you have nothing to lose bar some personal discomfort, a degree of embarrassment and a certain measure of privacy. Nothing worse than what you have already suffered at our hands, and judging by your responses that was not entirely disagreeable . . .'

Miss Kyle grinned as Vanessa blushed shamefully.

'And think of the sensational story you'll have to tell,' Shiller continued. '"MY MONTH OF HELL AS A PUPPET OF SEX TRADERS!" or perhaps: "SECRETS OF THE UNDERGROUND SLAVE WORLD!" I'm sure you can do better. I'm not asking you to like or trust us, merely to be pragmatic.' Shiller smiled almost mischievously and spread her arms wide. 'And you can still console yourself with the hope that despite our precautions you might be able to escape our control before the

66

month is up and bring this whole perverted edifice crashing down on our heads. That's worth a little inconvenience, isn't it?'

Vanessa thought furiously. It was a bizarre offer, but she didn't see she had any choice. It wouldn't be pleasant, but it was better than staying in this cell. Of course she knew they were playing for time, hoping she might have second thoughts about exposing them. They were clever – she'd give them that – certainly not crude thugs and no doubt good at manipulating people. Maybe they'd even convinced themselves what they were doing down here was acceptable. But they couldn't fool her.

'All right, I'll give you your month,' she said cautiously. 'What happens next?'

'First we shall eat. It's lunchtime and you must be hungry after your morning's exertions.'

Vanessa suddenly realised she was ravenous. It seemed a lifetime since she had last eaten.

'Then,' Shiller continued, 'we shall rehearse what you will say to your editor . . .'

Just after five-thirty, dressed once more in her overalls, Vanessa walked out of the main entrance of the Shiller building into the hazy sunlight of a London afternoon. She coughed as the dust and exhaust fumes caught in her throat. The air had been fresher down on level B3.

Taking a firm grip on her toolbox, its camera now wiped of all incriminating evidence, she made her way through the bustle of office workers heading for home. She kept her eyes lowered, acutely aware of the phalluses locked deep inside her, shifting slightly as she walked, and the blush the sensation brought to her cheeks. Of course it was illogical, since nobody would ever guess its cause, or that she was a living puppet controlled by unseen powers. That perverse thought conjured up a guilty twinge of pleasure that she hated to admit to herself was natural.

She turned down a side street and saw Enwright's car waiting as arranged.

'Remember, Puppet,' Shiller's voice spoke in her ear, 'do it just as we rehearsed.'

'Yes, Monitor,' she replied meekly.

She had toyed with the idea of risking punishment to try to warn Enwright something was wrong, but had decided against it. Shiller would be ready for such a move right now, expecting her to give into the natural temptation, and would no doubt react quickly. Better to wait until her invisible masters were off-guard. She would only get one chance, so it had to be a good one.

She opened the passenger door and slid into the seat. The dashboard was littered with discarded plastic coffee cups and fast-food wrappers. Enwright, half a doughnut in his mouth, almost choked.

'Vanessa! Are you OK? You've been in there all day. What happened?'

A sudden and unaccustomed feeling of elevated self-worth flowed though her. If only he knew. How would he feel with a couple of live-wired rubber prongs stuffed up him and twenty electric needles pressing into his nipples? No other reporter on the *Globe* could take what she had today and still be this cool.

But she said none of this. The signal tone sounded in her ears, warning her that she was to repeat exactly what she heard next. She let Shiller's words flow though her and out of her mouth. It was not so hard when she didn't try to resist.

'I'm fine, Mr Enwright,' she said brightly. 'Could you take me back home, please, instead of the office. I'll explain on the way.'

As the car wove its way through the traffic towards Richmond, Vanessa related the fiction Shiller had concocted.

'I got in all right and cloned a swipe card as planned. I spent a couple of hours poking my nose in everywhere possible, but didn't find anything. It's a big place. It might take days to search properly, let alone go through files and things. I was just about to give it up as a waste of time when I heard one of the women in the personnel department complaining about a glitch on her computer. Before she could call IT, I offered to look at it.

'The problem was nothing really. I could see how to fix it in two minutes. But I spun it out and got friendly with her. When she went to fetch us some coffee, I dug into the system. My application was still on file, together with the posts they were filling. I cancelled the offer they were going to make to somebody else and substituted my details. With any luck an e-mail offering me a job on Shillers' house magazine should be waiting for me when I get home.

'Working on the magazine is a good position. It means I can move around to all the departments pretty freely and nobody will suspect if I ask a lot of questions. I'll be able to find out for sure if Shillers have anything to hide.'

For a split second she resisted the urge to yell: 'They're slave traffickers!'

'You've got nerve!' he exclaimed with a chuckle. 'Sir Harvey was right about you. Bloody well done, Vanessa!'

The phalluses pulsed inside her as a reward for acting like an obedient puppet as she enjoyed the warmth of Enwright's praise. For a moment the sensual pleasure seemed to merge with Enwright's words and she felt wonderful. Then a reaction set in and her high became a low.

What had she been thinking? It was all false. She was lying to Enwright. How could she let herself be used like this? She realised her emotional state was going up and down like a roller coaster. She'd been shocked and caned and screwed too many times today. Now it was all catching up with her.

Shiller must have seen what was happening through the bio-feedback, for she found herself saying: 'God I'm tired! Do you mind if I close my eyes for a bit? It's been a long day.'

'Sure, Vanessa,' Enwright said. 'You rest. You deserve it.

Vanessa dozed uneasily, only rousing herself when Enwright pulled up the car outside the slightly shabby nineteen-thirties block of flats in Richmond where she resided on the third floor.

Vanessa wearily climbed the stairs and latch-keyed herself into her flat. Enwright followed at her heels, looking more eager than Vanessa now felt. When she had left that morning she had been so full of nervous excitement, but all she'd done was get caught and turned into a helpless, deceitful puppet. How did she know Shiller would keep her word? Would she ever escape her clutches? No, she must not give into that sort of thinking. She was back in her own home. Surely she could find some way of escaping her controllers.

'The e-mail should be waiting in your inbox,' Shiller said in her ear. 'Let Enwright see it for himself.'

Vanessa crossed to the desk tucked into one corner of the small sitting room and opened up her computer. In a few moments the letter from Shillers appeared on the screen. Enwright leaned over her shoulder to read it.

'Hmm ... New position in expanded department ... confirming salary and benefits ... blah, blah ... (Hey, that's not bad!) ... short notice ... can you go for an induction meeting tomorrow? They don't waste any time, do they? Well, the sooner the better. Looks like you're in.'

'I don't think you or anybody from the paper should call here while I'm working for Shillers.' Vanessa said, at Shiller's instruction. 'In fact, we'd better not meet at all. And I won't call you unless I've something worthwhile to report ...'

Vanessa trailed off.

Hanging on the sitting-room wall was a mirror set in a natural wood frame. It looked perfectly ordinary, except that it hadn't been there when she had left the flat a little over twelve hours earlier.

'That's sensible,' Enwright agreed. 'Can't be too careful now you're undercover. Well, I'll get back and report to Sir Harvey. And, once again, well done.'

'Thanks, Mr Enwright,' Vanessa recited somewhat distractedly. 'I'll do my best to find out the truth about Shillers.'

She showed Enwright out and with relief closed the front door behind him. There was, she now noticed, another new mirror hanging in the hall.

'Your neighbours believe you have just had a new security system installed,' Shiller said, anticipating her question. 'That's not too far from the truth, since our home security division did the work.'

Of course. Shiller had taken her keys out of the cell that morning and had asked if she lived alone. Knowing her name they could track down her address. There had been plenty of time to make copies of her keys, fix up her flat and return the originals to her.

'I suppose there are cameras hidden behind the mirrors?'

'Naturally. We must be sure you don't betray us in any way. I said you would only have to wear the close monitoring devices in public, but you could hardly expect us to allow you unrestricted freedom at home. In case you wonder, we have also installed taps on your phone and computer. You must also show us any letter you write before posting it.'

There was another mirror in her kitchen. With a sinking feeling, Vanessa made for her bedroom. Sure enough there was a new mirror on the wall facing her bed. The standing three-panel mirror on her dressing table had also been replaced; while on the table itself was an adaptor and battery recharger unit she'd never seen before. It was currently plugged into a black rubber collar.

'This power unit will also recharge the control and monitor devices you are currently wearing,' Shiller explained. 'The house collar is for use in your flat. It incorporates a self-contained, two-way audio link and will also monitor your speech and administer punishment if required. You have several high-necked tops or scarves which will conceal it adequately from any casual callers.'

'You've been through my wardrobe!' Vanessa exclaimed. It was quite trivial compared to the indignities she had already suffered, but at that moment it seemed a shocking invasion of her privacy.

'We had to check your flat and possessions to ensure our security measures will be adequate,' Shiller explained. 'This way your freedom of movement will only be restricted by the minimum necessary for our needs.'

'I'm supposed to be grateful for that?'

'We are not seeking your gratitude, Vanessa, only your understanding, though you may like to consider how much more onerous your situation could be. The house collar, for instance, is also fully waterproof, so you may shower or bathe with it in place.'

'I suppose I have to sleep in it as well?'

'No, though you will of course be secured to your bed while you sleep.'

'What do you mean: "secured"?'

'See for yourself.'

At first glance her pine-framed double bed looked to Vanessa as she had left it that morning. But when she felt around the back behind the headboard she found holster-like pockets containing cuffs connected to plastic-sheathed wire cords. More holsters had been fitted under the sides and foot of the bed, while some larger device concealed in a long casing was bolted to the bottom of the frame between its front legs. A power cable ran from under the bed to where it plugged into the nearest wall socket.

Vanessa sighed. She should have known escaping Shiller's clutches would not be that easy.

'I wish to test your house collar,' Shiller said. 'Remove your overalls . . .'

Vanessa stripped down to her new underwear. The locks of the earphone unit and choker band opened remotely, and she unhooked the devices with relief.

Shiller's voice now issued from the house collar. 'Put this on before removing your bra and thong.'

Vanessa unplugged the collar from the charger and gingerly closed it about her neck, where it locked with a click. It was sheathed in soft vinyl and was not exactly uncomfortable, but she could feel metal contacts pressing against her skin.

Electric needles stabbed briefly into her neck and she gasped in pain.

'The collar is active,' Shiller confirmed. 'Do I need to demonstrate its full power, Puppet?'

'No, Monitor,' Vanessa said quickly.

'Now you may remove your bra and thong,' Shiller said.

Gritting her teeth, only too aware of the hidden cameras watching her from behind the spy mirrors, Vanessa unhooked her bra and then awkwardly stripped off the thong. The front phallus slid out of its slippery sheath easily enough, but she had to tug to get the head of the rear plug free of the tight ring of her anus. By the time it popped out she was blushing furiously.

At no point in the change-over had she been free of one or the other control systems, but at least she was no longer carrying a spy camera around with her. Suddenly feeling exposed and oddly vulnerable, she grabbed her dressing gown from the back of the door and pulled it tightly about her.

Shiller's operatives had thoughtfully left a new pack of antiseptic wipes on her dressing table. Following Shiller's directions, she used them to clean the phalluses, still warm from their intimate contact with her, and then plugged the devices, linked by the spine cable, into the charger.

'If that's all, Monitor,' she said wearily when she was done, 'I really need to go to the loo.'

'You may go wherever you wish,' Shiller replied simply.

There was a new heated, self-demisting mirror hanging over the bathroom basin.

'No privacy!' Vanessa shouted. 'Not even when I'm on the toilet, or taking a shower?'

'No. Otherwise you might, for instance, try throwing a message out of the window. Hard though it may seem to believe, you will get used to it. For now, accept that you have no choice.'

Vanessa sagged, feeling utterly beaten and close to

tears. They still had her in their control as completely as though she was back in the cell.

She hunched down over the toilet with head bowed, eyes closed and thighs squeezed together. It took an effort to relax enough to let her water pass. It was less humiliating than her enforced disgrace in the cell, but not by much.

Vanessa microwaved a ready meal for herself, uncorked a bottle of wine and ate and drank in front of the television with the sound turned up a notch higher than usual, trying to drown her thoughts. She said and did nothing to invite any response from Shiller, kept her eyes turned away from the new mirror and tried to pretend her collar did not exist. She watched for four hours straight, and afterwards could not remember a single programme she had seen.

Following a brief shower and another embarrassing session on the toilet, she was mentally drained and desperately in need of sleep. Standing before her deceptively normal-looking bed, she asked aloud: 'What do I do now?'

Miss Kyle's voice came from her collar. 'I have taken over monitor duty from the Director,' she announced. 'I noticed you've been lax in using the proper responses. While this was new to you the Director was being lenient, but that period is over. Anybody controlling you is to be addressed as "Monitor", while you are "Puppet", remember.'

A warning flicker of pain coursed through her collar.

'Yes, Monitor,' Vanessa said quickly.

'What are you?'

'I'm your Puppet, Monitor.'

'From now on any slips will be punished, you understand?'

'Yes, Monitor.'

'Now take off your gown and turn back your bed covers . . .'

Vanessa obeyed.

'Pull the lower corner cuffs out of their holsters . . .'

The cables drew out easily after the cuffs. They were lined with rubber and banded in metal, fitted with integral locking catches.

'There's an anal lock-plug in a holster next to the left-hand cuff. Draw that out and lay it on the bed . . .'

Vanessa gulped as she drew out what looked a slim metal dildo ringed about its middle by a broad band of rubber, mounted on the end of a thick electric cable.

'If you open your bedside drawer you will find a pair of handcuffs, lubricating jelly and a new vibrator. The model you were using was far too small . . .'

Cringing in shame, Vanessa took out the items as instructed. The vibrator was a black rubber monster.

'Lubricate the vibrator and the anal plug . . .'

Vanessa did so. Was she going to have both these things inside her?

'Now sit on the bed with your legs spread and cuff your ankles . . .'

Trembling, Vanessa obeyed. The cuffs locked shut automatically.

'Cuff your hands in front of you,' Miss Kyle said.

Biting her lip, Vanessa clicked the handcuffs about her wrists.

'Take hold of the anal plug, bend your knees, lie back and push it well up your rear . . .'

Vanessa rebelled. 'No, please, Monitor! I can't escape. I can't give you away. You don't need to do this – uhhh!'

Her collar had stung like a ring of angry wasps.

'Stuff it up your bum-hole this instant or you'll get far worse!' Miss Kyle warned her.

Sobbing, Vanessa obeyed, forcing the metal slug up inside her rear. When it was fully inserted she felt the rubber band around its middle expand like a small balloon, filling the tunnel of her rectum and forming a plug too large to be expelled. The pressure was transmitted through to her vagina. Perversely she felt herself responding to this strange new stimulation.

'We can't allow you to become over-confident, Puppet,' Miss Kyle said. You'll be working in a subservient position in the company, so you'll have to show proper respect. Think of this as a lesson in humility . . .'

Vanessa yelped in pain as the bloated anal plug delivered a jolt of electricity to her rear passage. A warm slickness began to seep between her labia . . .

'Remove your collar, Puppet,' Miss Kyle said. 'Hang it over the bedpost where you can reach it in the morning . . .'

Trembling, Vanessa did so. Under the bed a motor whirred softly and her legs were drawn out wide, allowing anybody watching through the wall-mirror camera an unobstructed view of the cleft of her vulva and her plugged anus.

'Pick up the vibrator and lie back,' Miss Kyle said.

Vanessa started in surprise even as she obeyed. Now Miss Kyle's voice seemed to be coming from the bed itself. The whole thing had been wired up.

'Now you're going to give yourself a proper screwing for our entertainment. There are a lot of us watching right now. We can see every hair on your pubes. Does that excite you?'

Vanessa groaned and shook her head.

'Really? Then why are your nipples standing up and pussy lips wet? Now these are the rules: the faster and harder you screw yourself, the less often I'll have to give you a shock up your arse. They'll stop altogether when you come, but don't think you can fool me by faking it!'

The anal plug gave her a warning jolt. Desperately, Vanessa turned on the vibrator. Its head began to buzz and shaft pump and oscillate. Sobbing, she clutched it between her cuffed hands, screwed up her eyes and thrust it between her legs as though plunging a knife into her pubic gash.

Her vulva bulged as the thing slid up into her vaginal passage, pressing back against the bulge of her anal plug. Then she was completely filled, front and rear. Gasping and sobbing, she drove it in and out of her wet hole. Surely she could not come like this, knowing strangers were watching her every move.

Ahhh!

Another jolt up her rear made her pump the vibrator faster.

She had to pretend she was alone, playing a sex game. She'd put on the cuffs as a joke, to add a bit of excitement. A little bondage fantasy, that's all it was. Her unseen controllers were imaginary . . . this was all innocent fun.

Yes, that felt good! What nicer way to unwind after a hard day's work than a good screwing. This new vibrator was great.

She was making a wet patch on her sheets but that didn't matter.

A fresh jolt up her rear almost shattered her fantasy, but she rallied quickly.

That was her other new toy, a little electric butt-plug. It didn't hurt really, not mingled with the knot of pleasure tying itself about her pussy, which was going to burst at any moment . . .

She bucked wildly, hunching forwards, grunting and whimpering with pleasure, legs straining against her ankle cuffs, frigging herself frantically with the vibrator, trying to drain every last drop from the explosion of raw joy that was tearing through her loins.

'That was a fine show you put on, Puppet,' Miss Kyle's voice said, as though from a great distance.

Vanessa stirred groggily, her fantasy melting away with the last warm waves of the afterglow.

What had she done? How could she have come so intensely?

She felt the ankle cuff cables slacken, allowing her to close her legs and pull up the duvet. The anal plug remained locked inside her. Miserably she turned over, curled up and buried her face in her pillow, sliding her cuffed hands down to cup her sticky, aching vagina.

The bedside light went out by itself. They had wired up her whole flat!

'The monitor system is going on automatic now,' Miss Kyle said. 'If you were thinking of calling to your neighbours it will activate the anal plug, so I suggest you get a good night's sleep, Puppet. Tomorrow's going to be a busy day . . .'

Five

'Wake up, Puppet!'

It was a strange man's voice. It roused Vanessa from a crazy dream about slave traders under a London office building . . .

The anal plug gave her a jolt that brought her back to the awful reality. Cool morning light was edging the curtains. She was lying naked on stained sheets, duvet tumbled to the floor, with her wrists and ankles cuffed and a slug of rubber and metal stuck up her backside.

Her new Monitor didn't give her any time to gather her wits.

'Put on your house collar . . . now deflating anal plug . . . pull it out . . . ankle cuffs unlocked . . . get them undone and stowed neatly . . . wipe the plug clean before you put it away . . . move yourself, Puppet!'

In a daze she scrambled to obey, gasping out: 'Yes, Monitor!' at each command.

The key to her handcuffs was fastened to a chain screwed to the skirting board in the corner of the room, where she could not possibly reach it while secured to her bed.

'Get that exercise mat out of the wardrobe . . . into the sitting room . . . step proudly, chest out, nipples up, don't slouch!'

Still naked except for her house collar, Vanessa was marched into the sitting room. She dragged the coffee table aside and laid out her exercise mat in plain view of the mirror camera.

'I see from the records you didn't have your bowels open last night,' Monitor said. 'Can't have that. Got to keep regular . . .'

He put her through ten minutes of star jumps, toe-touching, running on the spot, squats and stretches. His relentless driving tone reminded her of a PE teacher she'd once had, except for his language: '. . . get those pretty tits bouncing, Puppet . . . legs apart, cunt wide, show me what you had for dinner last night!'

Finally, lathered in sweat, she was marched into the bathroom.

'Sit on the toilet, legs apart, hands clasped behind your neck . . . permission to relieve yourself . . . now!'

She had no time to think, only to obey. The pee gushed out of her, followed by the contents of her bowels, loosened by the exercise. A sick thrill coursed through her as she realised he was watching all of this.

'That's how I want to see you perform every morning,' Monitor said approvingly. 'Wipe clean . . . good. Now take the flush gun and greaser out of the basin cupboard and plug the adaptor into the shower hose . . .'

To Vanessa's dismay, a device similar to the one Miss Kyle had used to wash her out was resting under her hand-basin. At Monitor's direction she had to plug it in, then squat over the loo again. After flushing out her bowels she pulled the trigger that squirted a measured slug of special grease into her rectum.

'From now on, you do this without fail whenever you void your bowels,' Monitor said. 'A slave-girl

81

must keep every orifice clean and ready for use at all times, understand?'

'Yes, Monitor.'

'Now into the shower . . .'

She showered with the curtain back, so that he could see she washed herself thoroughly. 'Brush harder . . . use more soap!' Obediently she used a warm jet from the shower-head to wash out her vagina, followed by an ice-cold douche to tone and tighten. 'Turn round, bend over, pull back your bum cheeks . . . is the rim of that hole as clean as it is inside?'

'Yes, Monitor,' she said desperately.

'You don't want to have a dirty bottom first day in a new job, do you?'

'No, Monitor,' she agreed.

Towelled dry, teeth cleaned, but still naked, she was marched into the kitchen and directed to make a breakfast of fresh orange juice, two slices of toast and a small bowl of cereal. She ate sitting very straight, chewing every mouthful thoroughly before swallowing, nervously brushing crumbs from her bare breasts.

Breakfast over, she was returned to her bedroom, where she removed her house collar and put on her control underwear, choker collar and earphone. The pre-greasing helped, but still she strained to force its head through her anal ring.

'You can do it, Puppet,' Monitor said encouragingly. 'Even a tight bum like yours can easily stretch that wide . . . don't fight it . . . relax . . . tell yourself it belongs in there . . .'

At last the phallus popped into her, leaving her gasping in relief and for a few seconds feeling she had achieved a minor triumph.

Leaving her house collar recharging, she was directed to put on a blouse and light two-piece suit, but no stockings. A new pair of silver toe-post sandals now rested beside her own shoes. She didn't ask how they had got there. She put them on doubtfully, but they were her size and very comfortable.

Monitor directed her to use minimal make-up. 'You don't need it, Puppet.' She had to agree. The vigorous exercise and her continuing state of embarrassment had put what would pass for a healthy blush on her cheeks.

She gathered up her bag and keys, and stood to attention before the hall mirror so that Monitor could give her a final inspection.

'Now you look like a proper Shiller girl,' he said.

Staring at her reflection, Vanessa had to admit she was not the same woman who had left the flat the previous morning. She half expected to look shattered, but instead there was a subtle difference about her. Of course, the brightness of her eyes must be due to incipient tears, and the new tilt of her hips down to the phalluses plugging her front and rear, but perversely she looked more alive and alert than she had for a long time.

She got the shakes as she turned her red VW into the entrance of the Shiller car park.

She had no idea where to go or what would happen to her inside the building. Everything was a sham. How was she even supposed to identify herself?

But Monitor said: 'They're expecting you. Drive right in . . .'

Sure enough, the gate guard raised the barrier and waved her through without hesitation.

Vanessa blushed. Did he know who she was and what she was wearing under her suit?

The guard at the inner gate certainly did. When she pulled up by his kiosk he grinned broadly in at her

through the open window. 'Oh, yes, Miss Buckingham, isn't it?' He handed her a windshield sticker.
'Here's your car pass. I think you know the way.' He
looked her up and down with carnal approval. 'I'm
looking forward to seeing a lot more of you . . .'

She parked in level B2 and, directed by Monitor,
made her way to the lift. A new camera had been
installed overlooking the lift doors.

'One of the new security measures we've taken
since your visit yesterday,' Monitor explained.

The doors opened automatically and she stepped
inside.

'The magazine offices are on the fifth floor,'
Monitor said, 'but first you go down to B3.'

'The magazine job's real, Monitor?'

'The Director said so. She thinks it will give you
the best opportunity to see what we're really like.'

'Then why have I got to go down to B3 first, Monitor?'

'To change, of course. Go on . . .'

Vanessa pressed B2 three times. The lift descended.
'What have I got to change into, Monitor?'

'Appropriate dress for indoors, Puppet . . .'

The doors opened and she stepped out into the
secret level. There was no coffle of naked chained
slaves waiting for the lift this time, but as Vanessa
looked round, she saw a slave-girl tied to a railing
post on the veranda of the nearest chalet.

She'd been bound in rope from head to toe like a
mummy, so that she was utterly immobile. A strip of
cloth covered her eyes and a wad of it filled her
mouth, both held in place by more loops of rope
binding her head hard against the wooden post. Her
arms were drawn back until her elbows almost
touched. More ropes crossed her body between and
around her breasts, making them unnaturally prominent and cutting into her flesh. Her nipples stood out

in fat red-brown cones. A length of rope plunged into her vaginal cleft, forcing her outer labia to bulge and separate. It was stained dark with her juices.

How could they treat women like that, Vanessa wondered in despair? There was no way it could be consensual.

A warning jolt from her anal probe forced Vanessa to drag her eyes away from the unfortunate woman. She was directed to the block on the other side of the wide central alley from the cells and mews shops. Set in its end wall was a row of low openings closed by wire-mesh gates.

'You go in that way,' Monitor said. 'On your hands and knees.'

'Why can't I use a proper door, Monitor?'

'These are the doors slaves use,' he said simply. 'Inside you will stay on your hands and knees unless told otherwise. Mr Jarvis is expecting you. You will respectfully kiss his boots and announce yourself. He'll put you into something more suitable . . .'

Biting her lip, Vanessa got down on her hands and knees and pushed through the gate. Beyond was a short wire-mesh tunnel, carpeted with foam-rubber matting. Pushing through a second mesh gate, she found herself in a lobby with several exits leading off it, both slave-size gates and ordinary doors. A large, red-faced man in a security guard's uniform was seated at an open, glass-topped desk. Still on her hands and knees, Vanessa shuffled over to him, kissed the polished toes of his boots, and said: 'I'm . . . Vanessa Buckingham, Mr Jarvis.'

'Oh, yes. I've been expecting you,' he said, smiling not unkindly down at her through the glass top.

Monitor spoke in Vanessa's ear and she relayed the message: 'Monitor says he's handing me over to you, Mr Jarvis.'

She realised it made her sound like a parcel.

'I've got her, Monitor,' Jarvis said. He picked up a device like a TV remote and pointed it at Vanessa. Her front phallus tingled a warning.

'You'll give me no trouble, will you, girl?'

'No, Mr Jarvis.'

He took her bag. 'You won't need any of this. You'll get it back this evening. Right, now let's get you changed. This way.'

He got up and walked through a side door and she shuffled after him through the slave gate beside it. On the other side was a small changing room. Jarvis stopped before one of a row of metal lockers. Disconcertingly Vanessa saw it was already labelled with her name.

'You'll keep your street clothes and control kit in here,' Jarvis said, opening the locker and putting in her bag, then taking out a plain metal collar and belt linked to a set of slave chains. 'But inside the building you'll wear these.'

Vanessa gulped. 'Is that all, Mr Jarvis?'

Jarvis smiled sweetly. 'Oh, no. I could find a whole lot more chains and straps and tie you over a bench and give you a good hiding for cheeking me. Of course that's all, girl! Now on your feet and strip. Everything but your sandals.'

Hastily Vanessa obeyed.

Jarvis pressed a button on his controller and the locks of her underwear opened. He made her bend over and clasp her ankles so that he could pull out her anal plug. Keeping her in this position for a moment, he examined the glistening film she had deposited over the plugs and then patted and stroked her bottom appreciatively.

'If you weren't due to see the editor, I'd have some fun right now. Never mind. I'll have these all laundered and recharged for you by this evening, so you'll stay nice and fresh.' He gave her a smack. 'Stand straight, hands clasped behind your head!'

Vanessa obeyed and Jarvis locked the collar, belt and cuffs on to her. The chains linking the wrist cuffs to her belt allowed her just enough slack to reach her mouth. Snap hooks dangled from the sides and back of the belt. She realised her silver sandals matched her new restraints and wondered if it had been planned that way.

Jarvis clipped a key-card chain to her collar. 'This'll allow you to move between here and the secure zone offices upstairs, but it won't open any external doors. Your key code is 6969. Think you can remember that?'

'Yes, Mr Jarvis.'

'Every day, you report down here on arrival and last thing before you leave, understand?'

'Yes, Mr Jarvis.'

He put his big hand on her head and pressed her down on to her knees. 'Somebody's waiting outside to take you upstairs. Now off you go . . .'

Steeling herself, Vanessa bent and kissed his boots again. 'Thank you, Mr Jarvis,' she whispered.

Outside under the false blue concrete sky she rose gratefully to her feet. Standing by the bound girl on the veranda of the chalet, still dressed in her body stocking, was Miss Kyle. She was idly toying with the captive girl's taut breasts.

When she saw Vanessa emerge, she gave the girl's nipples a final tweak, pointed to Vanessa and crooked her finger. Miserably, Vanessa walked over to her. After the enforced intimacy they had shared yesterday and the remote ordeal she had put her through last night, she found being in Miss Kyle's presence both embarrassing and intimidating.

Miss Kyle looked her up and down in approval. 'That's better. You'll feel much more comfortable now you're properly dressed.' She turned and led the way back to the lifts.

Vanessa, instinctively trying to cover her breasts with one hand and pubes with the other, finally found her tongue and said: 'I don't call this dressed, Miss Kyle.'

'It's hardly less than I usually wear. Why are you covering yourself up? You've got a lovely body.'

Was she truly without shame or any degree of self-consciousness, Vanessa wondered? 'Thanks, Miss Kyle, but I'm not used to showing it off to strangers.'

'Not outside,' Miss Kyle agreed. 'But in here the rules are different. You'll only attract more attention like that.'

Vanessa took a deep breath and dropped her hands. She was probably right. But it wouldn't be easy.

Back in the lift, Miss Kyle punched the button for the fifth floor. As they ascended, she said: 'I think you'll like working on the magazine. That way you can snoop about and ask questions to your heart's content.' She smiled mockingly. 'That's what you planned to do here, isn't it?'

Once again Vanessa vowed she'd make Shillers pay. But first she had to get through day one in a new office, which was hard enough even if you weren't arriving naked in slave chains.

The lift deposited them in a lobby, which opened on to a floor of offices partitioned by panels of banded frosted glass and filled with people hunched over their desks, talking on phones or peering at computer screens. In the face of such mundane normality, Vanessa had a fresh attack of nerves and acute shame. If Miss Kyle hadn't been with her she would have turned and run.

But Miss Kyle was leading her down the corridor and she had to follow, meekly bowing her head. Her chains jangled as she swung her arms, so she held them straight down to her sides, drawing them tightly across her lower stomach. It seemed a horribly slavish posture but at least it was neat and silenced her chains.

Nobody made any overt response to her presence. Shiller staff were apparently used to having naked slave-girls running round their offices. Nevertheless, she was aware of many eyes following her progress and appraising her body. At least it's not as bad as what I was going through this time yesterday morning, she kept telling herself. Curiously, this thought gave her strength.

They stopped outside a door marked: ZARA FULTON: EDITOR. Miss Kyle pointed and Vanessa went down on to her hands and knees while she knocked. A woman's voice said: 'Come in,' and they entered.

Zara Fulton swivelled her chair round from her desk to look at them. She was a tall, full-busted woman in her mid-forties, still looking very attractive, with a mass of dark wavy hair and narrow blue-grey eyes.

'This is Vanessa Buckingham,' Miss Kyle announced.

'Thanks, Denise,' Zara said.

'Enjoy her,' Miss Kyle said, closing the door behind her.

Zara extended her legs to Vanessa and pointed to the toes of her shoes. Feeling slightly sick, Vanessa shuffled forwards and kissed the bright-red polished leather.

Zara patted her head, then stood up and walked round Vanessa, looking her over. Stooping, she ran her hands over her outthrust bottom, then slipped her fingers down her buttock cleft into the warm nest between her thighs, eliciting a stifled gasp. Grasping a handful of Vanessa's hair, she pulled her back on to her heels.

'Hands on thighs and legs apart, girl,' she said firmly, and Vanessa obeyed.

Zara cupped and squeezed Vanessa's breasts and examined her face. 'Well, you're a pretty thing,' she declared. 'You'll address me as "Mistress Editor", do you understand?'

'Yes, Mistress Editor.'

Zara raised an elegant mocking eyebrow. 'The Director tells me you want to destroy our company.'

'Only that part of it that turns girls into sex-slaves, Mistress Editor,' Vanessa said defiantly.

'And you don't accept they're all willing slaves?'

'I can't believe there could be so many of them, Mistress Editor.'

'Well, we'll see if we can't enlighten you on that score. Meanwhile, for the next month you're going to be a reporter for our house magazine. Actually there are two magazines: the public and the private, you might call them . . .'

She turned her computer screen round so that Vanessa could see it and called up a new file, which displayed a magazine front page. Under the title *Datumline* was an image of a white-coated scientist, with the sub-heading: 'Shiller researcher on course for Nobel Prize?'

'*Datumline* covers the official activities of Shillers and its subsidiaries,' Zara explained. 'New projects, personal interest stories about our staff, charitable work, future business trends, feedback and advice section, and so on. It goes out to all our subdivisions and a few of our larger customers. I understand you're a reporter on the *Daily Globe*. Still, you should be able to contribute something . . .'

From the distaste with which she had spoken her newspaper's name, Zara sounded doubtful whether Vanessa was fit to write for a school newspaper.

'However, your main concern will be reporting for our other magazine, with a more select circulation . . .'

Zara called up a new front page. Under the title *Girlflesh News* was a picture of a naked girl in a green collar. She was kneeling in much the same posture as Vanessa, except that her arms were bound behind her back and a chain was clipped to her collar that looped away out of shot. The sub-heading read: 'Lorna 7 of Jade Chain breaks One Hour record!' She was smiling shyly.

'*Girlflesh* is a newer title, of course, but it's very popular,' Zara continued. 'In fact the scope of the articles is not so different. New restraint devices and methods of training, personal interest stories about the girls, the amount they contribute to our charitable functions, projected expansion of the slave business, feedback from customers, personal advice, etc. So, do you think you're up to writing for it, girl?'

'Even the name of the thing makes me sick, Mistress Editor.'

'The Director said you were honest, though not quite how bluntly. Still, you should appreciate why the title is what it is. We trade in girlflesh, not euphemisms. It gives the girls a chance to read about themselves and things most relevant to their lives.'

Vanessa blinked. 'They read it, Mistress Editor?'

'Of course. Sportsmen read sports magazines, engineers read technical journals, so why shouldn't slave-girls read about slavery? And now we'll have one on the staff as well. Your byline might be:

"Vanessa: The Slave Reporter". I'm sure you appreciate the pun.'

Vanessa clenched her teeth. 'Very amusing, Mistress Editor.'

'But it's what you are. On the Director's orders, I'm treating you as I would any new slave. She assumes you would suspect we were trying to influence you if we made your time here too easy, and that you'd rather be treated honestly. Well, you certainly won't get an easy ride in this office. I expect professional work from you, whatever you think of the subject matter. Do you understand?

'Yes, Mistress Editor,' Vanessa said grimly.

Zara extended her leg and lifted Vanessa's chin with the tip of her shoe. 'It won't be all bad, girl. You might actually enjoy yourself if you let go of your prejudices a little.'

'I don't think of wanting people to be free as a prejudice, Mistress Editor.'

Zara grinned. 'It might surprise you to know I'm a great believer in freedom myself. Even the freedom not to be free. Now, I'd better show you where you'll be working. It's just next door. Follow me like a good pet . . .'

On her hands and knees, Vanessa shuffled out after Zara into the main office. Her chains seemed to be jingling loud as sleigh bells with each padding step. She fixed her attention on Zara's shoes as she felt a dozen pairs of eyes watching her. At least the outer windows of the office were mirror glass, muting the daylight and giving her some assurance that she was not exposed to the gaze of half the city.

In the middle of the office, Zara halted and announced loudly: 'We have a new temporary member of our staff: a somewhat reluctant trainee slave called Vanessa . . .' Zara grasped Vanessa by the hair and dragged her to her feet so that they could all see her clearly. 'You should all have read the memo about her exploits yesterday and the new security measures in place . . .'

Curious and angry mutters mingled as they circled the room. Vanessa cringed in sudden shame and fear.

'The Director's made a deal with her. Vanessa's going to find out the truth about our girlflesh business before deciding whether to report us. She'll be here for the next month. Treat her like any other slave-girl: firm but fair. Right, that's all.'

There was an empty work-station in one corner. Zara pointed and Vanessa scrambled into the chair, trying to huddle away out of sight of the other staff.

At Zara's direction, Vanessa turned on the computer and entered her access code. 'That won't allow you to post our secrets over the internet or send e-mails, in case you're tempted to try,' Zara warned her wryly. 'We use standard editing software. You should have no problem with it. I suggest you take until lunchtime looking through back copies of *Datumline* and *Girlflesh* to get a feel of our house style. Then I've got an idea for your first article.'

'Yes, Mistress Editor.'

'And address everybody here respectfully as Sir or Madam if they speak to you. Remember, in this building you're a slave.'

'I'm not likely to forget, Mistress Editor,' Vanessa said.

Zara smiled and left.

Vanessa tried to hide behind her screen and the small rack of tidy shelving that backed her desk. Maybe she could bring in a few plants to build a bigger barrier? Ten minutes went by and nobody came over or spoke to her. Apparently they were ignoring her . . . like you'd ignore any naked chained woman in the corner of an office.

She tried to focus on the magazine files.

Datumline was no problem. Bright and go-getting, yet ultimately reassuring and reliable, which was the normal goal of corporate identity projection. After half an hour's study she knew she could write articles for that in her sleep. *Girlflesh News* was something else.

It wasn't just the pictures of naked chained slave-girls being put through their paces, or the freaky bondage equipment it featured. She'd seen worse before. It was the underlying assumption that it was all perfectly natural and normal that was so disturbing.

There were features about 'assignments' that various 'chains' had been sent on, with names and places reduced to anonymous initials, illustrated by carefully cropped photos. Even more bizarre were the quotes from 'customer' feedback.

'Your girls were thoroughly enjoyed by one and all, and showed excellent endurance . . .'

'A wonderfully novel sex show . . .'

'. . . responded very well to punishment . . .'

Vanessa wanted to turn away in disgust, yet there was a horrible fascination about it all. And somewhere underneath, she knew, must be the truth.

Zara came back for her at lunchtime.

'Did you bring anything to eat with you?' she asked.

Vanessa realised she had completely forgotten about food. 'No, Mistress Editor. Isn't there a canteen or snack machines? Oh, my purse is in my bag . . . down in the locker room.'

'There's a restaurant and vending machines, but don't worry about money. I've already brought you something. I thought we'd eat in my office while I tell you about your first article.'

Obediently, Vanessa followed Zara back to her office.

There was a packed lunch opened on Zara's desk. On the floor was a large dog-food bowl, filled with diced cheese, apple, bread and a scattering of nuts.

'Now I want to see you eat neatly like a good doggy and not make a mess on the carpet,' Zara said, pulling Vanessa's arms behind her and clipping her cuff rings to the snap-hook on the back of her belt. She produced a rubber band and used it to tie back Vanessa's thick mane of hair, then pushed her down on to her knees.

Miserably, Vanessa shuffled forwards until her face was over the bowl. She had to spread her knees wide and stick out her rear to stay balanced. If anybody came in they'd have a view right up her bum-cleft, she thought. Dipping her head, her nipples brushing the carpet, she began to nibble carefully at the food. Zara sat down at her desk and watched her in silence, while eating from her own lunchbox.

'Good girl,' Zara said, after a few minutes. 'You see, it isn't that hard. Now, about your first article. This afternoon there's an induction ceremony for a new chain of girls who are going to start their basic training. That'll also take a month, so it ties in rather neatly with your time with us. They'll be graduating just when you'll be deciding whether to turn us all in. I hope all their hard work won't be for nothing.'

Vanessa gulped down a mouthful, looked up and said: 'Graduating? You make it sound like finishing college, Mistress Editor.'

'Well, they are awarded a diploma at a proper ceremony. Why not? Passing basic training is an important part of a slave-girl's life. It sets her up for the future.'

Vanessa shook her head in disbelief. It was all madness. She concentrated on clearing her food bowl.

'Anyway,' Zara continued, 'I suggest you follow the new chain through their training. You can interview them individually and find out for yourself why they chose to become Shiller slaves.'

Vanessa nearly choked. 'You're saying they really had a choice, Mistress Editor? They knew what they were getting into?'

'Of course. We selected them most carefully. What do you think we are: monsters?'

Vanessa lowered her head to her bowl again and said nothing.

'Maybe you'll accept the truth after you've followed the new chain through training. It'll be very exciting.'

Vanessa could think of other descriptions, but did not bother to voice them aloud. Zara knew by now how she felt. And if she really was allowed free access to the new girls, it would enable her to gather more evidence about how Shillers managed to recruit them and whatever deceptions they used.

'I'm sure it will, Mistress Editor.'

When they had both finished eating, Zara wiped Vanessa's mouth for her with a tissue, then asked: 'Do you need the loo?'

Vanessa realised she hadn't gone since she left her flat. Suddenly her bladder felt very full. 'Yes, Mistress Editor.

'Me too. I'll show you where it is . . .'

Leaving Vanessa's wrists cuffed behind her back, Zara produced a red-leather leash and clipped it to her collar so quickly and naturally that they were walking out of the door before Vanessa realised what was happening.

She was being led on a lead like a dog!

She lowered her eyes to Zara's twinkling heels once more. It was perverted and degrading and, what was worse, her nipples were standing up.

With Vanessa in tow Zara bustled into the toilets, which were clean and spacious, and selected a generously sized empty booth. She bolted the door behind them, lifted the lid of the bowl and sat Vanessa down, her hands still cuffed behind her.

'You go first.'

Vanessa blushed and clenched her thighs together.

Zara clicked her tongue. 'You should know better than to hide yourself by now. Slave-girls have no privacy. I want to see you make a pretty fountain for me.'

She reached down and pulled Vanessa's knees wide, then slipped a finger into her exposed furrow, teasing the hood of her clitoris. The sudden stimulation caught Vanessa by surprise and she lost control. Her pee hissed into the toilet bowl, to the accompaniment of Zara's light laughter.

'See, it's not so hard to please. All you've got to do is let go . . .'

When she was empty, Zara carefully wiped Vanessa clean with moisturising toilet tissue that was soft and cool. She dug deep into Vanessa's cleft with each stroke, trailing her stiff fingers slowly through her hot, intimate depths.

Vanessa groaned, willing herself not to feel anything, but nevertheless aroused by Zara's touch. Then Zara kissed her hard and masterfully, grasping a handful of her hair and tilting her head back. To her shame Vanessa melted helplessly under its intensity, opening her mouth and letting Zara's tongue play with hers.

When their lips finally parted, Vanessa knew she had lost whatever slight control she had over her situation. She was Zara's plaything now.

Zara pulled Vanessa off the toilet, turned her round and pushed her down on to her knees facing the loo. She lifted the toilet seat, passed the end of Vanessa's leash under it, drew it to one side, then dropped the seat again. The seat rests trapped the leash between them while still allowing it to slide freely over the rim of the bowl.

Lifting her skirt, Zara sat on the toilet, slipping her left hand through the loop of the leash as she did so. She wore no knickers. She opened her legs to Vanessa, exposing a full-lipped pubic mound framed by close-cropped dark curls. She slid her fingers into her vulva and spread her lips, revealing glistening pink depths and the dark tunnel mouth of her vagina. Two small thick gold rings pierced the soft folds of her inner labia, while a third framed the hood of her swelling clitoris.

Zara tugged on the leash running under the toilet seat, pulling Vanessa's face into her open groin. Helpless, Vanessa kissed and licked the hot, spicy-scented folds of slippery flesh, tonguing out the secret passage they guarded. Zara grasped a handful of Vanessa's hair, pressing her face harder into her hungry maw.

A spasm shook Zara, making her jerk her hips and sigh with delight while Vanessa's face was drenched in a spray of sweet exudation. Shamelessly, Vanessa tried to lick up every drop.

Suddenly hot pee spurted from Zara's tiny urethral mouth and over Vanessa's face, washing the orgasmic juices away and trickling into the toilet bowl. Held by her leash she could not pull back, and had to endure the golden shower.

'I said I wanted to go as well,' Zara reminded her with delighted laughter. 'Now you know how we treat girlflesh. I think you're going to make a perfect slave-reporter.'

Six

When Zara appeared at Vanessa's desk later that afternoon she had Miss Kyle by her side. After what had occurred in the toilets, Vanessa tried not to look her editor in the eye. She could not forgive Zara for using her like that. She'd even denied Vanessa her own release after arousing her, which felt desperately, if perversely, unfair. But, though she hated to admit it, she knew she'd been completely dominated by Zara. Now, to her shame, she could not muster the courage to respond. Yet there was evidently no mutual embarrassment. To Zara she was just a slave, to be used to satisfy her own pleasure.

'Miss Kyle will go down with you to B3 and show you where the new chain ceremony will take place,' she said. 'If it's not over before five-thirty, you can write it up at home and show me in the morning, understand?'

'Yes, Mistress Editor,' Vanessa said meekly.

'Are you ready?' Miss Kyle asked, as Zara went back to her office.

There were a couple of cameras, a digital recorder and an e-notepad on Vanessa's desk. It seemed that stories for the *Girlflesh News* were normally photographed and written by the same reporter. Vanessa had been checking over the equipment Zara had provided.

'Yes, Miss Kyle,' she said, hastily slinging a camera round her neck and gathering up her notepad. The recorder had a belt hook that she found fitted her slave-belt.

On the way down in the lift, Vanessa thought she'd better stop feeling sorry for herself and behave like a proper reporter – starting with some background details. She'd rather ask almost anybody else, but she had no choice.

'Do you mind, Miss Kyle, telling me how all these new girls are brought here?' She had visions of vehicles full of slave-girls like the one under which she had sneaked in. 'I mean they must come from all over the place. Doesn't anybody miss them?'

'They bring themselves by train and taxi, of course,' Miss Kyle said. 'And nobody misses them because it's all been arranged months ago.'

'They . . . really come here voluntarily?'

Miss Kyle sounded impatient. 'That's one of the facts we've been trying to make you believe since yesterday morning, girl. But I suppose you're going to have to find it out for yourself the hard way . . .'

Level B3 was bustling when they emerged from the lift. Slave-girls were scurrying about in excitement, mingling with oddly (or even minimally) dressed trainers. Vanessa saw the black man who had driven the pony-girl carriage stride by.

'If you want to learn a few facts, we call this the High Street,' Miss Kyle said, leading the way along the broad central corridor that ran the length of level B3. They passed the block where Vanessa had changed that morning and the turning to the cell mews. 'The shopping corridor is called the Mall, of course.'

There were doors and windows on either side opening on to who knew what strange things. It might only have a floor area the size of a large underground car park, but Vanessa realised there was still so much she did not know about the place.

They reached the very end block on the right and turned through a double gateway. It was the space Vanessa had looked in on through a viewing window the previous day that Shiller had said was a training area for new recruits. Now it was ringed about with a host of what Vanessa had to think of as off-duty slave-girls, their jewels sparkling and coloured ribbons fluttering. She'd never seen so much totally naked flesh of every hue paraded in one space before. There must have been eighty or ninety of them. It could almost be a crowd gathering for a talent show in a naturist camp – except for the coloured collars they all wore. Still, at least they made her feel a little less self-conscious of her own nudity.

Four slave-masters, three men and a woman, were assembled on a small podium. One man wore only boots and a posing pouch, the second training shorts and singlet, the last black-leather trousers and a harness top. The woman was a blonde dressed in thigh-length black boots and a matching black pvc bikini. They all wore belts from which hung an assortment of whips, crops and electric goads. Beside the masters, a small table had been laid out with a stack of red slave-collars and a cane. In front of the podium a dozen small rubber kneeling mats had been set out in a short arc.

Miss Kyle led Vanessa round the fringe of the crowd until they were just to one side of the podium.

'You should see everything from here,' she said. 'I'll be busy with the new girls from now on. I assume you can find your own way back to the office after it's over.'

'Yes, Miss Kyle.'

'Then you're on your own. What you make of all this is up to you.'

She turned and left to take her own place on the small stage.

I know exactly what to make of it, Vanessa thought as she watched her go.

She didn't want to witness whatever perverted spectacle they planned, but she had no choice. She might as well cover it as though she was a proper reporter for Zara's sick little magazine. The evidence would speak for itself later.

Vanessa snapped off several pictures to capture the atmosphere and then began jotting notes. But how could she describe such a bizarre scene? Concentrate on getting the bare . . . no, the basic facts and gut impressions down first, and put them into context later.

There was a stir among the slave-girls and Vanessa saw Shiller, still wearing the same conservative suit, come in through a side gate and make her way to the podium. Although smaller and slighter than anybody else around her, somehow it was obvious who was in charge. Shiller moved to the front of the podium as though to speak. Vanessa hung her notepad on her belt and held up her recorder to catch her words. More damning evidence, hopefully.

'We are here today to welcome twelve more special young women who wish to join our company. Bring in the new recruits!'

To waves of enthusiastic applause, twelve naked women were ushered in through a side gate by the black pony-girl driver and marched over to the arc of mats. Their hands were bound behind their backs but they wore no collars. They were blonde, brunette and redhead, large- and small-breasted, pale-skinned, olive and coffee-dark. But all were pretty, blushing, nervous and excited. They knelt down on the mats facing the podium.

Vanessa fumbled with the camera, trying to take pictures of the new girls and record what was said. She tried hooking the recorder on to her collar ring and it rested on her sternum.

.The pony-girl driver joined the others on the podium. Shiller smiled benevolently down at the new girls, before addressing the crowd.

'Many years ago I saw there was a need that was being shamefully served, partly due to long-established prejudice, and partly due to so-called enlightened modern morals. Many people sought sexual services of a nature beyond what society considered normal and reasonable, which were being satisfied often by cruel and criminal means. This led to the degradation of body and spirit of those who had unwillingly to fulfil those desires.

'Surely, I thought, this can be done both more efficiently and fairly, without the innocent and desperate suffering? Human beings are infinitely variable. Why not seek out those who enjoyed giving themselves for the pleasure of others, free them of guilt about their natures and so satisfy that demand for sexual submissives and masochists in a safe and profitable manner?'

Shiller looked at the twelve new girls.

'So I began the programme of psychological testing and evaluation that has brought you here today. Now you are ready to submit yourself to strict discipline, eager to experience sex in all its permutations and willing to suffer for the pleasure of others. You are special, never forget that. In the outside world these tendencies might make your lives difficult, since they are seen by some as aberrations. But down here it is the norm.' She opened her arms to encompass the watching slave-girls. 'These girls have all undergone the training process you are about to embark upon, and have graduated to the sisterhood of the chain. They are now, as you will be soon, proud to be slaves!'

There was a burst of spontaneous applause. The kneeling girls were smiling wondrously and some looked close to shedding tears of joy. For a moment even Vanessa felt uplifted by the wave of emotion. Hell, she thought, Shiller's almost got me believing in it.

The Director continued. 'Soon you will put on the collars that will bind you to the service of this company. They are the badges declaring your special natures. All Shiller girls wear them proudly. Our working unit is a group of twelve girls or "chain". Chains come in six basic colour bands: red, blue, green, yellow, orange, and pink and purple, with additional divisions within each band, so that no two working chains will ever have the same name. They serve not only as means of identification but as a bond between you.

'As part of a chain you will live and work together more intimately than you have with any other human beings, forming a companionship and trust that will stay with you for the rest of your lives. You new girls will join the red collar band as "Cherry Chain". While you work for us you will be identified by your Christian name, your number in the chain chosen alphabetically, and your chain name.

'Shiller girls are very proud of their own chains, and there's some friendly rivalry between them, as you will discover. But ultimately every girl here, whatever the colour of the collar she wears, is your sister in slavery. She will have undergone the same training and submitted herself to serving the same purpose. That is a bond stronger than any link of steel.'

There were nods and sighs of understanding from the assembly. Vanessa became aware of a growing closeness in the training compound. Underneath the fleshy warmth of so many bare bodies and the mingling of their perfumes, was a uniquely female scent of mounting excitement and anticipation. Nipples of all hues and sizes were visibly rising and spreading.

'Shortly you will make your public declarations and accept your collars,' Shiller continued, 'and then your training will begin.' She gestured to the people on the podium with her. 'These will be your trainers. Do not think it will be easy. For the next month their task is to break down any lingering inhibitions or doubts about your true natures. At times you may well be driven to tears. But it is all part of the process of forging you into self-confident, well-adjusted and above all happy submissives; finding pleasure in pain and humiliation, and eager to perform any sexual service required of you.'

The smell of sexual heat was getting stronger. Vanessa saw a few of the watching girls were quite openly rubbing their fingers through their pussy furrows.

'Now I will ask you to make your declarations of submission . . .'

Miss Kyle stepped up, holding a list in her hand. 'Amber Langford,' she called out.

Eyes sparkling, the first girl on the left of the line got to her feet and went forwards. She had short red hair and pale, freckled skin. Her large breasts swayed heavily as she moved.

She knelt again before Shiller at the foot of the podium and said in a tremulous but clear voice: 'I wish to become a slave. I surrender myself to the service of the Shiller Company to make whatever use of me they wish.' Then she bent forwards and kissed Shiller's shoes.

Miss Kyle handed Shiller a collar from the table.

'You shall now be known as Amber 1 Cherry,' Shiller said, closing the collar round the girl's neck.

Amber stood, turned to face the audience, spread her legs and bent forwards so that she presented her backside to Shiller. Miss Kyle handed Shiller the cane from the table, who used it to deliver three quick cuts across Amber's rear, making her yip in pain and sending ripples through her soft flesh.

'Thank you, Mistress,' Amber said huskily through her tears. She went back to her mat and knelt again, showing her now striped and glowing buttocks to the watchers.

More of the slave-girls were rubbing themselves now. Vanessa could see a pair of girls standing hip to hip, each fingering the other.

'Charlotte Powell,' Miss Kyle called out.

Charlotte was a slender blonde with small pointed breasts. She accepted her collar and became Charlotte 2 Cherry. The stripes from Shiller's cane showed lividly on her golden skin.

Almost all the watching slave-girls were masturbating now, filling the yard with the perfume of their arousal: the natural exudation of four-score exposed pudenda belonging to healthy young women trained to express pleasure without inhibition. They seemed almost unconscious of their actions as their eyes were locked on the scene before them.

Unsure where to look, Vanessa felt herself unwillingly caught up in the horrible fascination of it all. There was a deep perverted thrill in seeing each girl in turn voluntarily giving up her freedom, accepting bondage, receiving her first punishment, and then being grateful for it!

By the time a striking Indian girl with coffee-dark skin and a mane of honey-blonde wavy hair became Kashika 5 Cherry, Vanessa was having trouble concentrating on her job. Her own nipples were up and there was moistness in her pubes that, while squirming, she tried to ignore. Were all the female pheromones being sprayed around her turning her on? The mass enjoyment of such a degrading spectacle had to be wrong, but at that moment it did not feel so.

When Yvonne Jerrard finally became Cherry Chain girl 12, girls in the crowd were coming with little gasps and sighs. The air was saturated with their lustful aroma, and Vanessa was biting her lip as she tried to resist its allure, sliding her wrists and knuckles nervously about her crotch in a foolish attempt to pretend she was not actually toying with herself.

Shiller raised her hands and the crowd stilled. Fingers dipped in sticky holes ceased to rub and twirl. Even through her confusion Vanessa thought: she has some presence, I'll give her that.

'Cherry Chain is now complete,' Shiller declared.

There was a fresh round of applause.

'Now they begin their training.' She glanced at Vanessa. 'In one month I hope we shall gather again to celebrate their graduation, but for now please leave the yard . . .'

Obediently, the girls turned and began filing out of the yard, laughing and chattering, rubbing provocatively against each other, leaving the new recruits still kneeling on their mats. Vanessa followed after the rest. Looking back, she saw the masters descending from the podium to stand over the new girls, who looked up at them with excited, fearful eyes . . .

Then the yard gates were closed.

What would they go through now, Vanessa wondered?

Happy girls were milling about the High Street. Some in twos and threes were hurrying away hand-in-hand, with the air of having urgent business to be concluded. A few could not wait that long and were pressing each other up against walls and kissing passionately with an utter lack of inhibition or concern as to who was watching.

Vanessa still felt a little light-headed. Could being close to so much passion make you drunk? She knew it was both one of the most erotic and the most disgusting things she had ever witnessed, but at that moment she could not tell which prevailed. She was acutely aware of her still wet labia, and hoped nobody else would notice. Then she realised that at that moment none of them could care less.

It was gone five-thirty when Vanessa got back to the magazine office. Zara had left and the main room was half empty.

Vanessa spent a few minutes downloading the camera, notepad and audio files to her computer. She did not mind the delay, preferring the building to be as empty as possible before leaving to avoid having to share a lift.

She put her report data on to a CD to work on at home. Her computer station did not support any less bulky data transfer system, presumably as a security precaution. Even naked she might be able to smuggle out a data key, but it was not physically possible to do the same with a CD. As she worked, she thought about the trick that had been played earlier down in level B3, not just on her but on all those present.

Yes, there had to be a deception somewhere, of that she was certain. Shiller and her cronies seemed to have persuaded at least a hundred girls into accepting a life of slavery, but that was crazy. You didn't do such a thing in this day and age in the middle of London. Shiller had made a fine speech, making it all sound so reasonable, but at the heart of it all there had to be a flaw. And she would surely seek it out.

Vanessa collected the disk and turned off her computer. Now she'd have to go all the way back down to the B3 locker room and get her phallic spywear put back on. Well, she'd better get it over with. She got up to leave, looking automatically around her, then sat down again guiltily.

She'd left a shamefully dark wet patch on the chair where her pussy had leaked.

She fumbled about in the desk drawers but there were no tissues, or anything she could use to mop up the tell-tale mark. Her own travel pack of tissues was in her bag down in the locker room. Why hadn't she thought to bring some essentials with her? Too late now. She knew it was ridiculous, but at that moment she could not bear the thought of leaving behind such an intimate sign for anybody to find. She had at least to preserve one scrap of dignity.

There were only a couple of women left in the office now. Dare she wait until they'd gone and risk searching other desks? What time did the cleaners come round? Oh, hell! She sniffed loudly a few times, then got up and made her way over to the nearest woman.

'Excuse me, Madam,' she asked meekly, keeping her eyes lowered, but do you have a tissue, please?'

The woman, who had frizzy black hair and olive skin, looked her up and down calculatingly. She wore a necklace with the filigree name charm of 'Rona' dangling from it. Vanessa bit her lip but endured the scrutiny.

'So, Zara's toygirl wants a tissue?' Rona said with a thin smile.

'Please, Madam.'

'If I give you one, does that mean you won't mention my name when you turn us all in?'

Vanessa now knew she'd made a mistake. 'Sorry to bother you, Madam. I'll go . . .'

'No!' Rona said commandingly. 'Tell me why we should be nice to you?'

'You've no reason at all, Madam,' Vanessa admitted.

Rona looked thoughtful for a moment, then reached into a drawer and pulled out a handful of tissues. Dangling them in front of Vanessa she asked: 'OK. Here they are. What have you got to give in exchange?'

Vanessa realised as they'd been talking that the other woman, a blonde with her hair tied in a long single plait, had come up behind her. It was too late to back away. With a terrible inevitability she knew what was coming. All she could do was choose to co-operate or make a futile show of resistance.

'I can give you the same as Zara got,' she said.

The woman grinned.

'Share her?' the blonde-plaited woman asked, putting her arms round Vanessa and squeezing her breasts experimentally.

'OK, Pru, but I go first.'

Pru pulled Vanessa's arms behind her and clipped her wrists to her belt, even as Rona sat back in her chair and hitched up her skirt. Like Zara, she wore no knickers. Her vulva was plump and pouting, the crinkled tongue of her inner labia showing between her outer lips. As Vanessa was forced down on to her knees before her, she pulled her sex-mouth wide. Also like Zara, she was pierced by three gold rings.

Pru pushed Vanessa's head forwards, ramming her face into Rona's ready pubes. Almost smothered by warm, wet clinging flesh, Vanessa began to lick and nuzzle. At least she could get it over with quickly. Pru knelt between her spread knees, reached down and cupped her dangling breasts, pinching and squeezing.

'Come on girl, you can do better than that!' she shouted, thrusting her hips up against Vanessa's bottom to force her deeper into Rona's vagina.

'Maybe she needs some more attention at your end?' Rona suggested, grasping a handful of Vanessa's hair to control the bobbing of her head.

'Pass me that ruler . . .' Pru said.

The flat length of plastic smacked hard across Vanessa's buttocks. Her yelp of pain, half-smothered by Rona's vagina, made the woman laugh. Desperately, Vanessa redoubled her efforts.

'That's better,' Rona said. 'Ohooo . . . yes! She's using her tongue properly now. All she needed was a little encouragement . . .'

The ruler swished down and delivered a second blow . . .

By the time Rona came, Vanessa's bottom was a stinging blaze of scarlet. Hardly giving her a chance to catch her breath, the women switched places, and Vanessa's face was rammed into Pru's smooth-shorn pubes, urged on by a fresh round of swipes from the ruler.

And then the pain, disgust and shame became something else. It was as if all the arousal she had received that day had been stored up inside, and now it was about to burst out of her as punishment and temptation weakened her resolve. She could not help it, only surrender to its demands. As the wonderful immense wave of pleasure built in her loins, she slurped and licked her way round the sweet folds of flesh in which her face was buried with desperate new vigour.

'Oh . . . shit! She's getting good!' Pru exclaimed.

Vanessa was now glorying in every stinging, smarting blow of the ruler, which highlighted and intensified her pleasure. She was going to come and it would be huge . . .

Then Pru gasped, lathering Vanessa's face with her juices. Her hips jerked a few times, then she settled with a contented sigh. The ruler ceased its blows. Pru pushed Vanessa aside and she toppled to the floor.

She lay there squirming and flopping about like a fish out of water, her face shiny with sweat and female discharge, hair wild and straggling, her bottom bright-red from spanking. Her eyes were hollow and desperate, while her blushing pudendum, swollen with unfulfilled need, dripped on the carpet.

'Please . . . I want to come as well!' she begged.

The two women smiled down at her as they smoothed their skirts and tidied their hair.

'Underneath she's quite a slut, isn't she?' Rona said.

'She gives good tongue,' Pru added.

'But could she take it from a man?'

Pru grinned. 'Let's see if she's deep enough . . .'

They grabbed Vanessa's ankles and pulled her legs wide. Prising open her hungry vagina, they took the ruler and slipped it up inside her. Vanessa's eyes bulged. The ruler's edge and ends were rounded, but it still pierced her like a blade. Two-thirds of its length disappeared before it came to a stop somewhere around her cervix.

'Well, that should give them room to enjoy themselves,' Rona declared.

Vanessa groaned, her agony unabated. The unnatural intrusion of the ruler had almost brought her off, leaving her teetering on the edge – fearful of the hurt she might suffer if her vaginal tunnel went into orgasmic spasm.

'Look at the mess she's making on the floor,' Pru said. 'She's hot for it.'

'Still want to come?' Rona asked.

'Oh, yes ... please!' Vanessa gasped.

'Well too bad. We've had our fun and we're off home now.'

'Maybe we'll just leave you like this for the night?'

'No!' Vanessa pleaded.

'Perhaps the locker guard down in B3 would oblige her, if she asks him nicely?' Rona wondered aloud.

'That's a good idea ...'

'No ... please, just free my hands,' Vanessa begged. 'I've ... I've got work to take home to do for Zara ...'

'No problem ...'

Rona went over to Vanessa's desk. 'Hey, look at the pussy stain she's left on her chair,' she said. Vanessa screwed up her eyes in shame.

She brought the data CD back and tucked it under Vanessa's belt. 'Shall we send her down to B3 like this, just to show him what a hot slut she really is?'

'Good idea!'

'Oh God, don't do that – umphhh.'

Rona had clamped her hand over Vanessa's mouth. 'She makes too much noise.'

'Can't have that,' her friend agreed.

'Bring over that tape dispenser ...'

They closed Vanessa's mouth with criss-cross strips of clear tape, until the lower half of her face was covered and she could only make muffled squeaks and throaty gurgles.

'Mustn't have this slipping out,' Pru said, giving a twang to the end of the ruler protruding from between Vanessa's flushed pubic lips. Vanessa's nostrils flared as she snuffled with pain.

'She was asking for tissues . . .'

They stuffed wadded tissues into her vagina on either side of the ruler, making her pubic pouch bulge. Vanessa struggled feebly, grunting and gurgling and rolling her eyes.

'You don't want to drip all the way down, do you, girl?'

'I think we ought to tape it in place, just to be sure.'

'Yes, just to be sure . . .'

They wrapped strips of tape about the ruler and then out across her lower stomach and inner thighs, until her pubic curls were covered.

'Might be a bit painful coming off, still, that can't be helped.'

'I don't think she'll mind.'

They pulled Vanessa to her feet, and, holding an arm apiece, walked her down the corridor towards the lift. She stumbled along between them with her legs splayed, every step making the sticky tape crackle, pulling on her taped pubic hair and twisting the ruler inside her. Pushing her into the lift, the women pressed the button for level B3 and stood quickly back, waving to Vanessa as the door closed.

'Have fun!'

'We'll be thinking of you.'

Blinking the tears from her eyes, Vanessa leant back against the side of the lift as it descended, her legs splayed wide, the tormenting ruler jutting out grotesquely from between her thighs. She was half crazy with sexual frustration, mad at herself for utter stupidity, but above all deeply ashamed.

A truth she would not have believed just two days earlier was being driven home to her once again. What was even worse than enduring forced sex, was being roused almost to the point of orgasm, and then left cruelly unsatisfied. Was that some unsuspected sluttish side to her nature manifesting itself again, or was it all down to her unreal situation and bizarre treatment? She desperately hoped it was the latter, but she was no longer sure. All she knew was she had to find relief.

The lift stopped at Level B3 and she stumbled out. Uncaring what she looked like or who saw her, she half ran, half waddled across to the row of low slave-gates leading to the locker room. She shrieked as she bent over, the tape tearing hair from her pubes, and crawled through the wire-mesh tunnel into the lobby.

Mr Jarvis was still on duty. He chuckled as he saw her emerge and shuffle awkwardly over on her knees to his table.

'Oh, it's Vanessa. Wondered when you'd turn up. But not looking quite so smart as you did this morning. Not going to complain about your chains again, are you?'

Vanessa shook her head and made pleading sounds as she thrust her hips forwards, wiggling the impaling ruler.

'I see. Looks like you want something taken off you, right?'

Vanessa nodded desperately.

'Well you'd better follow me . . .'

She shuffled after him into the locker room.

A couple of girls were just finishing putting on street clothes. One was tying a scarf about her collar. They looked with curious interest but no great surprise at Vanessa's predicament. Briefly Vanessa wondered where they could possibly be going, but another yank at her pubic curls drove the matter from her mind.

'Hurry along, now, girls,' Jarvis said.

'Yes, Mr Jarvis,' they chorused. Quickly they gathered up their bags and left the room.

Jarvis had Vanessa straddle a bench and then lie back, leaving her feet resting on the floor on either side and opening her taped groin to his gaze. He straddled the bench facing her and began picking at the tape around her inner thighs, carefully peeling it back. His touch was unexpectedly delicate, and Vanessa began to relax.

'You see, there are two ways to do this,' he said. 'Just go gently or else –'

'Ahhheee!' Vanessa shrieked in pain through her tape-gag, arching her back, tears springing to her eyes.

Jarvis had yanked the ruler out of her and taken the tape with it in one go. It felt as if every hair had just been torn out by its roots. She sobbed and snuffled. Her pubes felt seared and raw.

He held up the ruler and its clinging collar of tape, to which adhered a fuzz of dark curling hair.

'But I don't have time for the gentle way. Don't worry girl, no harm done.'

He pulled the tissue wadding from her gaping hole. It was sodden with her juices. He smelt it and smiled. 'Got excited earlier, did you?'

Trying to catch her breath, her eyes filmed with tears, Vanessa nodded miserably.

'Nothing to be ashamed of . . .' He slid his finger inside her. 'Just checking to see you're not scratched. Silly thing to put up you. There are much better ways of plugging a hot little hole like yours . . .'

The need she had been denied flowed back into Vanessa as though he had turned on a tap. The pain in her groin became an exciting tingle, mingling with the liquid heat in her loins.

'Oh . . . still excited, are you?' he remarked with a smile.

Of course he was going to have her. She was gagged and bound and utterly helpless. It was perfectly natural. She nodded.

He stroked her crudely taped mouth, tracing the line of her jaw. She held absolutely still.

He was an overweight older man and a virtual stranger and she was not remotely attracted to him. But at that moment she wanted him inside her more than anything in the world.

She lifted her hips, shamelessly, offering herself to him.

He stood up and unzipped his flies, exposing a thick hard erection.

Kneeling over her, his weight pressing down hard, he mounted and entered her in one swift action without foreplay, because there was no need. She could not have been more ready.

Vanessa squirmed under him, accepting every hard, careless thrust, sucking on him with her vagina until the pent-up need exploded inside her.

And in that glorious, disgusting moment, she felt the last shred of her dignity being stripped from her. She had learnt what it meant to be a slave to the needs of her own body and, in turn, to those who could control those needs. They were the true masters of girlflesh.

Seven

The next morning, Vanessa knelt meekly on the floor in Zara's office while her editor read her article on Cherry Chain's initiation.

If Zara had noticed the lingering red blotches on Vanessa's bottom she didn't say so. Nor had she made any comment on the fact that overnight Vanessa had severely trimmed and cropped her pubic hair.

As Vanessa waited, she found herself marvelling that she had been in any state to write the article at all . . .

She had left the building the previous evening with a burning bottom, half her pubic hair torn out and Jarvis's sperm still oozing out of her vagina around her phallic controller. Apart from memories of Zara's humiliating treatment and the disturbing emotions of the initiation ceremony filling her mind, she was still dazed by the strength of her locker-room orgasm, which was either a triumph of her determination to find pleasure in adversity or else a shameful insight into her darker nature.

And then Shiller's voice came over the monitor earphones.

'I know you've had an eventful day, Puppet,' she said. 'You must be overwhelmed by new and strange sensations. I wanted to see how you were coping . . .'

Shiller continued to talk in the same understanding tone while calmly guiding Vanessa through the evening traffic, even advising her when to make a detour round a bad jam. Perhaps she was too exhausted to maintain her instinctive animosity, but in ten minutes she had almost forgotten Shiller was responsible for her current misery. It was more like having a sympathetic older friend travelling with her.

Back in her flat, Shiller suggested she change out of her control gear as soon as possible, easing her through its removal and the switch to her house collar, so that it did not seem half as awkward or embarrassing as it had the previous night.

'You need to run a deep bath filled with something foamy and relaxing,' Shiller suggested. Vanessa did so, washing away both female juices and semen, and letting the aches and soreness drain out of her. She almost forgot she was under continuous observation as she did so.

Shiller offered advice about tidying her ravaged pubic hair, and, when Vanessa was dressed again in nightwear of vest and shorts, spoke knowledgeably about recipes while she made herself supper. It was only when Vanessa at last sat down to work on her article that Shiller withdrew her virtual presence.

'This is your story, not mine,' she said firmly. 'You must report what you saw and how others responded to events. That in no way impinges on your integrity or implies you agree with what occurred. Remember that your readership does not feel as you do about our girlflesh business, but otherwise be honest.'

It was impossible for Vanessa not to be judgemental, but she did her best to give an impartial account of what she had experienced. Flicking through the file of her photographs in an effort to recapture the strange atmosphere of the ceremony, she found herself lingering on the images of the watching slave-girls openly masturbating. What was going on in their minds? Was it a perverted show of kinship with the newly enslaved Cherry Chain girls, or simple unrestrained hedonism? A bit of both, perhaps?

She enlarged the image, zooming in on the girls' hands busy in the wet clefts of their sexes and sometimes those of their neighbours. How was it possible to lack inhibition to such a degree? Was it the result of indoctrination, or a belief in total freedom within their controlled lives? How much of an alteration to normal behaviour did it take? She had to admit she had been caught up in the same erotic high the ceremony had generated, but that had been a response to the animal scent of arousal the girls were putting out. If they hadn't been there she would certainly not have reacted the same way. For God's sake, it was a celebration of enslavement.

She flicked on through the file.

By chance she had caught Kashika, the striking blonde Indian girl, exactly at the moment the third blow of her ceremonial caning landed. Vanessa studied the expression on her face, looking for answers. Pain and joy were there, but also, she imagined, a suggestion that she had in some sense 'arrived', that this was where she had to be. Was she really a natural-born slave? What else could make her voluntarily endure such pain? Her large dark eyes were clearly filling with tears, and it was obvious the blows were not playful smacks, because her neat brown-nippled breasts were blurred with motion as they bounced in response . . .

Vanessa froze, horrified to discover her hand had slipped under the waistband of her shorts and her fingers were sliding through the warm slippery wetness of her cleft. Blushing and angry, she jerked her hand away, wondering if anybody had seen her through the sitting-room mirror camera. But no comment came. Perhaps nobody was watching at that moment.

Surreptitiously she wiped her fingers on her shorts and flicked to another picture.

Shiller had delivered one last message when Vanessa was in bed and about to go to sleep. Her hands were cuffed in front of her and the anal cable lock was plugged in, but at least her ankles were free and she had not been forced to perform any more sex acts.

'I won't speak to you again while you are with us, unless it is absolutely necessary. I do have a large and complex company to run, and even you, Vanessa, must come second to that. Besides, if I give you too much personal attention, you may think I am trying to influence you. Probably you will believe that anyway by tomorrow.

'But accept one truth from me which may help you understand things that seem hard to accept. While you are in our care, you are never alone . . .'

Vanessa drifted off wondering how one might interpret that remark. She slept very deeply.

The 'PE teacher' voice was back as Monitor the next morning, putting her through the same exercise routine. He complimented her on her newly cropped pubes. 'That's better, Puppet. Clean and close. More hygienic. Shows off the line of your cleft better . . .'

Her nerves resurfaced as she entered the Shiller offices and descended to level B3. But it was not as bad as she had imagined.

As she kissed Jarvis's boots, she feared knowing leers and mockery, but he had simply patted her head, taken control of her from Monitor, and led her though to the locker room.

After putting her chains on he kept her bent over while he examined her trimmed pubes, but after a playful pinch and tickle he let her go on her way. To her surprise she found she felt no animosity towards him. He had used her for his own pleasure without spite or malice, and at the time she had needed, so very desperately, the relief he provided. He didn't seem to think any less of her. If anything, as he checked the packed lunch she had remembered to bring this time, he was more amiable. Any shame was all her own.

In the office, she saw Rona and Pru smirking at her, clearly looking for some show of embarrassment. She wondered how many of their friends they'd told about the fun they had with her. She couldn't hide her loss of pubic curls or the blush on her bottom, so she simply ignored them. She'd show them she could take it. Just because she was a virtual slave, didn't mean she was weak . . . which was, now she came to think of it, an odd concept.

Zara finished reading her article.

'There are a couple of redundant phrases we can drop, and I think we should inset this picture here instead of that one, but otherwise it's . . . not bad.' She sounded almost regretful at not having found more faults in Vanessa's work. 'You've captured the erotic intensity of the ceremony, but haven't let your own feelings colour your writing.'

'I just reported the responses of the people around me, Mistress Editor,' Vanessa replied, relieved she had passed her first hurdle. 'I didn't think you'd want a personal comment piece.'

Zara smiled. 'Not right now. Perhaps that's something you might write when you've got to know us better.'

'I don't think you'd like what I'd have to say, Mistress Editor.'

'As long as it's honest. But as I said, we'll give it a little time. You can start your follow-up articles about Cherry Chain's progress this afternoon. I've arranged with their trainers to allow you access to the yard. But you must report to them first and not get in the way.

'Meanwhile, try writing a few fillers for the next edition of *Datumline*. I've had a pile of titbits and minor personal interest stuff sitting around here for weeks . . .' she handed Vanessa a bulging file. 'Pick out the best ten. Fifty words min, three hundred max.'

'Yes, Mistress Editor,' Vanessa said, taking the file.

It was routine and rather boring work. The sort of thing junior reporters usually got stuck doing. But it made it easier to forget being naked in a corner of an office full of potentially unfriendly faces. She suspected that while she was seen to be working hard on a job for Zara she was less likely to be bothered. It also confirmed the scope of Shiller interests that her previous research had revealed.

Shillers controlled companies, large and small, all the way from the manufacture of abrasive materials to, for some inexplicable reason, a chain of yoga schools. There was even a 'zed' – a small city zoo – but that was run as charity, so perhaps it didn't count.

How many of those subsidiaries knew what was going on under their central offices? More than a few, perhaps. Shiller herself had said that the spywear Vanessa wore had come from one of their research departments. How many outwardly respectable companies supplied the needs of the girlflesh trade?

Somebody had fitted out level B3. Who made the special colour-coded collars the girls wore or those freaky horse-head masks for the pony-girls? Nobody could believe they were all being sold to bondage enthusiasts over the internet. When she blew the whistle on this lot, a whole house of cards would come tumbling down.

By the end of the morning she'd written short pieces about the minor triumphs and occasional humorous misfortunes of Shiller workers from all over the country, and found herself actually looking forward to going down to B3 to see how the Cherry Chain girls were doing. Well of course, she told herself, that was because they were in essence the true story she was after. The scoop of the year.

Recalling Zara's trip to the toilets yesterday, Vanessa sneaked a visit before submitting her filler pieces. Though she could simply order her to submit to her wishes, clearly Zara enjoyed finding excuses for having Vanessa to herself. In her turn Vanessa was going to do her best to see she gave her none.

Zara skimmed the items. 'Yes, that'll do.' She filed the copy and smiled broadly. 'Now, do you need to go to the loo?'

'I've just been, Mistress Editor.'

'What about some lunch?'

'I remembered to bring sandwiches today, Mistress Editor.'

She planned to eat quietly at her desk. While she was forced to walk around naked, she wanted as far as possible to avoid meeting anybody outside the magazine office and level B3.

Clearly determined not to be thwarted in her little game, Zara rallied. 'I think it would be a good idea if you saw our senior staff restaurant. It'll give you an insight into the sort of training Cherry Chain will be doing. My treat.' She held up the red-leather leash. 'You go as my pet, of course . . .'

The restaurant was on the tenth floor and offered a fine view over the city, with the Thames snaking away almost from under their feet to fade away into the distant haze. The interior featured a lot of stylish chrome work and was softly lit.

As they entered, Zara took a padded mat from a selection hanging on a large hook by the main entrance and pushed the handle between Vanessa's teeth for her to carry, as her hands were once again cuffed behind her. Resigned to her fate, Vanessa kept her eyes lowered and followed obediently after her editor as she found a single table and took her seat. Zara fastened the end of the leash to a hook hidden under the table-top and pointed to the floor by her chair. Vanessa bent over, dropped the mat, shuffled it into place and knelt down beside Zara.

A waitress came over to the table.

She moved with dainty steps due to the short hobble chain that linked her ankles. A slimmer chain lifted the middle of the hobble from the floor, preventing it from dragging or jingling unduly, and vanished between her thighs. Her face, except for eye and nostril holes, was covered by a mask of silvered plastic, moulded into an expression of serene prettiness. Integral with the mask was a moulded silver waitress-cap that perched on top of her head. The cap bore the number '7'.

Her wrists were rigidly cuffed a little apart so that her hands were held upturned before her. The metal spacer-bar of her cuffs was linked to her collar ring by a short chain running up between her breasts. Its length had been adjusted so that the bar nestled in the fleshy concavity of their undercurves. Another short

125

chain linked her upper arms behind her back. With her arms thus confined, it looked as if she was about to cup and lift breasts in offering. Between the two sets of restraints the girl was left with a small degree of movement and could, Vanessa supposed, carry things with care.

The slave-waitress went down on her knees beside Zara and handed her a copy of the menu, which was fastened to her wrist-cuff bar by a length of elastic cord. The menu was a plastic laminated scroll, fastened top and bottom to rounded wooden rods, and came with an attached marker pen.

After a little deliberation Zara ticked some boxes on the menu, then rolled it up tightly. 'Take my order!' she commanded.

The waitress stood and turned her knees outwards, spreading her thighs as far as her hobble chain allowed. Zara thrust the menu up into the girl's vagina until only the ends of the scroll rods were showing. Vanessa heard what might have been a moan of pain or pleasure come from behind the inscrutable mask as the girl bent over to ease the tension on the elastic cord that now cut through her soft sex lips and across her clitoris before running up inside her.

As the girl turned and shuffled away, bent over almost double, Vanessa saw how the hobble chain support was attached to her. A protruding metal eye-ring gleamed against the dark smudge of her anus. The support chain was snap-hooked to this.

Zara stroked Vanessa's hair and said, in that half-musing way people employ speaking to an animal when no response is actually expected: 'Cherry Chain will have its turn serving in here, but not until they've learnt poise and deportment. The regular waitresses are all fully trained girls.'

The waitress brought them wine on a small tray. Vanessa wondered how she could serve it while hampered by her cuff bar, but the designers of her restraints had thought of that. The stems of the glasses slid into slots in the tray rim, with the bowls resting on the tray top. She set one glass down on the table before Zara, carefully lowering the tray and pulling it back to disengage the stem. The slot rims were of different heights, Vanessa now saw, allowing the girl to set a glass down without disturbing the rest. She then knelt down beside Vanessa and set her glass on the floor. It had a straw in it.

As Vanessa drank, she glanced round the room, which was filling up. Peering between chairs and table legs she saw she was not the only pet there. There were seven or eight others, which made her situation seem a little less onerous.

Their owners, and she hated to use the word even in her thoughts, stroked and patted their heads like pampered dogs and fed them titbits from their own plates as treats in addition to the food in their gleaming bowls set out on the floor. Their girl-pets smiled affectionately back at them, rubbed against their legs or rested their chins on their knees, occasionally making plaintive whining sounds as they begged for more.

Vanessa blinked. Some of the girls seemed to be wearing elaborate prosthetic make-up. At least three had tails growing from the base of their spines. How were they attached? One slender creature with close-cropped ginger hair even had pointed ears and delicate feline whiskers. All she could see of another girl-pet was her upturned backside displaying plump sex lips that appeared to be closed by a zip fastener.

This was getting freaky . . .

More details struck her. Some of the girl-pets' collars did not match the regular colour range. There

127

were leather, silver and gold, some decorated with scrollwork and even studded with gems. Were they the private slaves of Shiller managers or the possessions of visitors to the building? The possibility would have seemed preposterous only a few days ago, but now she gave it serious consideration. How many places were there in London where you could freely take your slave out to dine?

There was so much she still did not know.

The food arrived: a plate for Zara and a bowl for Vanessa.

'Eat up like a good pet,' Zara commanded.

Vanessa buried her face in it, trying not to think about the strange unsettling people around her.

After a few minutes she felt Zara's hand slide over her upraised haunches. Her fingers circled the crinkles of her anus and then dipped into the soft cleft-pouch beneath.

Nearly choking, Vanessa glanced up. Zara was not even looking at her. She was casually eating with a fork in one hand while idly fondling her with the other. And nobody else appeared to be taking the slightest bit of notice. And why should they, Vanessa thought wretchedly? Here such behaviour was normal. She was the one with her instincts and sensibilities out of place.

She tried to ignore Zara's touch and focus on eating, but it was no good. Before a restaurant full of people she was being fingered and responding by getting wet. It was insane. What had they done to her?

The sweet course came and it was no better. Vanessa got cream on her nose and Zara, laughing, wiped it off with her napkin. As she did so she playfully tweaked her nipples. They were painfully hard. Zara grinned triumphantly and Vanessa stifled a moan. Once again the perverted need had been kindled within her. There was only one way to satisfy its demands.

It was no surprise that when they had finished, Zara led her not out of the restaurant but through the door into the lavatories.

Judging by the sounds coming from a couple of closed cubicles, other diners were also having some post-prandial fun with their pets. Zara dragged Vanessa into a free one, slammed the door, pushed Vanessa up against the partition wall and raped her mouth with her insistent tongue even as she gouged her fingers into the slippery depths of her pussy.

'Please . . . Mistress Editor,' Vanessa gasped. 'This time . . . let me come as well.'

'Well . . . if you're a very good girl and give me a really deep tonguing.'

'I will, Mistress!'

A few days ago the thought of striking such a bargain would have disgusted her. Now it seemed a minor triumph: an assertion that she still had some pride left. Or did she?

Zara hitched up her skirt and sat on the toilet. She pulled Vanessa round until her bottom faced her, then made her bend over, spread her legs and back up. Vanessa's head went down into the toilet bowl, the seat rim pressing into the back of her neck even as Zara's thighs closed about her cheeks and her mouth found Zara's wet groin. Meanwhile Vanessa's inverted pubes ground into Zara's face and opened to her tongue. Unable to resist any more, Vanessa surrendered to her instincts and licked her editor's cunt until she came, even as she herself was tongued to orgasm.

Zara held Vanessa in place with her head down the loo while they both recovered, kissing her sticky pubes and inhaling deeply.

'There's nothing like the scent of a girl who's just come,' she said wistfully. Then she seemed to recover something of her usual briskness. 'So, what am I going to do now?'

Vanessa knew. 'You're going to pee in my face again, Mistress Editor.'

'Why?'

'To remind me, even though you let me come this time, Mistress Editor, that I'm still your slave.'

'That's right, girl. And I hope you always will be . . .'

Her hot pee spurted over Vanessa's face.

Vanessa was still puzzling over her remark that afternoon, as, camera slung about her neck and notebook in hand, she descended to level B3.

Did Zara really think she enjoyed any of this? Couldn't she tell she was only giving in to her desires when forced? If she did not realise that in less than a month Vanessa would be helping to destroy all this, then she was deluding herself.

She stepped out into the High Street almost gratefully. It was a perverted place, but at least here it was natural to walk around naked, and slaves outnumbered masters. Almost a recipe for a revolution, she thought a little mischievously, except that the slaves seemed unwilling to revolt. But if she understood them better, perhaps she might discover the secret of the hold Shiller seemed to have over them.

She knocked on the door of the training yard. After a minute Miss Kyle opened it.

'Ahh, it's the Slave Reporter,' she said with a smile.

Once again Vanessa felt her resolve slipping in the woman's powerful presence. 'Yes, Miss Kyle,' she said meekly.

'If you're going to follow Cherry Chain through its training, these are the rules. You won't be allowed to talk to any of the girls face-to-face for a week. They've got to bond as a group and we can't allow any distractions. During that time you can photograph them if you want and ask us about the stages of their training. Otherwise you will keep quiet and stay out of our way, understand?'

'Yes, Miss Kyle.'

'Then you can come in. We're just helping the girls to get to know each other properly . . .'

The Cherry Chain girls lay on rubber mats in the middle of the yard. Six sprawled on their backs with their legs splayed wide, while the other six lay reversed across them, faces to pubes. Their arms were bound to their sides just above the elbows with black straps, while cuffs fastened to broad, garter-like straps that circled the tops of their thighs secured their wrists. Though they could not use their hands, judging from the snuffling, sucking sounds and the bobbing of their heads, their mouths were evidently busy enough deep within the pussies of their sister slaves, while their pelvises squirmed with equal vigour.

They had no choice, of course. Two of the male trainers stood over them with electric cattle prods. Any slackening of effort was rewarded by a jab in a softly rounded buttock.

'Change!' one of the men called out.

The girls on top all immediately rolled to their left and mounted the next reclining girl in the line. Only now did Vanessa see that round black pads strapped over their eyes blindfolded every girl. They could not even see whom it was they were being made to lick out.

The last girl rolling clear now had nobody to mount. She was dragged to her feet and taken round to the front of the line and made to mount the first girl.

It was darkly fascinating to see those blushing pretty faces, glossy with the juices of their sisters, blindly seeking another cunt to tongue each time they changed. The row of equally flushed pouting clefts, fringed with matted pubic hair, awaited them almost eagerly. The blindfolds reduced them to anonymous sexual playthings. Only the black girl, Olivia, and Kashika's blonde hair against brown skin were immediately recognisable. She was on top at the moment, her face buried in the red pubes of a pale-skinned girl. Amber, was it?

Vanessa supposed she would get to know them all properly when she had a chance to interview them, though how she could do that after seeing them like this she did not know. The seductive scent of unrestrained female arousal was permeating the yard once again. How could they let themselves be used like this?

'Reverse!' the blonde trainer commanded.

The girls on top all rolled to their right and lay on their backs, while the girls who had been underneath rolled over to mount them. Then the process started again. Vanessa realised that this way every girl would eventually have had every other girl both underneath and on top. But what was it supposed to achieve, apart from providing a degrading spectacle for the amusement of their captors?

She went over to Miss Kyle, who was standing a little apart from the male trainers. 'Excuse me, Miss Kyle. May I ask what is this meant to do for these girls?'

'They're learning each others' taste and smell, of course. They have to be totally at ease not only with their own bodies, but also those of their chain sisters. This way they get to know and love every bum, tit and cunt in the chain as though they were their own. It also teaches them to give and receive pleasure among themselves, so when they start working they'll perform any sexual act together without any inhibitions holding them back.'

The anger flared up in Vanessa again. 'And incidentally breaking their spirit and will to resist?'

Miss Kyle raised an eyebrow. 'Still speaking your mind, eh? And still just as wrong. No, you stupid girl, we're freeing their spirit. Be patient. You'll see . . .'

A break was called after another ten minutes of group oral sex. The girls were pulled apart and, still blindfolded, made to kneel in a trembling row. They were clearly desperately aroused, but the constant change of partners had not enabled them to come. Sweat glistened on their bodies and their nipples stood up painfully hard. A plastic watering can was taken along the line, the bare nozzle pushed into their mouths and they were allowed to gulp a few mouthfuls each. Then Miss Kyle went down the line pulling back each girl's head and slipping a ball-gag between her teeth.

Meanwhile, the two male trainers were wheeling out three identical rectangular, tubular metal frames from the selection arrayed about the yards. They stood over two metres tall. Sets of rubber-lined cuffs dangled from the upper rails, and a row of four telescopic rods with large black phalluses in their ends were mounted vertically on each base rail.

One by one, the girls were taken from the line and stood on the base rails of the racks, straddling the phallus rods. The straps binding their arms were removed and their wrists were lifted above their heads and cuffed, then pulled tight until they stood on tiptoe. When they were all in place, their legs were drawn apart and their ankles cuffed to those of the girl next to them, so that they hung from their wrist cuffs. The outside ankle of the girl at the end of each line was fastened to a ring in the side-post of the rack.

Soon the whole chain of a dozen girls was suspended from the frames, linked by their bounds like strings of paper dolls: blind, mute, helpless, trembling, nervous and expectant. The pink inner flesh of their still hungry sexes gaped, wetly waiting for their inevitable penetration.

Vanessa stared at them, unable to turn away. She knew it was wrong but the sight of the captive girls aroused her. Trying to focus on her job, she went over to Miss Kyle again.

'What are you going to do with them now, Miss Kyle?'

'They've had a lot of exercise with their mouths. Now they must start exercising their cunts and arses properly. They've got to learn to enjoy having a variety of objects inserted up them. When they're well stuffed and properly stimulated, we'll allow them to come. It'll reinforce the link in their minds between pain and pleasure. They can't be proper slaves without that.'

'But there is no link,' Vanessa blurted out.

'That's a stupid thing to say, girl, after the way you responded on the rack a couple of days ago.'

Vanessa blushed furiously, but persisted. 'You made me behave like that, Miss Kyle, as you are these girls. But it's not natural. Pain and pleasure are different things.'

'You mean you wish they were different things. Life would be so much simpler. Keep the emotions nice and tidy and separate. But it's not like that for some people. Not for these girls or for you. The sooner you learn to accept that the better.'

She left Vanessa to take up position by one of the racks. The men were standing one each by the others. They began raising the dildos on their adjustable rods, bending the ends slightly to slide them up into the waiting sheaths of flesh above them. The girls tensed and groaned as they were penetrated, throwing back their heads and biting on their ball-gags. Their pubes bulged as the dildos slid so deep inside them Vanessa thought they would burst. Then the rods were locked in place and the trainers stood back, leaving their captives grotesquely skewered.

They twisted in mid-air, their struggles making their sisters wriggle in turn. All they managed was to screw themselves about their impaling dildos. Vanessa saw trickles of clear fluid began to run down the black rubber shafts.

The raw scent of their need wafted over her, and she found herself losing her certainty.

They looked like primitive sacrifices to some pagan god of lust and perversion. She knew it was wrong and cruel yet they looked so ravishingly desirable it shamed her. At that moment they existed for nothing else but a celebration of sex and suffering, and try as she might she could not turn away from them. To hide her naked fascination she raised her camera and began recording their degradation.

The trainers moved to stand behind the three racks of girls. They were now holding what looked like slender paddles with wooden handles and flat black rubber blades. Of course, the stimulation . . .

The paddles swished down on bare soft bottom flesh, making sharp smacks as they struck. The girls yelped behind their gags, their taut, suspended bodies jerking in reflex, sending ripples down the line, grinding the dildos deeper into them. Vanessa saw Kashika's dark glossy breasts shivering and jiggling sharply, while Amber's heavier globes heaved in slower, more fluid motion. Their thighs tensed and knees turned inwards, trying to clench the rods on which they were impaled.

Feeling her own pussy weeping in sympathy, Vanessa kept the camera to her eye as she walked round the racks of tormented girls. From behind she saw how the trainers worked their way up and down the row of their charges, keeping up a steady stream of blows, changing the angle from which they struck, lifting bottom flesh and making it jump and shiver. The paddles did not cut the girls' flesh, but left broad stripes and blushes blossoming over twelve bouncing, clenching backsides.

It was a tie between Kashika and Olivia as to who orgasmed first. With drool running down their cheeks, both girls shrieked and jerked wildly, straining their arms spasmodically as they rode their dildos over the last barrier to relief.

As soon as they went limp their trainers concentrated their attention on the girls either side of them. Three minutes later, all twelve girls hung limp in their bonds, heads lolling on heaving chests, breasts glistening with sweat, vaginal juices dripping freely down the rods to the floor.

The trainers conferred in quiet voices for a minute, then they went to the racks and began lowering the dildos, pulling them out of sticky holes with sucking pops. The girls' gags were pulled out, the water can spout thrust between stretched lips and then the gags were reinserted. Vanessa sighed in relief. She did not know how much more she could have taken, trembling as she was with self-loathing and unquenched lust.

Then she saw the trainers sliding the now pussy-oiled dildos into the girls' rear passages. No, they

136

couldn't expect the poor creatures to come again so soon.

She went up to Miss Kyle. 'Please . . . don't do this to them!'

'Why not? They're willing. See for yourself!' She grasped Vanessa by her hair and pulled her forwards and on to her knees in front of Kashika's spread and impaled body. 'Tell me she's not hot for more,' she hissed, thrusting Vanessa's face into the girl's pubes.

The warm, rich, honeyed scent of the girl filled her nostrils. Her vulva was a dark cleft with contrasting coral-pink depths to her labia, which were wet and engorged by blood. There were beads of sweat in her smooth, deep navel. Her pubic curls were a darker honey-blonde . . .

Miss Kyle jerked Vanessa's head back out of Kashika's love-mouth and pushed her aside. 'Now don't you dare interfere again!'

Confused, Vanessa watched as bottom after bottom bulged with rubber prongs, and girl after girl gasped and groaned and then lifted her head. Were they truly ready to accept more punishment?

The trainers moved round to the front of their racks and began swiping their paddles across the girls' defenceless breasts and stomachs. They writhed and moaned, sore bottoms clenching as they squirmed and twisted on their anal mounts. Vanessa's mind filled with slaps and cracks of rubber on flesh, of breasts rebounding from paddle strokes, of straining nipples, tremulous navels, shafted rears and swollen labia. But above all was the animal scent of their desire misting the air. And helplessly caught up in the charged atmosphere she took picture after picture.

Then it was over. Once more the chain hung limp and drained. The floor beneath them splattered with a second shower of their juices.

Miss Kyle came over to Vanessa. She looked radiantly happy, her nipples standing up through the filmy material of her body stocking.

'This is going to be an exceptionally responsive chain,' she announced proudly. 'They'll make wonderful slaves. You should feel privileged to be covering their training.'

'No!' Vanessa gasped, shaking her head to clear the drug-like aroma of slavery from her mind. 'This is just disgusting. I've got to get out of here!'

An unexpected expression of sympathy crossed Miss Kyle's face. 'Of course. This is a lot to take in. Leave them to us for now. But you'll come back because you can't help it. You want to ask them why they need this. You want to see everything we do to them, however guilty it makes you feel. You can't help yourself. You have to know if it could be you hanging up there with a burning bum and dripping cunt, sobbing with pain but knowing this was what you were born to be . . .'

Vanessa heard no more as she slammed the yard gate behind her.

That night, curled up in bed, her hands cuffed, her bottom filled by her anal lock, Vanessa dreamt of Cherry Chain dancing on their impaling poles. One particular brown-skinned girl with blonde hair was the focus of her thoughts. She was trying to free her but she was chained up herself.

She woke the next morning to find her fingers sticky with her own juices.

138

Eight

Miss Kyle was right when she said Vanessa would come back, and not simply because Zara expected her to cover Cherry Chain's training for *Girlflesh News*. Hateful though it was to admit, she had become helplessly enthralled by the girls' responses. It was like nothing she had ever known before.

As the days passed, the outside world began to seem merely a mundane and rather drab background to the images and sensations of life at Shillers. She tried to rationalise the feeling by putting it down to her own state of enforced nudity and bondage at work, which was heightening and distorting her appreciation of events. This might have been at least partially true, but deep down she knew it could not account for the intensity of her response. It was almost like a drug.

Apart from short outings for essential shopping, she left her flat only to go to work. There were no friends she could imagine going out with in her current situation. How could she possibly behave naturally? Her life was no longer natural; it was a lie, both outwardly and inwardly. But she could see no escape.

Shiller herself contacted her briefly and, on her instructions and dutifully mouthing her words, she phoned Enwright to reassure him she was all right. At

the same time she gave details of a Shiller technical
subsidiary whose activities she thought were unduly
secretive and might warrant further investigation. In
fact, as Shiller explained, the firm in question was
working on classified defence contracts and had no
connection whatsoever with the girlflesh business.
The *Globe* could waste its time investigating the firm
while Vanessa would be seen to be conscientiously
doing her job.

The weekend came up but she worked through it.
The girls' training did not cease and she could not
bear the thought of being monitored in her flat for
two whole days. She was less closely observed at
Shillers. Nobody objected to her presence, and for the
most part it was oddly restful. The building was half
empty and she had the office virtually to herself. Most
of the time she spent down in B3, but she also found
herself daringly wandering along the deserted hall-
ways just peering into offices. What must she look
like naked and chained in such a mundane setting?
She supposed it was a perverse sort of freedom.

In one long utility corridor, she came across a
group of slave-girl cleaners.

There were four of them, their blue collars showing
they belonged to Cyan Chain. They were being driven
by a man in Shiller maintenance overalls working an
industrial-sized floor cleaner that had been modified
to incorporate slaves as part of its mechanism.

Instead of a single vacuum hose it had four, one
running to each of the girls, who shuffled forwards
ahead of the purring machine on their hands and
knees. They wore thick fingerless mittens on their
hands and foam shin pads. They were kept in line by
jointed rods snap-linked to large rings protruding
from their anuses. The hoses passed under their
bodies, supported by hooks from their anal rings, ran

140

freely through the clefts of their pudenda and then between their dangling breasts. Here they were supported by short rubber cords clipped to their nipples, which were pulled tightly inwards by the tension, turning their breasts into fleshy cushioned mounts for the hoses.

The girls held in their mouths the bulbous ends of the short tubular rods on which the actual brush heads were fixed. As they progressed forwards they moved their heads from side to side, as though they were grazing. Between them they swept the entire width of the corridor in one go.

Vanessa pressed herself up against the wall and lowered her head meekly as the extraordinary living machine passed. As she looked at the line of upturned bottoms receding from her, she saw the tell-tale glisten of female lubrication around the hoses where they pressed up into their vulvas, spreading their flesh-lips. The rubbing of the ribbed hose and the vibration of the machine transmitted through it was obviously exciting them. But was that compensation enough for such indignity?

She was just leaving the office after lunch when she had an altogether different encounter. The lobby doors opened and a pair of security guards entered. One she recognised as the main gate guard who always grinned at her as she passed on the way in.

'Hallo, Miss Buckingham ... or can I call you Vanessa?' he said, smirking broadly. 'I thought, as you were up here on your own, you might want some company, didn't I, Phil?'

Phil was also grinning, looking Vanessa up and down with unashamed pleasure. 'You did, Geoff.'

'I told you I'd be seeing more of you the first day we met,' Geoff said.

As they came towards her, Vanessa knew with sick certainty what they were going to do. She also knew that inside Shillers she had no reason to expect anything else. It was only a pointless conditioned reflex that made her turn and run back into the office. They followed laughing, as though it was great sport.

She dodged round the desks, her chains jingling, but they got on either side of her and she was cornered. It was almost a relief to feel the grip of their strong hands and let them take complete control of her.

They twisted her arms behind her back and clipped her wrist cuffs to her belt. How easy it was for them when she came ready-fitted with restraints, she thought dizzily. She made one last instinctive protest to satisfy what was left of her sense of honour. 'No . . . please don't –'

Geoff's big hand closed over Vanessa's mouth, silencing her.

'I'll take some oral, all right with you?'

Phil slid stiff exploratory fingers into Vanessa's vagina. 'That'll do me fine . . .' he withdrew his hand, his fingers now glistening. 'Look, the slut's already wet for it!'

They pushed her face down over a desk, so that her feebly kicking legs hung over one side and her head the other. Geoff held her down with one hand clasped about the back of her neck, while he unzipped his flies. His erect cock sprang out, foreskin already rolling back from its purple plum head. She could smell his musk. Phil kneed her thighs apart. Another zip came down. His thumbs sank into the soft flesh of her buttocks and pulled them open. Geoff prised her jaws apart and thrust his shaft into her mouth. Phil rammed into her vagina even as Geoff's cock plumbed the depths of her throat, almost choking her.

And because it was so much easier and seductively natural, she let her instinct take over.

In and out they pumped, grinding Vanessa to and fro across the desk, she cock-spitted between them, moaning and spluttering and squirming. When they came she swallowed greedily, trying to suck them dry with both her mouths even as pleasure boiled through her loins.

Recovering, they pulled out of her and tucked away their now drained and sticky cocks. Vanessa felt sudden emptiness. Unclipping her hands, they gave her bottom a friendly slap and left her sprawled across the desktop, sweaty, panting and soiled.

After a minute she got off the desk. There was a stain on the carpet where her juices and Phil's sperm had dribbled out of her slit. She scuffed it over with her toe. Clutching one hand over her pubes to contain any more drips, she stumbled out of the office and along the corridor to the toilets. She had discovered earlier that one stall contained a bidet. Now she understood why and used it gratefully.

She wiped herself clean, went to the sink and washed out her mouth, splashed her face off, towelled dry, and then examined herself in the mirror. It was hard to admit, but she didn't look freshly ravaged. Her cheeks were flushed, her eyes bright, her nipples still semi-hard. Her vagina was a little sore, but no more than she might expect from vigorous sex. Did that make her strong or weak?

She had just been treated like a slave-girl, and had ultimately responded like one. She'd had forced sex with two strange men and had responded with an orgasm. Not a big one but still an orgasm. That part of it had felt good. Why? Perhaps being here had unnaturally stimulated her needs, which had to be satisfied by the same brutal means. She should feel outraged but didn't. Why should she seek out grief? In the outside world she knew that was how she would react if something like this had just happened, but in here normal rules did not apply. Phil and Geoff evidently felt no guilt. They had enjoyed themselves and casually assumed she had too. In a way she had. What did that say about her? Was she really a slut?

Vanessa explored the rest of level B3, something she knew that as a reporter she should have done earlier. A lot of the girls were out on assignments over the weekend, so it was quiet there too.

Arriving early and staying late, she discovered that the ceiling lighting dimmed to a dull blue glow in the evenings, mimicking nightfall. Wall lamps came on, as did colourful strings of lights garlanded about the larger trees and shrubs. The air conditioning also shifted to a cooler cycle. At such times she could almost believe she was walking the narrow streets of some tiny village.

The six small chalets where the trainers lived she avoided, but otherwise she wandered at will. Paradoxically, in this underground haven of bondage, nobody stopped her and there were few locked doors.

Opposite the stables, which still gave her the shivers, was a plain building with fewer windows than the others. It turned out to be a storehouse of every type of bondage equipment imaginable – rows of hooks hung heavy with handcuffs, wheeled torture racks and suspension frames, and some devices whose functions she could not even puzzle out.

The huge array was mind-numbing. Overwhelmed, she sat down on a chair in the shadows to rest, only to find it was fitted with an array of hinged metal cuffs that could be closed about neck, waist, wrists and ankles. There was no proper seat but side legs where thighs could be held wide open, leaving the groin totally exposed and vulnerable. She got up quickly.

Backing the inner row of the Mall shops, so that it ran down one side of the High Street, was a long windowless block with heavy double doors at each end. Beyond them were lobbies with inner sets of doors marked with large red signs saying: QUIET PLEASE – GIRLS RESTING.

Inside were several warm, dimly lit chambers with rows of heavy hooks dangling from the ceilings. From these were suspended chains of sleeping slave-girls.

They were secured with their backs to wooden boards a little larger than coffin lids, their hands to their sides and feet slightly apart. Paired hooks bolted to the backs of the boards about one-third the way down from the top forced the girls to hang forwards at slight angles. They were fastened to the boards by broad rubber straps about their ankles, knees, upper thighs, waists, upper arms, wrists, and necks. Velcro pads were positioned on the back of the boards by the slots through which the straps emerged to fasten them in place. Wooden wedge blocks under their feet prevented them from slipping down the boards.

The girls' heads were enclosed in black rubber hoods, pierced only by a triangle for their nostrils and a soft plug for their mouths. Rings protruding from the crown of each hood were hooked to short rubber cords connected to the tops of the boards, ensuring the girls' heads did not droop forwards.

Marker memo pads hung on hooks by each chain. On them were written notes such as: 'Violet Chain. Assigned to Chudleigh Hall, Berks. Sat/Sun. Suspended 10.30. Take down 16.30. Depart 17.00.'

Vanessa walked between the aisles of suspended flesh, fascinated by the slight rise and fall of the sleeping girls' nipples. Despite the air of restful calm that permeated the chambers, she could not help thinking of sides of meat hanging in a butcher's shop.

After checking with Mr Jarvis that it was permitted, she explored the rest of the block beyond the locker room where she changed. She moved as a slave-girl was forced to do, through low gates and along low, mesh-lined tunnel corridors. These opened on to bathrooms, a large mess hall and dormitories stacked in galleries. None of the spaces were at all private, nor were any high enough to stand upright within.

Blocks of steps rested against the tunnels, so that anybody coming through the ordinary doors could climb up and walk along their reinforced mesh tops, looking down on the slaves under their feet. Vanessa could appreciate the psychological message such an arrangement reinforced. 'You are beneath me therefore you are inferior.'

At the end of the block she found something unexpected. A tunnel dipped down in a ramp, then along and up again, evidently going under one of the passageways above. It emerged into a perfectly tranquil walled garden containing a shallow blue swimming pool, grassy banks and low trees, and so artfully lit by sunlamps that for a moment she thought she had somehow wandered above ground. Then she realised this was the block across the High Street from the new chain-training yard.

As she emerged, half a dozen slave-girls were lazing about reading or splashing in the pool. They were perfectly friendly, if a little curious. Without a coloured chain collar she did not quite fit in. They clustered round in an unself-conscious knot of bare flesh. It was disconcerting. They only wore collars while she had slave chains as well. She was less free than they were. But evidently this was less important to them than who she was.

'Are you visiting? Do you belong to a friend of the Director's?'

'Wait, didn't I see you taking photographs at the new chain ceremony.'

'Yes,' Vanessa admitted. 'I've . . . er, just started working for *Girlflesh News* . . . as a sort of trial.'

At that they got excited. Some of them had the latest copy with them and wanted to suggest ideas for articles. That they seemed so utterly happy and at ease with their situation she could not believe. Had they been totally conditioned to accept their lot as slaves? It appeared they could not help the way they were. But perhaps the new girls might not be beyond saving.

Always Vanessa returned to the training yard and Cherry Chain. She no longer tried to interfere, but kept out of the way, recording each step they took on the way to total subjugation.

Miss Kyle seemed to be the new girls' permanent trainer, but Vanessa learnt the names of the others as they took their turn in the yard. The black pony-girl driver was Mr Winston. The blond man habitually dressed in shorts and a singlet, whom she had seen that first day driving a chain of girls into the lift, was Mr Tyler. Mr Hirsch preferred calf-length boots and a minimal leather pouch. Miss Scott was the blonde in the black pvc bikini, while Mr McGarry liked to wear leather trousers and a harness top.

Watching them work as they broke the Cherry girls in was at one and the same time revolting, fascinating and deeply arousing . . .

* * *

'Fetch!' Mr Hirsch commanded, throwing a handful of coloured rubber balls about the yard.

The girls chased after the balls on all-fours, snapping them up in their mouths. Rubber mittens confined their hands, while adhesive pads protected their knees and toes. Their wrists and ankles were linked by semi-rigid rubber bars snap-hooked to their cuffs, which meant they could only move in a series of bounding lunges that set their breasts bouncing and swaying. The motion further agitated the up-curving hollow rubber tails that had been plugged into their rear passages, setting them bobbing about in a parody of real dogs' tails. As they moved, Vanessa could see the fat tail plugs twisting and turning behind the girls' anal sphincters, which pinched tight about the narrow tail roots.

When the girls retrieved the balls they bounded back to Hirsch, sat back on their haunches with their constrained hands lifted up under their breasts in a begging posture and whimpered in their eagerness to present them. Like the pets in the restaurant, they had been instructed to speak only in canine yaps and whines. Hirsch allowed them to drop the balls neatly into his open hand and then patted their heads as he might real dogs.

Vanessa was not sure what disturbed her most: the degrading activities forced upon the girls or their apparent enthusiastic acquiescence. How could they enjoy such things? They all looked intelligent enough. They could not want this for themselves. But there was Amber, her pale face flushed and large breasts crowned with tumescent nipples heaving with her exertions, looking as though she would wag a real tail with pleasure if she had one. She saw Olivia, her dark glossy skin shiny with sweat, gazing up at Hirsch with soulful eyes. How could any black girl voluntarily accept a collar and chains? And as they all bounded off again to retrieve the balls once more, it was Kashika's smooth brown buttocks that were ahead of the rest.

'Although you'll be taught how to satisfy the needs of men and women equally well, over eight out of ten of your users will be men,' Miss Kyle told Cherry Chain, as if delivering a lecture. 'Over the past few days you've got used to having dildos inside you. Today you'll move on to the real thing . . .'

The girls had been divided into two sections and secured to a pair of wheeled frames resembling lengths of low fencing. The rows of girls faced each other, so that they could learn from watching their sisters' responses. With hands cuffed behind them, they were bent forwards over the fence rails and held in place with straps about their waists, so that their breasts and heads hung over one side, while their bottoms projected over the other. Their legs were spread, pulled inwards and tied to the lower bar of the frame, increasing the outthrust and exposure of their rears. Miss Scott, wheeling round a mobile douche machine, was giving the last of them an enema, leaving pink-rimmed and freshly oiled anuses in her wake.

Winston, Tyler and McGarry stood to one side of the group. All three were totally naked. Each was stroking a rampant erection. Vanessa swallowed at the sight of them and hid behind her camera, ashamed of her own shameful response to such a blatant display of masculinity. The girls wriggled in their bonds, fearful yet eager, as their eyes flickered between the man and Miss Kyle.

'You must get use to the feel of cockflesh inside you,' Miss Kyle continued, 'no matter what orifice it enters. Each has its own special appeal to the man using you. Your bum-holes are hotter and tighter, your cunts juicier, your mouths more mobile. You'll do your best to please with each one. The only difference to you is that when your mouths are being used, you can taste where that cock has been previously. This sometimes troubles girls so that they do not perform properly. You will learn not to let it bother you. It doesn't matter if you can taste your own juices or those of another girl on the cock, or if it's just been up your rear or one of your sisters. That's why we've flushed you out so thoroughly, and why you will never be sent on any assignment without being completely clean inside and out. You must learn how to give pleasure without guilt or hesitation. That's what this exercise is designed to teach you.'

The men moved forwards and took up position. Winston stood between the rows of girls in front of Amber, who goggled at his thick erection. Tyler stood at the other end on the outside of the same row, his cock pressed up against Lisa's already wet cleft. McGarry had the other row to himself, his rod nuzzling Yvonne's bottom cheeks. Vanessa smelt the girls' anticipation filling the air.

'The exercise will continue until the men are satisfied,' Miss Kyle said. 'Whether you come once, twice or not at all during the time is for the moment unimportant, as long as you continue to please. Any unsatisfied desire must be contained until you are allowed to couple with your chain sisters later. They will always be there for you. But for now, it's men you must please . . .'

The trainers rammed their cocks into their chosen fleshy holes. Three or four quick thrusts in each and then they moved on down the line. They had thirty-six orifices to fill between them so they did not waste any time. Cheeks briefly filled with hard penis meat, labia spread and bottoms bulged. The girls were used impersonally, almost brutally, their dangling breasts swaying as the men pumped into them from front and rear.

Cocks that had been up bottoms were now in mouths, saliva was mingling within vaginas and girlish lubrication was oiling anuses. Eyes misted with tears as they squirmed in the bonds. Were they straining to escape or to please? Vanessa could not tell.

The rotating penetration continued until the men were all drained and their cocks hung flaccid. The girls' labia and anal rings were reddened with use, and sperm, saliva and vaginal juices splattered the floor beneath them. Some looked at their masters hollow-eyes with need, silently begging for more. But they knew they would have to wait for their release. Was that the cruellest part of it?

The following day Vanessa saw the girls at their most peaceful.

Zara had kept her late finishing an article for *Datumline*, which she had found unexpectedly heavy going. On an impulse she dropped in on the training yard before going to the locker room. It was very quiet and the yard sky-lighting had already been dimmed in advance of that in the rest of the level.

Miss Kyle, padding around clearing up the equipment, put her finger to her lips and whispered: 'They're already asleep. You can look at them if you want, but be quiet. They worked very hard today and deserve the rest . . .'

Cherry Chain were housed in a hutch-like structure in one corner of the yard, its wood and wire-mesh frame covered by external roller blinds. Edging a blind aside, Vanessa could see the interior illuminated by a dim red nightlight.

The girls lay on a bed of straw huddled in pairs face-to-face and sleeping in each other's arms. Short chains, holding them close, linked their collars. Kashika was entwined with a dark-haired girl Vanessa recognised as Victoria. Their breasts were flattened together in soft pancakes, bellies almost touching, pubic hair mingling. She saw a gleam of metal between Kashika's buttocks and realised the pairs were also linked by anal locks, similar to the one she wore at night. The air in the hutch was warm with their body heat . . .

'Pretty, isn't she?' Miss Kyle whispered, peering through the blinds beside Vanessa and following the direction of her gaze.

Embarrassed, Vanessa quickly lowered the blind and stepped back from the hutch. 'Why do you make them sleep like that, Miss Kyle?' she asked, trying to sound matter-of-fact.

'To teach them to love and trust each other, of course. We change the pairing every night. Once they've got used to this arrangement we'll put them in the kennels for a night on their own.'

'Isn't that cruel, Miss Kyle?' Vanessa said quickly, before she realised that by implication this arrangement of chained flesh in the hutch before her was in some way kinder.

Miss Kyle shrugged. 'They know they have to suffer to become Shiller girls. They must get used to being treated as proper bitches occasionally. But the isolation also makes them value each other's company more. They'll learn chain love. There's nothing like it. That's worth a little suffering.'

Nine

Vanessa knelt submissively before Zara in her office.

'Right,' Zara said. 'Denise says you can start your interviews with Cherry Chain tomorrow. I'll leave the angle you take up to you, but I suggest one thing. If you want them to be forthcoming and open, don't tell them the real reason you're here. You may not believe it, but they aren't looking for rescue by a crusading investigative reporter.'

'I've already talked to some of the other girls, Mistress Editor,' Vanessa admitted. 'I just said I was here on trial.'

Zara chuckled drily. 'Whereas in fact it's us who are on trial. Why did the Director ever make that bargain with you? Still, she knows people better than anybody, so I suppose it'll work out for the best. All right, that's all . . .'

She lifted her dress, exposing her knickerless crotch. It was a new rule Zara had invented to be applied whenever Vanessa entered or left her office. Vanessa dutifully shuffled forwards and kissed Zara's moist, fragrant love-lips in their soft nest of hair.

'Thank you, Mistress Editor . . .'

Back at her desk Vanessa found herself experiencing a little illicit thrill of anticipation. She knew it was ridiculous, but she was getting excited at the thought of talking to Kashika. God, it was like having a juvenile crush rewarded. So the girl was strikingly pretty, but still she should be over such things by now. Get a grip on reality, she told herself. This is not a game.

Her emotions flipped, suddenly filling her with a sense of acute embarrassment and inadequacy. How could she possibly talk to Kashika, to any of the Cherry Chain girls, after having seen them so completely degraded? Did she even have the confidence to conduct a proper interview naked and slave-chained as she was? Most of these raw girl-slaves were younger than her, if only by a few years. They'd expect some show of self-assurance. She didn't even have the strange sense of inner composure the other slave-girls possessed.

She needed a prop, a distraction, something to boost her confidence. Then it came to her. Yes, that was it. There was a shop she knew that stayed open late. Tomorrow she'd be ready to do her job.

As Vanessa knelt before her the next morning, Zara raised a quizzical eyebrow at the new white fedora perched on her head. Tucked into its black silk band was a folded card marked 'PRESS'.

'Well let's hold the front page,' she drawled. 'Who do you think you are: Hildy Johnson?'

Obviously she had recognised the allusion to the classic film comedy drama about journalists. 'It doesn't hide anything, Mistress Editor,' Vanessa said defensively.

Mr Jarvis had thought it was very fetching when he checked her in that morning. After examining the hat he had her walk up and down a few times to show it off, and she had found herself unexpectedly rolling her hips and flicking the hat brim provocatively. It was true that sometimes a part-dressed girl can look sexier than one totally nude.

The fedora was a gesture of independence. It was true that it concealed nothing, but it drew attention away from her exposed body, at the same time accentuating her nakedness by contrast. She had made a statement and it was emboldening. She was showing off and not hiding any more. If she had to be a slave reporter then it would be with style.

'Wear it if you like,' Zara said, to Vanessa's relief. 'You can interview Cherry Chain after lunch. But finish that chemistry piece for *Datumline* first.'

'Yes, Mistress Editor.'

Zara lifted her skirt. Vanessa briefly took of her hat to bestow her ritual kiss.

Zara patted her bared head. 'Perhaps you can be my girl Friday . . .'

Yes, she did watch old movies.

Miss Kyle smiled archly at the fedora when Vanessa entered the training yard, but said only: 'They're still eating, but they've got a rest period coming up. I've told them about the interviews and shown them a copy of *Girlflesh News* and they're really excited about it.' She added with what sounded like genuine concern. 'They're still learning to be confident with what they are so don't do anything to disappoint them!'

'I won't, Miss Kyle,' Vanessa promised.

Miss Kyle considered the hat again. 'Find it empowering, do you? Makes you feel more confident?'

She understood! 'Yes, Miss Kyle,' Vanessa admitted.

'It suits you.'

The chain were arranged in a ring on their hands and knees, heads facing inwards, showing off their pretty bare bottoms and pudenda clefts pouting out from between their thighs. They ate out of metal bowls. Their wrists were not cuffed but their hands were encased in fingerless rubber mittens, so that they rested the weight of their upper bodies on their elbows and ate with their faces buried in the bowls, as Vanessa had been made to do by Zara in the restaurant. Was that even more a mark of a slave-pet than enforced nudity or collaring, she wondered? To be made to eat like an animal . . .

As she got closer she saw their bowls were neatly numbered and inscribed with their names and chain number. They really were being treated like animals, or at least, like pampered pets.

When the girls had literally licked their plates clean, they turned to their neighbours and licked each other's faces as well. Then they were led over to a corner of the yard where some mats had been laid out. A long chain fastened to a wall-mounted ring was passed through their collars. Then the trainers withdrew, leaving Vanessa smiling down at a ring of bright, expectant faces.

Perhaps the hat helped, for she sounded more confident than she felt as she said: 'Hallo, my name's Vanessa. I'm the slave reporter for the *Girlflesh News*.' God, I've actually said it out loud, she thought.

Some smiled back uncertainly, while others submissively lowered their heads, clearly unsure, despite her slave chains, if she was their equal or not. Kashika was one of them. Quickly Vanessa sat down cross-legged on the mat facing the half-circle of naked girls.

'It's all right, I'm a slave as well,' she said, trying to reassure them while not choking in disgust at her words. 'My editor's given me the job of covering your progress. Now, so far I've learnt your names and watched you train –'

'Have you been taking pictures of us?' Victoria interjected hesitantly, eyeing the camera slung round Vanessa's neck.

'Um, yes, but I promise nobody else will see them until –'

'Will they be published in *Girlflesh News*?' Olivia asked.

'Yes, some of them, but I'll try not to show . . .'

Vanessa trailed off as a dozen pairs of nipples perked up and hardened before her eyes. Their faces displayed not shame at the idea but excitement. What had they done to these girls? She recovered and pressed on, trying to treat it as an ordinary interview despite the unreal circumstances.

'I want to find out what it feels like to live down here for a month, how you're being treated, what you think of your trainers, and so on. If you don't mind I'd like to record your answers.' The girls nodded and she switched on her recorder.

'To begin with, there's one big question I think any ordinary person would want to ask all of you. In this day and age, in any day and age, for that matter, why would anybody choose to be a slave?' She couldn't leave such a question hanging there, so she added: 'I mean, the careers adviser never suggested taking a course in it when I was at school.'

That set them laughing and giggling.

'I knew one teacher who'd have been happy to talk to me about that sort of thing,' Charlotte said with a huge grin.

The others chuckled knowingly. Vanessa asked anxiously: 'You weren't abused? He never made you do anything . . .'

'No. He never touched me. But I knew he'd like to. It was sort of exciting thinking about it even though he was a creep.'

'When I was young I used to like playing games when you were tied up,' Holly admitted. 'I suppose that shows I've always had a thing about bondage.'

Several of the other girls nodded.

'Is that something you all felt?' Vanessa asked, trying unobtrusively to catch Kashika's eye and encourage her to join in.

Kashika said almost shyly: 'I tried tying myself up a few times. I didn't know why it made me feel good. But I was too frightened to tell anyone. Nobody would have understood, and if my parents had found out I don't know what would have happened! It did make me move away from home as soon as I could, so I would have more privacy.'

Her voice was clear but softly pitched, her large liquid brown eyes demurely downcast. Vanessa had to drag her gaze away from her as Olivia spoke.

'I had a boyfriend who spanked me once. Just for fun on the bum, you know, but it really turned me on. The thing was when I wanted the same on my tits . . .' she stroked her full, chocolate-brown nipples '. . . he started calling me names. Said I was weird. So I dumped him. But I knew I wanted more of it.'

'I think a lot of men dream of having a harem but don't know how to handle a real submissive,' Tina suggested to a round of assenting nods.

Vanessa said: 'But it's a big step from spanking and playing at bondage to letting yourselves become full-time . . .' she sought for a better word but could not think of one '. . . professional slaves. As though it was a career. How did you make such a jump?'

'It was answering the survey that started it for me,' Fiona said.

'And after going to the Fellgrish Institute, I knew for sure it was what I wanted to be,' Madelyn added. Again they all nodded.

Vanessa tried to look as though she knew what they were talking about. 'Oh, yes, the Institute. Tell me about that.'

Yvonne, a flush forming on her pale cheeks, said: 'Well, it was embarrassing at first. All those tests and questions about sex. Having those devices stuck up inside you as you watched those videos, and so on. But as I went through the stages and the stricter it got, the better I liked it. You know what I mean.'

The other girls were nodding and grinning. Vanessa could not admit her ignorance now, so she had to phrase her next question carefully. 'Didn't you worry, while you were at the Institute, that you were being manipulated in some way? Led on?'

'Oh no,' Yvonne said quickly. 'They were very careful to explain what would happen in each stage before I signed the consent forms. I knew exactly what I was doing. I wanted to keep going to find out how much I could take. When I passed the final test they told me about this place. Then it all made sense.'

It couldn't be as simple as that, Vanessa thought. She said: 'But how do you cope with the pain, the humiliation. Don't you find it degrading?'

The girls looked slightly puzzled. 'I suppose it is,' Amber said, 'but that's part of the fun.'

'You're chained up right now,' Vanessa persisted. 'You're locked up in a cage at night. You're being taught how to give yourself to people as sex-slaves. You get beaten and abused. Most ordinary people would think you'd want to escape, that what was being done to you was wrong!'

There was an awkward pause, then Charlotte said: 'It's all about wanting not to have the choice, isn't it?

The thrill is in being helpless, thinking of what you're going to be made to do. I can't speak for anybody else, but for me it feels . . . right.'

'What does it matter what ordinary people would think?' Holly said. 'We're not ordinary, we're special!'

Kashika spoke up, her voice as soft as before but carrying deep conviction. 'A year ago I thought I was sick or something. Then I went to the Institute and found out I was not a freak, just different, and that I was not the only one who had these feelings. Now I'm here, being myself. I think it's destiny.' She clasped the chain running through her collar, joining her to the other girls. 'For the first time in my life, I feel really free!'

Back in her flat that night Vanessa replayed her recording and tried to make sense of it all. The girls sounded so sincere, but then they would in such surroundings. Away from B3 it might be different, if they were not already too far gone to be saved. And what about this Fellgrish Institute? If that was where their conditioning had begun, the actual lure that drew the girls into slavery, then it was even more important than Shiller HQ. It was certainly worth investigating further. And who knew what chance she might have to escape her continuous monitoring if it involved travel outside the capital?

When she raised the idea with Zara the next day she responded more positively than Vanessa had hoped.

'Yes, it might be an idea for you to visit the Institute,' Zara agreed. 'It's on the outskirts of Oxford, so you could do it in a day. It ties in with the Cherry Chain articles: "Where it all began for the new girls", perhaps. But the people at Fellgrish don't like visitors interfering with their research schedule, so it might take a while to set up. I'll see what I can do. Meanwhile, you'd better get that interview written up, then start on the thermal glass article for *Datumline* . . .'

The next issue of *Girlflesh News* came out a few days later, carrying her coverage of Cherry Chain's initiation and the group interview. It was distributed to its highly select readership as a download, on disk or as limited hard-copy run. These were given away as a free-sheet in the B3 mews beside the other regular papers and magazines. Passing through on her way to the training yard, Vanessa could not help stopping to look through the issue.

Under the heading: 'A new chain take their first steps', was written: 'by Vanessa B. your Slave Reporter'. What a feature to have her name associated with, Vanessa thought. Yet on display in this flesh-lined thoroughfare, it looked almost commonplace.

Several other girls who had been reading *Girlflesh News* stopped her to say how they liked the piece. Despite everything she felt flattered by their words. She picked up a few copies of the *News* to show Cherry Chain. On an impulse she also bought them a large selection box of sweets.

With glowing cheeks and vulvas still pink and puffy from whatever the latest sexual exercise they had been performing, the girls pored over the paper in their rest period, eating chocolates while admiring the graphic images of themselves. Vanessa looked on, both touched and dismayed by their reaction. What sort of madness was this when young women got excited reading about their own subjugation?

'Will you be writing more about us?' Holly asked.

'I expect so,' Vanessa said.

'Will you do a special feature on our graduation?' Amber asked.

'Er . . . we'll see,' Vanessa said.

'If you want any more treats you must duck for them,' Miss Kyle announced, coming up quietly behind them.

In a minute she had cuffed the girls' hands behind their backs and then pushed one chocolate each up into their vaginas. The chain had soon dissolved into a squirming, giggling mass of girls with their faces buried in each other groins and their tongues probing hot wet depths as they delved for the melting sweets.

Vanessa watched Kashika's cheeks getting ever more smeared with chocolate as she slurped and sucked at Amber's gaping love-mouth and felt a wild pang of desire and urge to join them. They seemed so innocently happy. No, she would resist. But she knew the longer she was part of this madness, the more it would seem normal.

At the end of Cherry Chain's second week of training, a notice was posted on the training-yard door. Copies had already been posted in all the offices above.

CHERRY CHAIN
BREAKING IN TODAY
2 TO 6 PM
ALL WELCOME
FIRST SERVED,
FIRST COME

Vanessa found herself smiling at the last lines before she remembered what was going to happen.

A long tent had been erected in the yard. Cherry Chain waited nervously outside in a coffle, collars chained together in number order, wrists cuffed behind them, blindfold straps and ring-gags hanging ready about their necks.

Vanessa's appearance was greeted with sudden smiles. She was the only person besides their trainers that the girls had had any real contact with since their initiation. As both a sister slave and reporter of their personal story, she had become a confidante and minor celebrity in their eyes, which made her feel uneasy.

'Please wish us luck,' Amber begged.

How could she do such a thing? It would seem as though she condoned what they were about to do. But she could not disappoint them.

'Of course,' she said. 'Good luck . . .' And on an impulse she hugged Amber, feeling her large breasts press against her own, and then kissed her on the lips.

Then of course she had to hug and kiss them all in turn, working her way down the line. She tried not to linger when she reached Kashika, but she was acutely aware of the special scent of the Indian girl's body, the hardness of her nipples, the moist willing warmth of her full lips. She let her hand slide briefly across the smooth curves of her buttocks, giving them an extra squeeze, then reluctantly broke her embrace and moved on to Lisa next in line.

With a final wave she turned quickly away from them, trying not to show her own arousal. Horrible as it was to admit, nervous as they were, the girls were ready and eager for sex and it was impossible not to respond in kind.

But now she had to do her job. She was not going to be allowed in the tent while the chain girls were serving, so she had to record the scene before the customers arrived.

Inside the tent was divided down the middle by a long low continuous wooden rail, which had been crossed by post and canvas partitions, forming twelve narrow compartments with curtains at either end.

The upright posts in each compartment were hung with cuffs and chains. A length of canvas rolled up like a blind hung across the middle of each compartment directly above its section of railing, which had foam padding bound around it. A second canvas screen also hung from the rail to the floor. Set to one side in each compartment was a swivel chair mounted on castors.

The attendants for Cherry Chain were already in place. Two dozen hooded girls wearing the green and pink collars of Apple and Carnation chains respectively, were tethered one on each side of the long rail. They were sitting cross-legged on little rubber mats with sponges, wipes and hoses by their sides. They were there to clean and freshen a girl's mouth, vagina or anus as required between each user. It was very like the service Sandra had performed for Vanessa while she was on display in the mews cell. The thought deepened her arousal and she felt the familiar exciting warm slickness begin to ooze between her labia.

She tried to cover her body's treacherous reaction by taking a flurry of pictures and making scribbled notes. Why was she responding in this way? What was planned here was almost an orchestrated gang rape. Yet the girls were pathetically willing. Was it the big tent that made it worse, lending the event a pseudo-public air, as though it were some bizarre sideshow at a fête?

Miss Kyle was walking round the tent making last-minute checks. Vanessa went over to her.

'Why do they have to perform in a tent, Miss Kyle? Couldn't you put them in cells in the Mall? At least they'd have a bit more privacy.'

'I thought you understood by now that chain girls don't expect privacy,' Miss Kyle said curtly. 'This way they can feel the movement of their sisters' bodies through the rails, and know they are all experiencing the same sensations and serving the same purpose. But if it's any comfort, they'll get their chance to serve one-to-one in privacy next week. We'll be holding a lottery and twelve lucky members of staff will be able to take a Cherry Chain girl home with them for a night. It's a test of their confidence for those occasions when they have to serve individually.'

'And I suppose being treated as raffle prizes is also good training, Miss Kyle?' Vanessa said, an edge of sarcasm in her voice.

'Of course. It teaches them that they belong to Shiller to do with as we wish – yet also that they are prized and have value. Who wouldn't want such a gift?' She grinned mischievously. 'Even you might enjoy having a Cherry Chain girl as your sex-toy for a night. Or at least, one particular Cherry girl . . .'

Vanessa turned aside, blushing shamefully. She knew!

Cherry Chain was brought into the tent. Their coffle chains were unclipped and they were taken to their assigned compartments. The blindfold straps were pulled up into place. They not only held circular black-cushioned pads firmly over their eyes, but where the broad bands covered their ears they had integral foam plugs on their inside faces.

'What they see and hear is unimportant from now on,' Miss Kyle said. 'It'll also help them focus their attention . . .'

The girls were bent over the low padded rail and straps went across their backs to hold them in place. Their legs were spread and ankles cuffed to the upright side-posts. Their arms were unfastened, pulled up and back and cuffed to rings set in the posts above their waists. From the same rings hung a pair of light spring chains, the ends of which were hooked to moulded rings set in the back of their blindfold straps, supporting their heads and keeping them centred.

The enforced posture was similar to the one they had been put in when the three male trainers had used them front and rear. It might have been a rehearsal for this event. Now their mouths, breasts and genitals were positioned at the ideal height for male and female users alike, who might sit or stand to use them as they wished.

The canvas blinds were unrolled, dropping down around the girls' waists. Semicircles cut out of the fabric enclosed them tightly. The trailing ends were tied to the cross-rail dividing the compartment in two, with a girl's legs and body from the waist down on one side and from the waist up on the other. By this means two people could use her simultaneously without seeing each other.

With Vanessa trailing after her, Miss Kyle moved between the compartments, checking the girls' bonds. She said: 'For the next four hours they must pleasure any cock or cunt that's presented to any of their orifices, singly or two at a time. It's a test of their endurance and commitment, but I'm sure they'll all pass.' She looked at Vanessa. 'Don't you think they look incredibly fuckable right now?'

'No, Miss Kyle,' Vanessa said

'You're not tempted at all? You don't wonder what it would be like to use them?'

'Of course not!'

Miss Kyle suddenly reached out, grabbing a fistful of Vanessa's hair in one hand and cupping her pubes with the other.

'Liar! You're hot and wet. You're a slut at heart, just as I said the day we met. This turns you on.' She thrust stiff fingers up Vanessa's moist vagina. 'Admit it!'

Vanessa gasped. 'All right . . . I'm aroused! But it's wrong!'

'No it's not, you stupid bitch! They want this . . .'

There was a growing murmur of voices from outside the tent. The first of the office staff were beginning to arrive.

'Find out for yourself, then you might believe me . . .'

She pulled Vanessa's arms behind her and clipped her cuffs to the back of her belt. Pushing her forwards she propelled her into one of the compartments and sat her down in the swivel chair.

Kashika's upper body was spread out before Vanessa, seeming to burst out of the canvas screen. Her arms pulled back and behind her accentuated her neat, perfectly ripe breasts as they hung from her taut ribcage. Her brown nipples stood out in hard cones ready to be pinched and sucked and played with. Blindly she seemed to stare out at Vanessa, her lips slightly parted. The ring-gag dangled from her neck, there for any man to push between her teeth and force her mouth wide for his cock.

Still holding Vanessa by the hair, Miss Kyle tilted back the chair. Pinching Vanessa's left nipple between finger and thumbnail, she hissed in her ear: 'Open your legs or else!'

Trembling, Vanessa pulled her legs up and back, hooking her knees over the arms of the chair, exposing her pubic mound and shamefully glistening cleft. Looking down between her breasts she was horrified to see her clitoris swelling up from the gaping valley of her already engorged labia. Miss Kyle pushed the chair forwards, ramming Vanessa's pubes into Kashika's face. Immediately, the Cherry

Chain slave-girl began to nuzzle and lick her way deep into the sheath of wet, perfumed flesh.

Vanessa groaned and shuddered, unable to resist her touch. Kashika's tongue was like a darting snake, slithering into every fold, teasing her clitoris into painful hardness. She had never felt such a powerful response to another girl. Her juices streamed from her, wetting her bottom and glistening on Kashika's dark skin. Kashika gasped as somebody on the other side of the canvas divide started using her from behind, but she continued dutifully licking Vanessa out.

Too soon it was over. Vanessa arched her back in orgasmic spasm as she came, grinding her vulva into the face of the girl she now knew, in that stark moment of perfect release, she adored utterly and completely.

Ten

Vanessa had never known such guilt as she felt the day after Cherry Chain's breaking-in. Though it was wrong, she could not forget Kashika's tonguing and the power of the orgasm it had ignited. She had to face the fact that she was becoming dangerously obsessed with Kashika, and that it was distorting her judgement. She must escape before she was swallowed up in this twisted world of slavery and submission and no longer knew right from wrong. And, if possible, get Kashika out as well. But how?

Zara apparently sensed nothing of her inner anguish and sent her down to B3 to record the Chain's reactions to their marathon sex-session. Vanessa went with dragging feet. How could she possibly face Kashika after what had happened? Just because she did not know Vanessa had been her first user did not diminish her own sense of shame. Yet at the same time that part of her unhindered by conscience longed to see her.

She found Cherry Chain had been excused any sexual training to allow them to recover and were out on to the exercise track to do laps. Making her way to the perimeter she soon saw them coming into view.

They were not running because coffle chains linked their collars and they had wooden yokes bound across their shoulders. As they appeared she saw they were gazing about them at the vistas of the secret level, which they had hardly seen since their initiation. Catching sight of Vanessa they smiled and called out to her, and she fell into step beside them.

Their arms were held outstretched by the yokes, strapped to them at the wrists and elbows. Chains ran down from the yoke and crossed their chests, dividing and lifting their breasts. Pairs of lighter chains clamped to their nipples ran forwards to snap on to a link midway along the chain joining their collars. If the heavier chain grew tight it would deliver a warning tug, encouraging them to keep in step and not lag behind.

They had been arranged according to their Chain number, so Amber was in the lead. As she had no girl in front, her nipple chains ran back over her shoulders to link with the coffle chain at the point where they joined with those of Charlotte.

Trailing last in line by number order, Yvonne had been fitted with a lap counter wheel that clicked away the distance the Chain had travelled. The upward-curving handle of the wheel was plugged into her rear. Vanessa noticed their pubes and bottoms were blotched and sore and glistened with salve. They looked tired but undeniably content.

'We all passed!' Amber declared. 'Miss Kyle said she was very proud of us.'

'But are you feeling all right?' Vanessa asked anxiously, trying not to look directly at Kashika yet desperate for reassurance. She received a chorus of replies mingled with rueful grins:

'Yes, but I could hardly walk afterwards.'

'You'd never believe how that much oral makes your jaw ache.'

'I think I've got a sandpapered cunt, but OK otherwise.'

'My bum-hole feels like it's one big bruise.'

When they had quietened down, Amber asked tentatively: 'Can we ask you to take a message to Miss Kyle? Something isn't quite right.'

At last, Vanessa thought. Despite what they've just said it's becoming too much for them. They're rebelling. Aloud she said: 'Of course. What do you want me to tell her?'

'Well, it's not fair Yvonne has that counter wheel handle stuffed up her arse when she's as sore as we are. We were wondering if we could take turns being rear girl . . .'

Miss Kyle beamed in satisfaction when Vanessa relayed the Chain's request.

'That's just what I was hoping they'd do.'

'What have you done to them to make them want to share the pain, Miss Kyle?' Vanessa demanded.

'It's what they've done to themselves. It's called chain love, Vanessa.'

The next couple of days passed as uneventfully as was possible inside the Shiller building. The Cherry Chain girls swiftly recovered and were returned to a full programme of demanding and degrading training, in the perversity of which they seemed to revel. Zara kept Vanessa busy recording their activities in between writing worthy but bland articles about the doings of Shillers' numerous subsidiaries for *Datumline* magazine. It was all becoming frighteningly routine, and occasionally Vanessa forgot she was working in an office naked and slave-chained. At nights in her flat she masturbated under her bedclothes and thought about Kashika.

Then one morning Vanessa walked out of the lift into the fifth-floor lobby and saw Kashika on display in front of her.

It was as though she had become part of a living sculpture. She was encased in a double interlocking spiral of gleaming tubular metal that rose from a black marble plinth. A bright metal strap circled her head, holding a ball-gag in her mouth. Her arms were raised and secured with matching metal cuffs to the apex of the spiral above her head. The inside curves of the spiral bristled with metal spikes that seemed to menace Kashika with their points. Her legs were spread and cuffed to the base of the spiral arms. A tongue of ribbed metal curved up from the plinth between her legs, as though licking at the exposed pouch of her sex. It was wet with her juices.

Beside her was a notice:

I AM ONE OF THE PRIZES IN THE
CHERRY CHAIN RAFFLE.
PLAY WITH ME AT HOME FOR A NIGHT!
PROCEEDS TO THE CHARITIES ALLIANCE.
BUY YOUR TICKETS NOW!

Kashika was facing the lift doors and grinned around her gag when she saw Vanessa. She worked her hips back and forth suggestively over the arch of the metal tongue lapping at her pussy, as though offering herself. Vanessa goggled at her stupidly for a moment, drinking in her perfect figure, gave a nervous smile and half-wave, then hurried past her to Zara's office.

Had somebody specially chosen to put Kashika on display on her floor? It might be a joke of Miss Kyle's. But was it meant to tease or subvert her?

'One girl's been put on display on each floor,' Zara explained when Vanessa reported to her. 'You'd better take a picture of each girl in case we want it as a background to coverage of the draw itself.'

'Why not a run a competition?' Vanessa said. 'Choose the best piece of modern art to include a living slave-girl!'

She was being sarcastic but Zara seemed to take her seriously.

'That's an idea. Get several shots of each girl and we'll run a gallery of them.'

So Vanessa had to go from floor to floor taking pictures of each Cherry girl. She soon realised they had been put out in chain order, with Amber on show in the first-floor lobby and Yvonne in the twelfth. It was just chance than put Kashika on floor five . . . she hoped.

The girls were displayed in varied and degradingly ingenious ways.

Amber had been bound like a mummy in strips of clear plastic and was suspended from a gibbet-like frame. Charlotte was hung on the wall inside a large gilded picture frame, to which she was tied in a squatting position with thighs splayed wide by dozens of cords. Fiona had been set on her hands and knees on a waist-high plinth, held in place by a dozen adjustable clamps, whose metal jaws closed about her legs, arms and neck, squeezed her breasts, and even reached into her mouth and held her tongue in check. Holly was suspended like a puppet by heavy chains that also looped between her legs, diving into the furrow of her vulva. Lisa had been tightly wrapped in chicken wire, so that her nipples squeezed through its lattice, and laid on her back on a long narrow black table like an offering. Madelyn stood contorted within a series of asymmetric horizontal bars that forced her bottom out, her stomach forwards and pinched her breasts between them. Olivia was bound tightly to a polished wooden 'X' cross by numerous loops of white rope in contrast to her dark skin. Rachel had been tied to what looked like a large cartwheel mounted flat on the floor, so that the hub pressing into the small of her back lifted her hips invitingly. Tina was trapped upright and spread-eagled between two wire lattices strung within a large metal hoop, the tension on the wires digging into her skin and squeezing her breasts between them. Victoria stood imprisoned and rigidly erect within what looked like a free-standing wooden shelving unit, formed in two halves with scallops cut out for her neck, chest, waist and wrists, knees and ankles. Finally Yvonne lay on her back, weighed down by concentric rings of heavy black chain, across a large white plastic dome.

The girls were gagged but none were blindfolded and all could be freely handled by anyone who cared to do so. They were living artworks; there to be enjoyed as much for the tactile pleasure they gave as their visual appeal. They responded to the strokes, pinches, prods and fondles with helpless squirming, muffled grunts and whines and bright excited eyes.

Vanessa found the sight of them displayed so publicly both erotic and disturbing. She wondered who had designed the settings. Some thought had evidently gone into them. Did Shiller include among its subsidiaries some firm of perverted sculptors? She had a sudden crazy vision of the imprisoned girls being put on display in the Tate Modern and having art critics arguing whether they were art or pornography. Both or neither? She was not sure any more.

When she delivered the pictures to Zara she could not help speak out.

'Do they have to be shown off like this, Mistress Editor?' she asked.

'Now they've gained confidence they like being shown off to people. The attention makes them feel important. Being on display excites them.'

'But raffling them off as though they were prizes in some show! It's sick!'

'I heard from Denise that you suggested they be put in individual cells for breaking-in. Being taken home is far more secluded than that. It's wonderful experience for the girls to serve one or two people in an intimate domestic setting for hours on end. Afterwards they'll swap stories about how they were treated with their Chain sisters. They'll enjoy it!'

'How would you know, Mistress Editor?' Vanessa retorted sharply.

Zara looked at her in thoughtfully for a long moment, then picked up her phone and dialled. 'Hallo Jude ... You know that girl spy I told you about ... Yes, the one with the lively tongue. Well, I'm bringing her home tonight to play with, so get the toy box out.' She rang off and gave Vanessa a wicked smile. 'Now you'll find out what the Cherry girls will be feeling ... and maybe one or two other things as well.'

Zara took Vanessa home in the boot of her car. For the first time in over two weeks she left the Shiller building without being locked into her spywear. But there was absolutely no chance of escape.

Vanessa lay on her side on a blanket, curled up in a ball with her wrists cuffed to her ankles, which were in turn secured by heavy cuffs linked by a short rigid bar. An additional chain ran from the bar up between her thighs to her collar, preventing her from straightening out. Bungee cords ran from her collar and cuffs to eyelets set in the floor, holding her firmly in the middle of the boot space. A blindfold covered her eyes and a broad gag-strap with an integral pear-shaped rubber plug filled her mouth. She could neither call out nor move enough to bang on the side of the car in the faint hope some passer-by would hear her. She was totally helpless, her stomach churning at the thought of what Zara had planned for her.

Eventually Vanessa felt the car turn into a short drive and enter what she took to be a garage. The engine was switched off and she heard the whine of a powered door. The boot was opened, she felt Zara unfasten the bungee cords and then her collar chain. Her wrists were freed from her ankles and she was seated upright. Zara pulled the blindfold off, leaving Vanessa blinking in the white strip light that illuminated a garage lined down one side with tidy shelves.

Zara took a fistful of Vanessa's hair and twisted it hard. 'While you're in our house you won't speak a word, because play-bitches don't talk! You've had enough to say for yourself so far, now it's time to listen and learn like a proper reporter. Understand?'

Vanessa nodded and whimpered.

Removing her ankle hobble, Zara led Vanessa through a side door into a well-fitted kitchen. A woman who had been seated at the kitchen table got up as they entered.

'I'm home, Jude,' Zara said cheerfully.

Jude was an attractive, fortyish blonde with a shining creamy smooth skin. She was shorter and plumper than Zara, with prominent breasts. She came forwards and kissed Zara on the lips with uninhibited affection, then looked Vanessa up and down.

'So this is Vanessa. You're right, she is pretty. Let's have a proper look at her . . .'

Leading Vanessa by her cuffed hands, she bent her backwards over the kitchen table. With her free hand she squeezed and pinched Vanessa's breasts and tested the firmness of her stomach. A casual slap on the inner thigh made Vanessa spread her legs wider so that Jude could examine her pubes. She stroked Vanessa's soft curls, flicked the swelling nub of her clit, making her yelp behind her gag, and probed the mouth of her vagina.

'Already juicing, that's good,' Jude said, withdrawing her wet and sticky fingers. She smelt the exudation. 'Nice . . .' she offered her hand for Zara to sniff.

'I know,' Zara agreed. 'She's a natural slut at heart, but she won't let herself admit it.'

Jude grinned. 'Then we'll have to see what we can do to change that.'

Jude flipped Vanessa over on to her front so that she could view her bottom, cupping and kneading the pliant hemispheres, then pulling them apart to examine the rose of her anus.

'You didn't have her washed and greased?'

'I thought we could do that.'

Jude grinned. 'That'll be fun.' Suddenly she slapped Vanessa's bottom sharply three times in quick succession, making her soft flesh jump, leaving her handprint emblazoned across both buttocks and bringing tears to her eyes. She bent her head close to Vanessa's ear. 'Tonight you belong to us. You're our slave-slut and we'll do what we like with you. Nothing else matters but your absolute obedience and our pleasure, understand?'

Vanessa nodded, trembling both in fear and in shameful excitement.

'Right, let's get some paws on you and then you can start acting like the bitch you are . . .

Vanessa was on her knees and elbows in a corner of the kitchen, her rear facing Zara and Jude as they sat and drank coffee at the kitchen table.

They had removed her gag but she was too cowed to think about making a sound out of turn. They had put tight, fingerless rubber mittens on her hands similar to those she had seen the Cherry girls wearing. Their supper was still cooking; meanwhile Vanessa was eating a simple diced slave-meal out of an old metal dog bowl. In a similar bowl beside it was a dessert of chopped fruit and cream. It was going to be messy to eat, but she knew she had to finish every last bit.

Her bottom still burned and her eyes were still misted with tears. She was once again being sucked into that frightening paradox of disgust and arousal. She had been denied the use of her hands and her voice, and was being made to eat like an animal. It was shameful degradation. So why was she feeling so excited? Her pussy was wet and swollen and she knew in her current posture she was showing it off to her mistresses like a bitch in heat.

When she had licked her bowls clean, she turned to the two women, bowed her head and made a diffident whimper.

'Looks like she's finished,' Zara said. 'Time for a shower before we eat . . .'

Hands now cuffed behind her, they sat Vanessa on the toilet and made her pee and void her bowels. With an enema gun like Miss Kyle had used they flushed her out and left her rectum lined with grease. Then they stripped off and pulled her into the shower stall with them.

In a tight press of bare flesh they soaped Vanessa and each other, rubbing their slippery bodies against hers. Jude's large pink breasts swayed and wobbled, her red nipples standing out like organ stops. They pushed Vanessa on to her knees, fingers locked into her wet hair, and ground her face into the streaming clefts of their vaginas. Jude had gold rings set in her labia and clitoral hood like Zara. Vanessa licked about and between them with increasing desperation as the women twisted her round to share her favours, trapping her head between their thighs and hungry sexes as they embraced and kissed each other passionately.

First Zara then Jude came in her face, rubbing her nose deep into their slippery slots. Clasping handfuls of her hair, they used it to wipe themselves clean and then let her slide discarded to the floor of the shower where the spray washed their juices from her.

Dried and robed, Jude and Zara sat on the living-room sofa eating their dinner off trays while they watched TV. They rested their feet on Vanessa.

She was their footstool now, doubled over with her face almost touching the carpet. Her elbows were drawn backwards and held tight to her sides by a rope that passed between them and around the backs of her knees. Her ankles were tied together and held pressed up against her bottom by loops of rope going over the tops of her thighs. Another rope ran from her ankles under her body between her clenched thighs to her collar ring, pulling her head down and bowing her back. Two short lengths of rope linked her collar ring to her wrist cuffs, pulling her lower arms forwards and adding tension to the bond between her elbows and knees.

They had turned her into a piece of furniture, using the bow of her smooth back to rest their heels. She was utterly helpless and degraded. So why was a dribble of clear fluid trickling from her vagina between her thighs and on to the carpet?

Jude slid her foot out of its slipper and probed the oozing slit of Vanessa's pouting pudenda. Vanessa shivered and groaned with frustrated need.

'I think this little hotpot'll soon be coming to the boil,' she observed.

The posts at the foot of Zara and Jude's big brass-framed double bed telescoped upwards until they stood two metres high. They had handy rings on them to which slave cuff chains could be clipped.

Vanessa was splayed wide between the tall posts. Jude knelt on the bed in front of her while Zara stood on the floor behind. Both women were as naked as Vanessa. Each held short scolding paddles that they had taken from a large box stowed under the bed. This was the 'toy box' Zara had told Jude to prepare. The smack of rubber on flesh filled the room as they methodically beat Vanessa front and rear, creating a rosy glow on her skin from the back of her knees to the upper slopes of her breasts. They had put a rubber bit in her mouth for her to bite on so that she could moan and yelp and whimper and squeal freely, which she did. Drool ran down her cheeks and on to her breasts as Jude happily smacked them from side to side, setting them bouncing and quivering. From behind, Zara's paddle not only drove shivers through her bottom flesh, but curled up between Vanessa's spread thighs to slap against her pouting mound.

Under this onslaught Vanessa jerked and writhed, straining at her bonds, her eyes running with tears and bulging as the harder blows fell. But she knew there was no escape or release until her mistresses permitted. She would do anything they wanted. She was ready to please, she wanted to please and she needed to please!

When the last blow had fallen and her body was throbbing and tingling and alive to the slightest touch, they freed her arms. She fell forwards across the bed, trembling and sobbing. From the toy box they produced a broad belt that they buckled round her waist, chained to garter-like straps going round her upper thighs. They clipped her wrist cuffs to the straps. Another strap was buckled just above her elbows, linking them across her back and pinioning her arms to her sides.

Jude and Zara took out a bundle of thick bungee cords and strung them between the four bedposts and the rings set in the sides of Vanessa's belt. The tension countered most of her weight, lifting her middle off the bed. Next the toy box supplied them with a pair of double-headed black dildos curiously shaped in a broken 'V'. One arm was moulded like a huge penis, while the other was half its length and ended in a fat bulb. They pushed the shorter ends into their vaginas, leaving the fake erections bobbing rampantly before them.

Zara raised Vanessa and parted her legs so that Jude could slide underneath her, then lowered her on to Jude's dildo. Her breasts pressed into Jude's full glossy globes, hard nipples indenting soft flesh, as the rod of rubber filled her shamefully eager vagina. The tension of the elastic cords meant she did not bear down on Jude with her full weight.

Vanessa felt Zara pull her legs further apart and then mount her from behind. She bit on her gag-bar, whimpering as her anus was stretched wide and the length of the shaft slid into her, filling her rectum until it was painfully tight. Then she was doubly plugged and fit to burst, sobbing with desperate need.

Zara began to thrust up Vanessa's rear, grinding her body over Jude's soft fleshy form, the two dildos so close together inside her, sucking and pumping within her most intimate spaces. She was a slave-girl filling between the two lesbian lovers. A girlflesh plaything. A nothing, or an everything?

With a choking shriek she jerked her hips frantically as she came and came. It was the most intense thing she had ever known.

The next morning, stiff and sore inside, Vanessa ate breakfast bent over the bowls set out as the previous night in the corner of the kitchen. She felt herself in a half-dream state, still shattered by the intensity of her orgasm. She was fearful of what they had done to her yet knew she would react the same way if they did it all again. She really was a terrible slut.

Jude and Zara sat at the kitchen table. Suddenly Vanessa realised they were talking in increasingly louder and clearer voices about her.

'. . . and she accused me of not understanding what the Cherry Girls would be feeling after their raffle night out,' Zara was saying.

Jude chuckled. 'Silly girl. Doesn't she realise yet?'

'Nope.'

'And she's supposed to be a reporter?'

'Yes, but what sort of reporter can't see clues even when they're literally right . . . under . . . her . . . nose?'

Vanessa stopped eating. What? She lifted her head and for the first time looked properly at her food bowls.

Worn and chipped but still readable were the inscriptions: JUDITH 7 SAFFRON and ZARA 12 SAFFRON

Her dominating mistresses had both been Shiller slaves!

Eleven

The Cherry Chain raffle took place the next morning. Zara said she would cover it, so Vanessa was spared the degrading spectacle. It suited her as she was still coming to terms with the idea of Zara and Jude having been former Shiller slaves.

Vanessa glanced round the office with searching eyes. Were Rona and Pru former slaves as well? How many others? What percentage of women in the whole building had once served in chains down in level B3? Half of them? More? It might explain Shillers' low turnover of staff and their obvious familiarity with slaves. But they were clearly not controlled and monitored as she was out of the office. They were free to do what they wanted.

Even if that was working for the company that had formerly enslaved them?

Was it conditioning and brainwashing on a huge scale? Or were Zara and Jude and their conveniently named and numbered bowls simply clever plants? Or had she been wrong all along? Could there really be such things as willing slaves, not as sad isolated cases, but by the hundreds? Where did the truth lie?

'Look what I've won!'

Zara strode proudly into the main office. Everybody turned to look at her. She held the end of her red leash in one hand. On the other end, shuffling along on her hands and knees with a flush of excitement on her lovely face, was Kashika.

For the rest of the morning, Zara sent Kashika scurrying about the office delivering messages and carrying notes and files in her mouth like a dog. She was playing with her raffle prize by showing her off to the rest of the staff. As Kashika passed her desk she flashed Vanessa bright smiles, as much as to say: 'Look at me, I'm a proper slave now!'

At lunchtime Zara took Kashika on her red leash up to the restaurant, leaving Vanessa to her packed lunch. Briefly Vanessa felt a perverse twinge of jealousy at the thought of Kashika up there eating from a bowl beside Zara's table and then she firmly quashed the idea. How could she be jealous of Kashika? It was Zara who was playing games, taunting her with her new girl-toy.

When they returned, Kashika's face was even more flushed and suspiciously shiny. Vanessa knew Zara had taken her for a trip to the bathroom. She hoped it hadn't been too much of a trial for her. Then she thought of what she knew Kashika had already endured in training and realised her concerns were ridiculous. The hardest thing to accept was that the girl appeared to be enjoying herself. But that could not be right!

It was mid-afternoon when Zara sent Kashika out with a message summoning Vanessa to her office. Mystified, Vanessa followed her back.

Blushing slightly as she delivered her customary pussy-kiss in front of Kashika, Vanessa sat back on her haunches expectantly. Kashika had taken up a position by Zara's chair, crouching on a blanket and resting her cheek against Zara's leg, as she had no doubt been instructed. Vanessa ached at the sight of her.

Zara considered Vanessa thoughtfully before speaking. 'I was looking forward to taking this pretty thing . . .' she stroked Kashika's hair '. . . home to play with tonight. But something's come up and I've got to go out of town. Jude's also busy this evening, so it looks like I'll have to pass. Now, I could raffle her again around the office, but then I thought of you. Everybody can see you've got wet knickers over her.' Vanessa lowered her eyes in acute embarrassment. 'Yes, you want her and don't dare try to deny it!'

Vanessa looked up again and nodded mutely. She saw Kashika staring at her in wonder and delight.

Zara grinned mischievously. 'But I was wondering just what you'd do for a night with her? How much are you prepared to give?'

Vanessa's mind whirled. Zara was playing one of her games, wanting to see how far she could make Vanessa humiliate herself. Yet that knowledge was nothing in the face of the hot, liquid lust filling her loins at the idea of a night alone with Kashika. Then another possibility struck her. A harder choice but perhaps her last chance to test the truth.

Vanessa slowly smiled, shuffled forwards, nuzzled under Zara's skirt and kissed her pussy again, flicking her tongue-tip into the wet cleft. 'I'd do whatever you want, Mistress Editor . . .' she said huskily.

Bent over Zara's knees, Vanessa yelped and sobbed and moaned as the ruler smacked repeatedly into her bottom, turning it into a blaze of burning scarlet strips. Kashika looked on with wide fascinated eyes, her hand slipped between her thighs, her fingers busy.

'What are you?' Zara demanded.

'Aww! . . . a slutty . . . eeek! . . . bitch, Mistress!' Vanessa gasped.

'What are you good for?'

'Screwing . . . ahhoww! . . . and licking and . . . owww! . . . beating!'

'Again, what are you?'

'Your slave, Mistress . . . uhh! . . . your piece of girlflesh . . . aaah! . . . your sex toy!'

'What do you want to do?'

'I want . . . ahhh! . . . to please you . . . owww! . . . in any way you . . . aww! . . . want, Mistress!'

Abruptly Zara pushed Vanessa off her knees on to the floor.

Vanessa snivelled and wiped her streaming eyes, then resumed her normal submissive pose and looked up appealingly at Zara. 'Your bitch needs to go to the bathroom, Mistress. Will you take her?'

Inside the toilet stall, Vanessa laid her neck across the rim of the seat, her nose brushing the pubic hair of Zara's moist pussy. She could smell the older woman's excitement. Her heart was thudding and she felt dizzy with her wild purpose. The knowledge that it was the height of perversion to ask to be treated like this was teasing the back of her mind. Even so the pulse was swelling in her vulva at the degrading thrill of it. She had to get away, she had to get away!

She raised her eyes to Zara's triumphant face. 'Pee on me, Mistress,' she begged. 'It's all I'm good for.'

Zara smiled. 'Open you mouth . . .'

And Vanessa did so.

A little later, washed and cleaned and back at her desk, the chair seat feeling like sandpaper against her smarting bottom, Vanessa tried to think clearly. When the moment came she would only have one

186

chance to get it right. Could she rely on Kashika to react quickly enough? The girl was so ingrained to her slavish way of thinking she might not respond. But how to prime her without being seen or heard? There was no guarantee of having sufficient privacy before leaving to tell her, and once she was plugged into her spywear there would be no chance. She could write a note for Kashika now easily enough, but how and when could she pass it to her? Zara was going to be playing with her until the last minute. Besides, they would be searched before leaving the building, and even a note secreted in that most feminine of hiding places would be found.

It took several minutes before the solution came to her.

At five-thirty Zara appeared with Kashika on her leash trotting along obediently at her heel. She handed Vanessa a black holdall.

'There are a few things in here you might like to try on Kashika when you get her home,' she said, adding with a knowing grin: 'I think you'll both enjoy using them.'

Kashika smiled shyly. Vanessa said meekly: 'Thank you, Mistress Editor.'

'And you promise to take good care of her?'

Poker-faced, Vanessa said: 'I promise, Mistress Editor.'

Zara travelled down with them in the lift to B3 and walked as far as the slave doors leading to the locker rooms. 'Have fun,' she said. 'And don't be afraid to be strict . . .'

As she followed Kashika's perfect bottom through the short tunnel Vanessa congratulated herself on her foresight. There had been no chance to pass verbal instructions. As long as Jarvis didn't find her note.

Jarvis was at his desk as usual. They shuffled over and kissed his boots. 'Please, Mr Jarvis,' Vanessa said. 'I have permission to take Kashika home with me.'

'So I've been told, girl. You going to write another of your articles about it?'

'I might, Mr Jarvis.'

He led them through to the locker room. Commanding Kashika to stand first he looked her up and down, then tweaked her nipples in a playful fashion, making her giggle. 'No need for a bra to hold these titties up,' he said.

From a locker Jarvis took out sandals, panties, jeans and a tight white T-shirt, with a light scarf to cover her collar.

'Want her hobbled?' he asked Vanessa as Kashika dressed.

'No thank you, Mr Jarvis,' Vanessa said. 'I'm sure that won't be necessary.'

Kashika watched with intense interest as Jarvis removed Vanessa's slave chains and began fitting her with the spywear.

'It's a special range of remote slave control gear I'm testing out for the Director,' Vanessa explained quickly, as she bent over and held her ankles while Jarvis slipped the panty phalluses into her.

She saw Jarvis smile but he did not contradict her.

Making the most of the opportunity she added, while Jarvis cupped her breasts into the control bra: 'With this lot on everything I look at or say can be monitored. The bra and phalluses can deliver punishment shocks and the choker can stop me saying the wrong things.'

Kashika's nipples were standing up through the thin material of her top. 'That's amazing!' she exclaimed, looking impressed. 'Do you think I could try them sometime?'

Please let me get away from here before I begin to believe that's a normal thing for a girl to wish for, Vanessa thought desperately.

When they were both dressed, they took the lift back up to B2 and Vanessa led Kashika to her car. Vanessa's heart was thudding as they passed through the barriers but they were waved on with no more than a wolfish grin from the guard.

Kashika looked about her as they threaded their way through the evening traffic. 'I'd forgotten how busy the city is. I'm not sure I like it so much now. It's so much more peaceful down in B3.'

Vanessa was only half listening. Her objective wasn't far. With her eyes still fixed on the road ahead she reached behind her seat to where she had been careful to put her hat and pulled the Press card out of the band. Unfolding it with her fingers she slid it across into Kashika's lap and eased it into her open hand.

'Yes,' she said loudly to cover any sound Kashika might make, 'it can be a pain getting into work sometimes. I know I should use public transport more often, but I like my car . . .'

Suddenly she pulled over and stopped. Just beyond a parade of shops ahead was the blue lamp of a police station.

'Get out now!' she shouted to Kashika, bracing her hands on the steering wheel, expecting the paralysing pain to course through her at any second.

But Kashika was frowning at the message written on the inside of the card.

'What does it mean? Is it a game?'

DON'T SPEAK BECAUSE I'M BUGGED.
YOU'RE FREE, NOT A SLAVE!
WHEN I STOP RUN TO THE POLICE STATION.
I WON'T BE ABLE TO FOLLOW.
YOU MUST TELL THEM EVERYTHING!

'Go!' Vanessa snapped, wondering why she could still speak.

Then Shiller's voice sounded in her ear. 'Kashika is not going to run to the police, Puppet. Hard as it clearly is for you to accept, she's a natural slave. She has nothing to escape from. She is happy just as she is.'

Vanessa looked at Kashika's mystified face and realised the truth of it. The poor girl was not going to move. It was all over. She slumped forwards, feeling empty, defeated.

'What do I do now, Monitor?' she asked miserably.

'Continue on to your flat and enjoy Kashika as she expects you to, of course,' Shiller said. 'Take the opportunity to talk to her. Convince yourself of the truth.'

'But . . . aren't you going to punish me, Monitor?'

'For what? You have not attempted to escape yourself, only to save another human being you thought, however misguidedly, was being oppressed. Why would I punish an act of compassion? But we will talk further in the morning. Now, I think you are parked on a double yellow line, Puppet, so I suggest you move on.' And her voice cut off.

'Please,' Kashika asked plaintively. 'Who are you talking to? What's all this mean?'

With a sigh, Vanessa started the car again and pulled back out into the traffic. 'You'd better know the truth. I really work for a paper called the *Daily*

Globe. A few weeks ago I broke into the Shiller building . . .'

Vanessa finished her story as she opened the door of her flat. Kashika looked about her curiously as they passed through to the sitting room.

'So, all these mirrors have cameras and microphones hidden in them?' she said.

'Yes.'

'And you wear a control collar all the time you're here?'

'That's right. I suppose I'd better put it on. It's a bit less uncomfortable than all this gear.'

Kashika followed Vanessa through to her bedroom and watched with interest as she stripped off, donned her house collar and plugged in her spywear to recharge.

'Can I strip as well?' Kashika asked, as Vanessa reached for her gown. 'I've sort of got out of the habit of wearing clothes.'

'Of course,' Vanessa smiled.

Kashika gratefully peeled off her clothes and they sat side by side on the bed, naked except for their collars. Vanessa became aware of the warmth radiating from Kashika's body. She could smell her scent. She was so lovely . . .

'You really let Zara spank you and risked getting the Director angry just to save me?' Kashika asked.

'Well, I hoped it would mean I'd get free as well,' Vanessa said quickly to hide her embarrassment. 'But I did hate the thought of you being treated like a slave any more. Or the rest of Cherry Chain.'

'But couldn't you tell we were loving it? We're submissive masochists. We enjoy pain and bondage.'

Vanessa sighed. 'I found it so hard to believe. I still do to tell the truth. I thought you'd all been brainwashed or something, but if you were taken away from Shillers you'd snap out of it. That sounds pretty stupid now. Sorry.'

'I think it sounds kind and brave,' Kashika said, kissing Vanessa lightly on the shoulder. Then she slid down off the bed to kneel before Vanessa, thighs spread wide, hands folded neatly behind her back. Her eyes were sparkling with anticipation and her nipples stood rigidly erect. 'Maybe the best way to prove I enjoy what I am is a practical demonstration. What do you want to do with me first . . . Mistress?'

Vanessa swallowed hard. 'I'm . . . not your Mistress.'

'You are for tonight, Mistress. I was given to you to be your pleasure slave. Make me please you.'

'You know everything we do will be watched?'

'I think that makes it more exciting, Mistress. Would you like me to see what Mistress Zara put in that bag? There's bound to be something interesting. A big vibrator, maybe, or a spanking paddle . . .'

'I don't want to hurt you!'

'It won't hurt, Mistress, I promise!'

As Vanessa hesitated, Miss Kyle's voice sounded from the bed speakers. 'If you don't know what to do with her, girl, I'll tell you!'

Kashika lay on her back on the bed, her limbs drawn out to its four corners where the integral cuffs held her tight. Her knees were slightly bent and drawn both up and out by broad cuffs whose unyielding wire cables extended from holsters in the middle of the bed sides. This tension forced her legs to turn outwards from the hip, the sides of her feet pulled flat to the covers and displaying the soft flesh of her inner thighs.

Her honey dark mound of Venus and its sparse crown of tight dark curls were totally exposed. Her swollen inner labia rose out of her gaping love-mouth, whose coral-pink depths glistened with her juices. A trickle from her weeping sex ran down to her anus, whose dark crinkled well-pit bulged about the girth of a large silver vibrator that purred softly as it tormented her entrails with its promise. Elastic cords looped about her thighs and clipped to rings on the vibrator base ensured it stayed firmly in place. The sheet under her bottom was damp with her spilled lubrication.

Metal clamps linked by a short chain painfully compressed the hard cones of her dark-brown nipples. A bar-gag filled her mouth, stretching her lips back to expose her white teeth, which clamped hard on the rubber bit. Her large brown eyes were locked on to Vanessa as she stood over her, swatting the rubber paddle once more down on her helpless body.

Vanessa had an anal lock plugged into her, trailing the cable behind her like a tail as she moved round the bed. Warning jolts had been needed at first to encourage her to use the paddle, and she had flinched at the smack it made, the darkening mark it had left on the smooth tan flesh and the tears it had brought to Kashika's eyes.

But the thrill of mastering Kashika had taken over, and her own juices made a slippery sheen on her inner thighs. Now she understood what Zara and Miss Kyle felt when they had chastised her. Kashika was hers to do with as she wished, hers to dominate, to celebrate her loving submission in the only way possible.

Little by little, by tweak, caress and smack, she brought Kashika to a state of almost deliriously frustrated need, which under Miss Kyle's expert direction she had been careful not to allow the release of orgasm. Kashika squirmed and tugged at her bonds, gurgling and whimpering round her gag, her eyes full of pleading. 'Please let me come, Mistress!' they begged.

'Is your little cunt hungry now?' Vanessa asked, fondling Kashika's mound and revelling in its soft pliancy.

Kashika nodded, straining to lift her hips as far as her bonds permitted.

'Does it want feeding?'

Again the mute nod.

Vanessa tossed the paddle aside and took another item from Zara's gift bag. It was a shocking pink double dildo of huge proportions, with large fake testicles where the roots of the two members joined. In place of pubic hair was a bristle of soft rubber prongs for clitoral stimulation.

Feeling her own need could not be long delayed, Vanessa pushed one end up into herself, gasping as the monster filled her to the brim. She glimpsed herself in the bedroom spy mirror, with plastic balls and a fantastic pink cock standing proud, almost reaching to her navel.

An incredible sense of potency infused her. She was the master and Kashika her slave. This was her moment.

Scrambling on to the bed between Kashika's wide-spread thighs, she rammed the head of her pseudo-cock into the dark mouth of Kashika's waiting screw-hole and lunged with her hips, forcing a stifled squeal of pain from the girl which she endured because she was there to suffer. Her nipples ground painfully against Kashika's clamped teats and she revelled in her own pain.

She rode Kashika with wild abandon, feeling the buzzing of the anal vibrator transmitted though the

194

dildo and the teasing of the clit prongs. She smothered Kashika's helpless gagged mouth with rough kisses and called her a hot, shameless, slave-slut. Then she came wildly even as Kashika bucked under her and their bodies spasmed again and again until they sank together into blissful exhaustion.

Vanessa awoke in the small hours.

Kashika was stirring in the cradle of her arms. They each had an ankle cuffed to the foot of the bed and anal lock cables trailing from between their buttocks. Was it standard Shiller practice to cus-tomise beds with two anal locks, Vanessa wondered fleetingly, or had somebody anticipated just this situation? At that moment she did not care.

Vanessa kissed and stroked Kashika sleepily. Monitoring would be on automatic at that time of night, so she murmured softly: 'There was something I meant to ask you. "Kashika" is a lovely name, but does it mean anything?'

'It means: "The Shining One", Mistress. Because of my hair.'

Vanessa chuckled softly. 'Well, you've certainly illuminated my life. And changed it. I won't be the same girl walking into the office tomorrow. Oh, and please don't tell the other girls what I really am.'

'If that's what you want, Mistress.'

'Yes. I must see out your training period without any more complications, so I can be sure I'll make the right choice when my agreement with the Director ends.'

'But you won't give us away now, Mistress?' Kashika asked anxiously. 'Not now you know we want to be slaves.'

'It's not that simple. I know I'm getting a taste for this sort of life and it's clouding my judgement. Even if you are all consenting slaves, what Shiller is doing is still illegal. I've got to be sure it's not truly wrong. Do you see?'

Kashika seemed to accept this and was silent for a moment, then said: 'Will you get into trouble for trying to free me, Mistress?'

'Maybe. I don't care.' She kissed Kashika. 'It was worth it.'

'The Director won't ... take you away from us, Mistress?'

Vanessa kissed her again, more passionately. 'I hope not ...' Abruptly she rolled on top of Kashika, pinning her down, and felt for the cuff holsters in the bedhead. 'But just in case, I'd better make the most of you right now ...'

Twelve

Vanessa could see by the look on Jarvis's face the next morning that she was not in his good books. But he waited until Miss Kyle had led away Kashika, casting one last loving smile at Vanessa, before speaking his mind.

'You slipped one past me last night, girl. Sneaking a note out like that. Made me look as though I can't do my job properly.'

'I'm sorry, Mr Jarvis,' Vanessa said as she knelt before him on the locker-room floor. He had removed her spywear but not yet put on her slave chains. 'I was doing what I thought was right. I wasn't trying to get you into trouble.'

'Maybe not, but it's the principle that matters, girl. This place works on discipline and obedience. You've all got to be a bit afraid of us in charge. That's natural for slave-girls. And even though you're not properly one of them, the rules have got to be enforced. The Director may let what you did pass, but down here I can't afford to . . .' He undid his belt and pulled it free of its loops. 'So you know what I have to do now?'

Vanessa knew. It seemed so clear and obvious she felt no surprise. 'You've got to punish me, Mr Jarvis, in case any other girl learns what I did and gets the idea she can smuggle something past you as well.' Despite her lustful night, she felt the now familiar sluttish response stirring in her loins as her body prepared for the inevitable. She held her arms out before her, wrists crossed. 'Would you like me up against the wall?'

And then she added something that surprised even herself, but came out quite naturally. 'If you're going to give me a punishment fuck as well, Mr Jarvis, please could you use my bum-hole because my cunt's still sore? I douched and greased myself before breakfast so I'm perfectly fresh . . .'

Jarvis tied her wrists to a ring on the wall, leaving some slack in the tethering rope. Then he arranged two benches so that they extended out from the wall on either side of her. To these he tied her spread ankles. He looped a rope about her waist and drew the free ends down on either side and tied them to the benches behind her ankles. This pulled her belly down, putting tension on her arms and forcing her to stick her haunches out and back, offering their smooth curves to him to do with as he wished.

The belting was not that severe, just six lashes, but he laid each one neatly across her buttocks and paused between blows to stroke her bottom and feel its growing heat, building the anticipation inside her. When he was done he unzipped his flies and vigorously sodomised her, thrusting his thick cockshaft hard and deep and making her squeal in a satisfactory manner.

When he had spent himself inside her with a grunt and had pulled his cock out of her now reddened bum-hole, she blinked away her tears and said huskily: 'Thank you, Mr Jarvis. I won't be a bad girl again. I've learnt my lesson.'

He grinned and patted her sore bottom. 'And don't you forget it, girl!'

And that was it. He'd reasserted his mastery of her and all was back to what passed for normal at Shillers. He untied her, flushed her rectum clean in the adjoining shower room, and put on her slave chains.

'Now, I think the Director's sent somebody down for you . . .'

A slim blonde slave-girl in a white collar was waiting in the lobby. Though she did not recognise her bright open face, Vanessa felt there was something familiar about her.

'Here she is, Sandra,' Jarvis said.

'Thank you, Mr Jarvis,' she replied.

They both kissed his boots and crawled out of the slave hatch. Standing up again outside, Vanessa said: 'You cleaned up after me the first day I was here.'

Sandra smiled cheerfully. She hardly looked eighteen, but she carried herself with the unconscious grace and self-assurance of somebody older. 'That's right. And even though you were confused and frightened you remembered to say thank you. I liked that.' She led the way to the lifts, which she opened with her own key card dangling from her collar. Inside she pressed the button for the top floor.

As the lift started up, Vanessa said: 'You're the only girl I've seen so far in a white collar. I guess that's something special.'

'It means I belong to the Director's personal chain,' Sandra said, with a distinct touch of pride.

'And do the Director's own slaves often have to mop up pee and wipe girls' pussies clean?'

'A Shiller slave does whatever she's told,' Sandra replied simply.

'Like telling the Director how an inconvenient reporter was coping with being screwed on a rack?'

'That's right,' Sandra admitted.

'Yet you wore a hood all the time.'

'But I could still hear you, and smell your juices and touch you when I cleaned you up. That was quite enough.'

Vanessa blushed at the thought of such an intimate appraisal being carried out without her knowledge. 'And what did all that tell you about how I felt?'

Sandra smiled. 'That's between me and the Director.'

The lift stopped and they stepped out into the penthouse level.

It was a light, airy foyer, with glass doors opening on to a lush roof garden. A double row of glass-topped desks ran down each side of the room occupied by half a dozen women working at computer keyboards, who were naked save for white collars and sandals and wore slave chains and ankle hobbles.

Sandra led the way down the middle of the room to a large frosted-glass double door. She knocked on it and then went down on to her hands and knees. Vanessa copied her.

When the doors slid silently apart, the girls shuffled into the room beyond and the doors closed behind them. Glancing sideways Vanessa saw that a pair of hooded slave-girls operated them, facing away from each other like bookends and crawling back and forth on their hands and knees.

Eye bolts were set low down close to the glass-door panel edges where they butted together, and from these ran chains which hooked into anal rings protruding from between their upturned buttocks. By pulling on them the girls slid the doors open. A second pair of bolts was set in the outer edges of each panel. From these ran chains that ended in figure-of-eight loops that were tightly bound about the girls' pendant breasts. Vanessa saw the pair backing up to pull the doors closed and winced in sympathy as their breasts bunched and stretched under the strain.

The room was as airy as the outer chamber, with sliding glass doors opening on to the same rooftop garden. Between the windows were two small trees growing out of large pots. Planted in front of them and bound to their slender trunks, as Vanessa had seen Bethany the day she first arrived, was a pair of naked hooded slave-girls.

Shiller herself sat behind a huge leather-topped desk, empty except for a single slim screen and keyboard. She was the darkest thing in the room in her black suit. A pair of backless stools stood in front of the desk.

'I've brought Vanessa as you ordered, Director,' Sandra said.

'Thank you, Sandra. Come up here, both of you.'

Without actually standing upright, Sandra shuffled up to the desk and used the right-hand stool to climb gracefully on to its green-leather top. Vanessa copied her using the left-hand stool, sitting back in the display posture on the other side of the computer console. They must look like a pair of exotic executive toys, Vanessa thought.

Shiller considered Vanessa thoughtfully for a moment, then said: 'When I was young I found I had a liking both for women and discipline that was hard to satisfy in the conservative community where I grew up. So I moved to a large city where I was able to better satisfy my desires. But at the same time I saw too many women forced to prostitute themselves in a manner alien to their natures, while also being exploited by those who controlled them. And so I decided to find an ethical solution to the problem. And now you would destroy all that.'

Once again Vanessa felt her resolve wilting in the Director's commanding presence, but she forced herself to speak clearly.

'I believe now that all the girls I've seen are happy to be slaves, Director. But is it right that you encouraged them to come here in the first place?'

'It is in their natures. They were destined to be slaves. We give them the chance to live that life in a safe, controlled environment. Left to themselves many of them would end up in far less scrupulous hands. Remember that.'

'Maybe that's true, Director, but you still charge for their services, or whatever you want to call it.'

'A fair proportion of which is paid into bank accounts for their use when they retire from our employment.'

'But it's still illegal and probably immoral. I'm just not sure if it's wrong or not, in the deepest sense of the word.'

Shiller smiled coolly. 'That's quite a complex philosophical problem you have set yourself. And on its resolution hangs the existence of my girlflesh company.'

'I suppose it does, Director.' She bit her lip, thinking of the plea Kashika had made. 'If I do decide against I'll give you the chance to close down the business first and get rid of all your slaves. If you do that, then I'll keep quiet.'

Sandra gave a fearful shiver, while Shiller bowed her head slightly. 'That would be very considerate, Vanessa.'

'Assuming you'll still let me make my choice freely, Director.'

'I gave my word I would not hinder you. That promise still stands.'

'But that doesn't stop you trying to influence me, does it? Trying to suck me into your world.'

Shiller smiled. 'It would be strange if I did not try to do so, would it not? But reflect also, that your own treatment could have been much gentler. I could have ordered you to be given a show of false courtesy and consideration. Instead you have been treated in every way as a probationary slave might expect.'

Yes, that had puzzled her. 'But why?'

'To allow you to know the truth, of course. What it is to be girlflesh.'

The thought made her shiver. Quickly she asked: 'Was it really chance that Zara won Kashika in the raffle and then gave her to me, Director?'

Shiller shrugged. 'Does it matter? Kashika is exactly as she seems to be. You will find no falsehood in her.'

'And why did you put Sandra in my cell to spy on me that first day?'

'To confirm my initial assessment of your nature. Which she did.'

'Which was?'

Shiller smiled. 'I think I shall reserve that answer until after you make your decision as to our fate. Now, you had better go back down to your office. I believe Zara Fulton wishes to talk to you . . .'

Vanessa had expected Zara to punish her immediately and personally for her escapade with Kashika as Jarvis had done, but it was not quite as simple as that. While Vanessa knelt before her in her office, Zara delivered an angry rant.

'You promised me you'd take good care of Kashika. That does not include upsetting her by trying to make her run into a police station!'

'I thought I was doing it for her own good, Mistress Editor!' Vanessa protested.

'But you know better now?'

203

Vanessa sighed. 'I believe she is a natural sub-missive here of her own free will, Mistress Editor.'

'Like the other Cherry Chain girls?'

'Yes, Mistress Editor,' Vanessa conceded.

'And how long has it taken you to reach that blindingly obvious conclusion? You should have worked that out in the first week! You had every chance to interview other girls or members of staff for background. You must have seen girls changing into street clothes in the locker room at times. Didn't you think it odd, if we were holding them against their will, that we'd allow that?'

She had seen them, she now recalled, but she'd been too preoccupied to take proper notice. 'I . . . didn't think,' she admitted lamely.

'You didn't think to follow it up because you'd already made up your mind what we were!'

'This is a weird situation, Mistress Editor. It's taken me time to accept the facts.'

'No, you let your prejudice interfere with gathering the facts and facing up to them. That's why I'm going to punish you. Not for trying to help Kashika escape, but for being a bad reporter and thinking you needed to help her in the first place!'

She pulled Vanessa to her feet, clipped her wrists behind her back and led her out by the hair into the main office.

'Right, listen up!' she said loudly. The buzz in the room died away as every eye turned to her and Vanessa.

'Our pet Slave Reporter hasn't been doing her job properly and nearly caused the company a lot of trouble. She needs to be reminded what the penalties are for careless work. I've booked her into a fully kitted private cell in the Mall. She'll be there all day

204

so you can all take a turn. You don't have to go easy on her ...'

'Faster, girl, faster!'

The cane swished across her bottom again. With a shriek Vanessa jerked her hips faster. She was straddling a square balk of timber carried horizontally on a single heavy post, so that its edge was uppermost. This edge had been carved into a series of notches and ridges that ground into her soft cleft, spreading her labia wide as though they were sucking at its faces. The wood was stained dark with the juices of the numerous slave-girls who had ridden it before her.

Her wrists were cuffed via a heavy spring to a ceiling hook above her head, while her legs were spread wide and tethered to the outside of the base that supported the post and timber. There was just enough slack in her ankle bindings to allow her to stand on tiptoe. Her arms took some of the strain, but this still meant most of the weight was borne by her groin.

An office woman, stripped to the waist, was standing behind her wielding a cane. Every time Vanessa slowed the frantic jiggling of her hips she would add another stripe to the collection growing across her haunches.

'Get on with it, you slut!' she shouted. 'This doesn't end until I see you come ...'

The naked man grinned at Vanessa as he pressed himself up against her and shoved his hard cock into her gaping vagina. She gasped as the slug of tumescent flesh filled her passage, but the ball-gag in her mouth stifled the sound.

She hung flat against the painted breezeblock cell wall. Her wrists were clamped into a thick, padded cuff-bar that hung on a large wall hook above her head. Her legs were outstretched horizontally on either side of her and held almost flat to the wall by cuffs and short chains clipped to large ring-bolts. The big tendons of her inner thighs stood out like cables as they framed her exposed and gaping pudenda. Directly under her suspended and open groin was a stand and an adjustable vertical rod on which was mounted a large black rubber dildo. Its head and half its shaft were sunk into the wide-stretched mouth of her pink-rimmed anus. Discharge from her vagina ran down the sides of the dildo.

As the man entered her she felt his cock squeezing the thin walls of flesh and muscle that separated her vagina from her tightly stuffed rectum. Slowly he began to pump away inside her, not hurrying but savouring every moment of his total possession of her body . . .

The blood pounded in Vanessa's ears as she twisted and swung upside down from her ankles. Her hands were cuffed behind her back and a ball-gag filled her mouth. Two naked office women were beating her with rubber paddles, the smack of flesh ringing back from the hard walls. The hopeless flinches and writhing she made in response to the stinging blows only added to her torment. Loops of cord had been wrapped about the roots of her inverted breasts and lead weights hung from them. More weights hung from the silver clamps that pinched her nipples so tightly, drawing her breasts out into swelling, elongated cones of tortured flesh.

Only when she was finally sobbing with pain and dribble from around her gag splattered the floor did the women stop beating her. Drawing up two chairs they sat facing each other with her dangling body between them, the chair seats putting their crotches level with Vanessa's head. Each taking a nipple weight, they tugged at her breasts, pulling them in opposite directions and swinging her between them until Vanessa screamed through her gag for mercy and her eyes bulged.

Tearing out her gag, one of them rubbed her inverted and flushed face into her scented pubes. 'We'll only take you down when you've made us both come,' she told her.

Desperately, Vanessa began to lick and suck at her fleshy cleft . . .

The last man to have her left Vanessa bound over a punishment horse.

She lay along the length of its narrow padded top, her wrists and ankles cuffed together and stretched down to where they were clipped to the side struts linking the horse's splayed legs. Her breasts hung down on each side of the top beam and a cord passing underneath it tied her nipples together. The man's sperm still dribbled out of her anus between her reddened buttocks, where they projected over the end of the beam.

But after what she had endured that day the position almost felt comfortable. She was utterly pummelled and drained and had lost count of the number of orgasms that had been forced out of her. All she wanted to do was sleep . . .

Then somebody lifted her head by a handful of hair and slapped her cheek. She opened bleary eyes and saw it was Zara.

'Not yet, girl,' she said. 'I've still got to have my go . . .'

She turned Vanessa's limp and unresisting body over on to her back and refastened her wrists and ankles to the side struts. Taking a tapered bracing strap from the selection hanging on the walls, she buckled it about Vanessa's neck and the padded beam, ensuring she could not turn her head aside. Then she stripped off her own clothes and climbed on to Vanessa so that her thighs straddled her upturned face. She bent and kissed Vanessa's ravaged and swollen pussy.

'I can taste everyone who's used you. That takes me back . . .'

She began to ride Vanessa's face as one would use an inanimate object for pleasure.

'Have you learnt your lesson?' Zara asked, giving Vanessa's clitoris a warning nip between her teeth.

'Ahhh . . . yes, Mistress Editor!' Vanessa said indistinctly from between Zara's sticky love-lips as they slithered up and down her face.

'Good. I've arranged for you to visit the Fellgrish Institute the day after tomorrow. You can see for yourself how carefully we select our girls.' She nipped Vanessa's clit again. 'And this time get your facts right!'

Thirteen

The Fellgrish Institute nestled in one corner of a science park south-west of central Oxford off the Henley Road. It was a low, slab-like building with a façade that mingled red brick with tinted glass and polished steel. Under the Institute's name on the plaque beside the main door it said: 'Human Response Laboratory'.

Apart from not having to consult a map for directions, another advantage of being under constant monitoring, Vanessa realised, was that people knew who she was and when she had arrived. She didn't even have to announce herself. The woman behind the reception desk looked up as she approached and said: 'Miss Buckingham? Dr Gold is expecting you. Through that door please . . .'

Monitor guided her along a corridor and through a second set of security doors to an office bearing the nameplate H. GOLD MD.

Sitting behind an untidy desk framed by shelves crammed with books and file folders, Dr Gold was an almost perfect cliché of a traditional scientist. He was short, balding and bespectacled, wore a white lab coat and had a slightly distracted manner. In his hand, however, he held a remote controller like the one Jarvis used.

'Ah, yes, the reporter girl,' he said, blinking owlishly at Vanessa. 'Thank you, Monitor, I have control of her now . . .'

He pressed a button. 'I've unlocked your collar, girl. You'll wear one of ours while you're here. Now get those clothes off . . .'

In two minutes Vanessa was naked but for her sandals and an Institute collar, which was similar to her house collar except that it seemed to have more contact points on its inside. It fitted closely round her neck. Gold looked her up and down with an approving smile, then pressed a button on the controller. Vanessa felt the familiar stinging pain, making her wince. Gold smiled at her distress.

'I don't have to demonstrate what will happen if you make a nuisance of yourself, do I, girl?'

'No, Dr,' Vanessa said quickly.

'You will call me "Master"'.

'Yes, Master.'

'Now, you were told you could not take pictures or make live recordings? You will work from notes only and not use real names in any article you write. We must maintain our subjects' anonymity until they have consented to become Shiller slaves. Is that understood?'

'Yes, Master.'

'Good. I've scheduled ten minutes for you to gather background, as I believe you call it, and then an hour to tour our facility. You may begin . . .' he patted his knee '. . . sit here.'

Clasping her notebook she seated herself on his lap. She felt slightly foolish as she was half a head taller than Gold. His hand slid up her between her thighs and began to fondle her pubes. She gritted her teeth. This was not going to be easy.

'First, Master, how would you describe the aims of the Fellgrish Institute?'

'Oh, to investigate and codify the full range of female emotional responses to varied visual, physical or emotional stimuli, with special reference to their influence on the sexual urge. Also to identify those individuals with behavioural patterns suggesting an inherent predisposition to what is commonly known as "submissive" or "masochistic" behaviour. Through a process of graduated selection and testing we aim to focus on those women with both a higher than average sex drive and a positive response to imposed order and discipline.'

Vanessa struggled to get all that down while Gold's fingers were busy teasing her clitoris. 'And how exactly do you go about selecting girls for slave training, Master?'

'Initially we survey women of suitable age, health and appearance, via detailed personality question-naires circulated through colleges, magazines, social centres and so forth. We send out a few thousand every month. Those women who give responses suggesting they have above average submissive or masochistic tendencies are invited here for closer investigation and testing.'

'And how many of those turn out to be suitable for slave training, Master?'

'It averages perhaps three or four a month.'

Vanessa gritted her teeth as Gold's fingers slid up her vagina. 'Not many out of thousands, Master.'

'There are undoubtedly many more we miss. Prob-ably the majority of what one might call natural slaves never fully achieve their potential. It is a matter of being given the opportunity we provide. Many would never express their true natures or suspect they had such a desire if it were not for us.'

She was making a stain on his trousers now. 'Do you encourage them to become slaves, Master?'

'No, there are no inducements of any kind. We only pay their travelling expenses and a token fee to cover their time. The testing programme is entirely voluntary and may involve sessions spread over two or three months. If they did not enjoy it they would simply not attend. And they do not graduate to the next stage of testing without knowing what degree of personal discomfort or intrusion it may involve.' He indicated a filing cabinet. 'We have the waivers they sign on file if you wish to examine them, together with videoed interviews.'

'Perhaps later, Master.'

'We do not say we are looking for natural submissives, of course,' Gold said with a smile. 'At first they believe they are participating in a series of experiments to test responses to sexual imagery. If they react favourably to those they move on to testing certain sex toys. Later, if they are willing, they graduate to what we tell them is an examination of their reactions to combinations of physical, emotional and sexual stimulation. We say this has applications in understanding the effects of long-term hostage situations and military anti-interrogation training.'

'You lie to them, Master.'

'Not really. The data we collect is valuable and is submitted to many reputable journals. Only our ultimate purpose is withheld. Most of our subjects probably think they are using us as an excuse to do things in the name of science that they would never dare do in ordinary life. We create an environment where they feel free to explore the limits of their sexual desires by providing an excuse to bypass traditional inhibitions.' He smiled cheerfully, twirling his fingers inside her. 'In other words we free them from guilt.'

'I see, Master. May I ask, on a personal level, do you find your work fulfilling?'

'I find the workings of the human mind endlessly fascinating and its study a continual challenge. In addition, I have the natural male interest in the female of our species, plus a taste for seeing her in situations of confinement and libidinous activity. It is both intellectually and emotionally satisfying.'

He pulled his fingers out of Vanessa's now dripping vulva and held them up to display the wet sheen that coated them.

'For example, in how many other occupations could I, a man of modest physical appeal to the opposite sex, have an attractive woman sit naked on my lap and accept my toying with her mons veneris less than five minutes after meeting her?'

Before taking Vanessa on a tour of the facility, Gold took out of a drawer a phallic object of transparent plastic with complex circuitry visible within it, together with two flat rings of black plastic with fine metallic contacts clustered about their undersides.

'A vaginal probe and nipple sensors,' Gold explained. 'They work in conjunction with your collar. Via short-range radio circuits they relay measurements on your state of sexual arousal. We use variations of this system on our test subjects. I thought it might be interesting to measure your responses to our work. Bend over . . .'

The probe was held in place by a pair of rubber-jawed clips on its base that clipped to her inner labia. In comparison to some of the objects that had been inserted into her vagina over the last three weeks, it was quite comfortable. The nipple sensor rings were lightly self-adhesive and covered her areolae, leaving her hardening teat tips poking through the hole in the middle. Gold chuckled at this display. 'It seems you do not require much in the way of stimulation, girl . . .'

He clipped a leash to her collar and led her out into the corridor. Vanessa shivered nervously, wondering how well used the corridor was and who might see her naked and leashed like a dog. A couple of white-coated men passed, nodding to Gold but hardly paying her a second glance.

Double doors at the end of the corridor opened and a man dressed like a hospital porter appeared pushing a metal-topped trolley. On it was a naked girl lying on her back with her arms strapped down to her sides. A crepe bandage covered her eyes and she had a vaguely medical-looking tube plugged into one side of her mouth and held in place by tape, forming an effective gag. Wires trailed from electrode pads adhered to her chest and groin. Her knees were bent, her feet spread and ankles cuffed to the trolley frame. This left her dark-haired, full-lipped vagina spread wide by a metal speculum exposed for all to see.

Gold drew Vanessa aside to let the trolley pass.

'This is part of an ongoing psychological test,' he said quietly. 'She's been told she has to be moved to another room as there's been an equipment break-down just before she was to have a deep vaginal sensitivity scan. In fact we are determining how she responds to being casually exposed like this in a semi-public situation. She'll be wheeled around and then left unattended for a while. We find any shame usually gives way very quickly to arousal. Occasionally they fear having being forgotten or even suffer frustrated boredom. Afterwards we explain it was deliberate and all part of the test. They quite understand.'

Gold led Vanessa through a set of security doors into a long, dimly lit corridor. On either side of it and running its entire length were pairs of doors and large windows. Vanessa recognised the speakers beside the window frames and the slightly misty look of the glass. They were one-way mirrors like in level B3.

'We have a variety of subjects undergoing tests at the moment,' Gold said. 'They represent most of the stages in the process. We'll start with a new girl ...'

They looked into a small room holding a couch and a large TV. A slim red-haired girl, dressed only in a sensor collar and light hospital gown, lay on the couch watching the images flicker across the screen. Commonplace scenes were interposed with shots from porn movies. On the arm of a couch was a pad with a selection of buttons, which she pressed after each image.

'We're testing her reaction to sexual imagery,' Gold said. 'She's wearing a vaginal probe and nipple sensors as well, of course. We record her deliberate responses together with her unconscious ones. Comparing the two later on will help her begin to free herself of any habituated shame and guilt.'

Vanessa peered more closely at the girl's collar. It had a tag with S14 embossed upon it.

'I assume there's another reason you use collars, Master,' Vanessa said. 'It must be useful to see how they react to wearing them when you're looking for potential slaves. And tagged like dogs as well. Let me guess; they're only referred to by their collar number while they're in here.'

Gold favoured her with a smile. 'Very good. Yes, we tell them the collars are less obtrusive than a lot of wiring and the alphanumeric codes are to ensure confidentiality, but as you deduce, there is a secondary purpose.'

A string of porn images were flickering across the screen. The girl had slipped a hand under her robe and was rubbing her groin. Gold chuckled at the sight. 'I think she shows promise . . .'

Next a woman with close-cropped dark hair, naked apart from collar and nipple sensors, was lying back on a bed while using a large silver vibrator on herself. She was working the device back and forth in her equally close-shaven sex with evident enthusiasm. Her ankles were confined in broad rubber cuffs and pulled out to the corners of the bed, though they were obviously only fastened by velcro straps and easily releasable.

'She's testing a new design of vibrator for the sex-toy market,' Gold said. 'We tell them their legs must be held apart at a regulation distance for consistency.'

'While actually getting them used to associating sexual gratification with bondage, Master?'

'We allow her to make the association. Her readings show a distinct elevation of arousal while she is strapping her ankles in place, before she's even touched the vibrator.'

'So you're conditioning her, Master?'

'No. She's conditioning herself . . .'

In the next room, a hooded blonde girl was kneeling on all fours on a low, padded bench, her wrists and ankles secured by heavy cuffs. Under one hand was a button pad. A rod rose up at an angle from the bench under her and pressed a padded bar against her hips. This bracing was necessary because on a stand behind her was a rotating wheel sporting half a dozen very realistic-looking, erect rubber penises of different sizes, with a number of transparent tubes plugged into their bases. Between it and her was a clear plastic shield that covered her buttocks, pierced only by a hole in line with her pouting, eager-looking vagina.

As they watched, the wheel rotated, bringing a new penis opposite the hole in the shield. The penis was extended on a hydraulic rod even as the stand carrying it tilted forwards. The fake cockhead slid into the woman's vagina, penetrating her to the root. She tossed back her hooded head in apparent pleasure. The stand began to rock back and forth in a realistic rhythm, setting her breasts swaying with every thrust.

'This is one of our more advanced subjects and a near certainty for slavehood, I think,' Gold said with a twinkle in his eye. 'She has already admitted a liking for sex and bondage combined, and has asked to try more unusual experiments just for the pleasure it gives her. Together we have concocted a spurious scientific excuse for a test where she has to try to tell the difference between a real penis and a fake one, without any other clues save vaginal contact.'

The phallus wheel, which had been oscillating at increasing speed, suddenly tilted back, pulling the rubber penis out of her even as it spurted out jets of white fluid that splashed over her vagina and the shield. The woman squirmed in frustration.

'A synthetic substitute for sperm heated to body temperature,' Gold said. 'We try to make it as realistic as possible. In fact this might be a good time . . .' He clipped Vanessa's leash to a ring on the wall by the viewing window, opened the door and slipped into the room.

She watched him pull the phallus wheel aside, part his lab coat, unzip his flies and release a good-sized erection. This he slid through the hole in the shield and into his captive test-subject's hungry vagina.

Vanessa became aware of the sympathetic wetness of her own pussy oozing round her embedded vaginal probe. What a voyeur she had become! She supposed that this reaction would be registered and relayed with all the other intimate data for Gold to examine at will later. What would he make of her?

Gold pumped away for a minute, then his small body hunched over the shield separating him from the naked woman as he came inside her, while she jerked and strained against her straps. Collecting himself, he pulled out of her and swung the phallus wheel back into place.

He left the room wiping his glasses, his cock still jutting out of his trousers. 'Most satisfactory ...' he muttered. 'Now lick me clean, girl ...'

Vanessa got down on her knees and obeyed. She could taste his sperm mingling with the nameless woman's juices.

'Not all our subjects are as brazen and open as that one,' Gold said as she lapped away. 'Some seem to be testing themselves and are surprised by their own needs and capacity for both pleasure and pain. Like our next subject ...'

She was dark-haired and olive-skinned, and she was reclining naked in a padded chair. Broad straps crossed over her wrists, neck, chest, waist, thighs and ankles, holding her firmly in place. There was a rubber bit clenched between her teeth. Crocodile clips trailing electric wires were clamped to her large brown nipples and outer labia. Each clip had a small light-bulb mounted on it. Fitted to the armrest of the chair under her right hand was a pad with a large numbered dial.

The bulbs on the crocodile clips suddenly flashed red, the woman's eyes screwed up, her fists clenched and her body jerked against her straps.

'Of course we are careful to keep the actual current to safe levels and the clips on her nipples are not inter-connected to prevent heart stimulation,' Gold said, 'but it is still quite painful.'

The woman's agony went on for ten seconds, then the light faded from the bulbs and she sagged limply in her chair. Vanessa could see the sweat on her body. A voice came from a speaker inside the room said: 'Give your rating, C37!'

With trembling fingers the woman turned the dial under her hand.

Next a buzzing, pulsating vibrator rose up between her spread legs and slid into her vagina, making her stomach bulge. She groaned and rolled up her eyes as it went to work inside her. The lights flashed and her body convulsed with pain once more. After ten seconds the light went out, leaving her panting heavily, the vibrator still buzzing inside her.

'Give your rating, C37!' the unseen voice demanded, and again the woman adjusted the dial.

'Her task is to assess the intensity of each shock on a pain scale,' Gold said. 'Typically they rate it as lower when their pussies are occupied, even if it is the same as the preceding shock or higher . . .'

The next window looked in on a room with a row of cages set out on a waist-high ledge. They were about the size of a typical desk and built of metal angles and flat metal bars riveted into square grid sheets. Three of the cages contained naked, collared girls lying curled up on straw bedding. Their hands were encased in black rubber mitten-paws.

'This is one of our longer-term experiments,' Gold explained. 'We put them in here for two or three days to test reactions to confinement, prolonged lack of privacy, being denied speech by their shock collars and, in short, being treated like animals.'

Vanessa could see where the design for the slave dorms in level B3 had originated.

A skinny young man in a slightly grubby tan

workcoat entered the room through a side door. Immediately the girls scrambled on to their knees and pressed their faces up against the sides of the cages as they reached through with their paw-hands. They made faint throaty sounds while plaintively opening and closing their mouths, as though begging to be fed.

The young man just chuckled at their antics and methodically went about refilling the water bottles hanging on the side of each cage and changing the waste-pans under the cage corners. Only when he was done did he dip into his pocket and bring out a handful of sweets.

The girls ground their hips against the cage sides, fluffing up their pubic bushes and squeezing their breasts through the lattice so that they bulged between the bars. Their keeper pinched and squeezed and tickled the fruits of their bodies so eagerly offered. He unwrapped a sweet, rubbed it into the first girl's pubic cleft framed between the bars, then popped it into her open mouth.

'As you can see, they soon form a close and affectionate bond with their keeper,' Gold said. 'Accepting the discipline of confinement is an essential characteristic for a life-slave.'

Vanessa imagined Kashika in one of those cages, and had a fleeting sense of the power and satisfaction it would give to hold the key to that cage. Or would she rather be in the cage next to her?

They were close to the end of the observation corridor when they looked into a room resembling a prison cell. The door was of solid riveted metal pierced only by a peephole and the walls were bare concrete blocks. The furnishings comprised a bucket in a corner and a low metal-framed bed with a sagging mattress and scrap of blanket. A naked woman with hands cuffed behind her back sprawled on the bed as though in exhausted sleep, her dark hair straggling and tangled.

'This subject is in a final-stage test,' Gold said. 'A little bit of extended role-playing. Supposedly she is a captive spy under interrogation to reveal the code word "Midnight". When she does so the test ends.' He checked his watch. 'The next interrogation session should start very shortly. Each gets increasingly harsher, of course. So far she has been in there for nearly three days. She is certainly proving one of our more masochistic subjects . . .'

The cell door suddenly banged open and a large unshaven man in military-looking dark-green fatigues strode in. In one hand he held an electric cattle prod that he jabbed into the sleeping woman's buttock. As she yelped and struggled into wakefulness, he grabbed her by the hair and dragged her to her feet.

'Ready to talk now, bitch?' he growled.

Resolutely she shook her head. Her eyes were shadowed but very bright.

The man grinned evilly, drawing the shaft of the goad up between her legs and through the furrow of her sex. 'Then you know what I'm going to do to you?'

Trembling, she nodded. Vanessa saw her nipples swell and harden.

The man dragged her out of the cell. Gold led Vanessa along to the next window. It was another bare concrete room with a heavy metal door, this time furnished with a very small but solid bench, with many lengths of rope hanging from heavy rings screwed to its sides. The walls were hung with an array of whips, canes, tongs and other devices whose purpose Vanessa could only guess.

The door opened and the man and his captive came in. The girl's eye widened in horror as she saw the bench and she began to struggle, but it was quite futile.

He pushed her face down across the bench top, so that her head and breasts hung over one end, then lifted her feet off the floor and bent her legs over until her heels pressed against her bottom. With lengths of the dangling rope he tied her ankles down, the tension also pulling them outwards so that she was forced to keep her thighs spread, and leaving her exposed sex pouch hanging over the other end of the bench.

He took a huge tubular metal hook from the wall. She whimpered as she saw it. Gathering and twisting her long hair into a rope he knotted the end about the hook's large hanging ring, then pulled her head backwards until he could insert the bulbous tip of the hook into her anus. She gasped, her body bowed by the tension, her eyes bulging in disbelief as she impaled herself.

'Did you say anything, girl?' he asked.

She shook her head a fraction.

In the observation corridor, Gold clipped the end of Vanessa's leash to a wall-ring and moved behind her, cupping and squeezing her breasts. 'Remember, all she has to do is say "Midnight" and the test ends,' he said. 'It's entirely up to her how much she suffers ... if you can call it suffering.'

The man in the cell had attached screw clamps to her nipples and was now hanging weights on them, stretching them out into pink cones, turning her breasts into fleshy stalactites. Her eyes filled with tears and she gritted her teeth.

'What's the code word, girl?' her inquisitor demanded.

She bit her lip but said nothing.

He took down a cane and slashed it across the stretched and unnaturally drawn upper slopes of her breasts, briefly flattening them against the edge of the bench and setting the weights swaying. She sobbed in pain, shaking her head.

Vanessa heard Gold's zip go down. He pushed her forwards until her breasts pancaked against the mirror glass, her hard nipples in their sensor collars pushing back into her, and kicked her legs apart. She felt the tip of his cock burrowing between her buttocks. He was stiff again so quickly!

The inquisitor walked round the bench until he faced his captive's soft, exposed inner thighs, engorged sex and plugged anus. Vanessa heard the relayed swish and crack of his cane as he struck her. Gold's cock found Vanessa's greased anus and forced its way into her, so her grunt and gasp at his entry mingled with the captive girl's shrieks of pain.

'Talk to me, talk to me!' the inquisitor commanded.

Tears streaming down her flushed cheeks, she shook her head.

Gold began to pump up and down the hot tunnel of Vanessa's rectum.

The inquisitor threw his cane aside, tore open his trousers and rammed his cock up into his captive's pussy, making the bench jerk and her tortured breasts jiggle. Instead of more pain, Vanessa saw a look of perfect bliss pass across her face. Was it also a look of triumph?

Horrified and fascinated, Vanessa could not turn away from the tormented girl as Gold's cock pummelling up her arse synchronised with the thrusts of the inquisitor into his victim's helpless cunt. Any lingering sense of pride or dignity left in Vanessa melted away as her simmering arousal came to the boil and orgasmic release tore through her.

This was submission to a need too powerful to be denied.

This was what Cherry Chain had undergone.

Was it also what she darkly craved for?

Fourteen

Vanessa brooded over her experience at the Institute for several days.

After the tour, she had watched a selection of videoed interviews with the girls who passed the final test stages. Once they had viewed a video of life in B3 showing other slave-girls at work and were convinced Shiller was making a genuine offer, they had been eager to join their ranks. In some cases tearfully so.

She now accepted that all Shiller's slave-girls were natural submissives and had not been coerced in any way into slavery. But that still left her with the matter of whether it was right or wrong to exploit and sell their services for money. And always in the background was the memory of her own helpless responses to what she had seen and felt. She had been drawn so deeply into a life of slavery that she was beginning to regard it as normal. Was she still capable of making the proper choice?

Then, late Friday evening just as she was packing up, Zara called her into her office.

'Cherry Chain are being field-tested tomorrow,' she announced briskly. 'They've been assigned to provide the amusements for a big house party in Surrey. You'd better get in early to talk to them before they're rested. Then you can go with them and see how they do. Think you can manage that?'

'Yes, Mistress Editor.'

The Cherry Chain girls were already making circuits of the exercise track when she saw them at eight the next morning.

They had weighted packs strapped to their backs and their glistening breasts bounced prettily as they ran, but they wore none of the usual restraints or stimulations. Instead their hands were constrained by rubber paws and they wore wire-mesh chastity belts, through which the fluff of their pubes peeped. They looked exhausted but their trainers, ranged around the inside of the track, were still driving them on with flicks of carriage whips across their bare bottoms.

'We haven't allowed them to touch themselves or each other since they were bedded down early last night,' Miss Kyle explained, when Vanessa asked her about the preparation process for Cherry Chain's first assignment. 'Now we're tiring them out so that they get six or seven hours' solid sleep through the day before we ship them out. By the time they're ready to entertain this evening they won't have had any sex for over twenty-four hours.'

Vanessa thought of the effect such enforced abstinence would have on a dozen lustful and uninhibited young women. 'Putting it simply, you want them gagging for it, Miss Kyle.'

Miss Kyle grinned. 'We want them eager to please, as slave-girls should be.'

'How do you think they'll do tonight, Miss Kyle?'

'I think they'll be fine. They're the hottest chain we've had for a long time.'

Vanessa smiled and waved to the girls as they jogged past. Kashika, sweat-streaked and bedraggled but somehow even more beautiful for all that, flashed her back such a look of joy and yearning that it set butterflies of lust fluttering about her loins.

When the girls were finally allowed off the track, Vanessa watched as they were hosed down and watered, then strapped to the wooden pallets and suspended in the dim calm of the rest chamber. She took one last lingering look at Kashika hanging beside the others, perfectly at ease in her straps and already asleep, then tiptoed out to leave them in peace.

Vanessa fretted the next few hours away making notes for her article. She wanted the girls to be happy following the course their natures clearly intended for them, yet she was still faced with a dilemma. That evening they were going to be set out as sex toys for a lot of, presumably, wealthy people, to play with. Could that be right in any circumstances? On the other hand, if those clients did not employ the services of well-cared-for and naturally slavish Shiller girls, would they find less willing and oppressed alternatives elsewhere? Was it better this way?

To kill time and get some further background for her article, Vanessa took herself down to the B2 loading bay where the assorted vehicles that transported the girls to and from their assignments were housed. She had often seen the vans and lorries with their secret human cargo coming and going, but she had been so absorbed with Cherry Chain and level B3 that she had not investigated further. Was it because she had initially dismissed them from her mind as minor cogs in what she had then thought of as the evil Shiller slave machine? But now she saw they also had their part to play. Perhaps she should suggest to Zara doing a feature on the drivers and staff who actually transported the girls to the clients, presented

them for use and saw that they gave satisfaction . . .
Oh God, she was at it again!

By chance or design, the lorry assigned to transport
Cherry Chain was the very vehicle she had hidden
under weeks before. Fortunately its crew, two solid-
looking middle-aged men named Graham and Des,
and a younger woman called Nina seemed to bear
Vanessa no ill will. In fact Nina asked: 'When are you
going to write about all the hours we have to put in
shipping the girls back and forwards, doing all the
rigging and making sure they're used properly?'

'I was just thinking of doing an article about that
very thing, Mistress,' Vanessa was able to reply quite
honestly.

They showed her round the back of the lorry.
Three of the equipment boxes had already been
loaded and were lined up down the middle of the
compartment. Along each side were the narrow
mesh-walled alcoves she now saw were to hold girls
standing upright with their backs facing the sides of
the van. They were held in place against padded
boards by strips of elasticated webbing, which could
be quickly pulled across and secured. These not only
supported them for long journeys but gave them even
more protection than seat-belts. On hooks above the
alcoves were slung two long aluminium ladders to
assist with rigging displays.

At the far end of the compartment backing on to
the driver's cab, a section of panelling had been
folded back to reveal a compact bank of flat-screen
monitors and remote surveillance camera controls.
Three swivel chairs were bolted to the floor in front
of the display.

'This is where we keep an eye on the girls while
they're working,' Des explained. 'Don't want anybody going too far with them.

Graham took a tiny video camera out of a metal case holding a dozen more. 'We put these out when we're rigging the venue. The clients never know they're there.'

'Tonight we've got to make doubly sure we see everything,' Des added. 'The trainers want a copy of it all to see how well Cherry Chain perform.'

At four o'clock, Cherry Chain were taken down, fed, cleaned and watered. As they knelt before her in the training yard, Miss Kyle gave them some final words of advice and encouragement.

'You've been assigned to provide additional amusement for a large party at Mansley Park in Surrey. You'll be fully restrained in exposed postures at all times so you won't have to put on any special display. Just react naturally. Remember that for tonight whoever uses you is your master or mistress and you are their slave. Be that to the best of your ability and be proud to be Shiller girls!'

Gagged to prevent any nervous chatter and to concentrate their minds, and still in chastity belts, they were chained in a coffle, hands cuffed behind them, and marched into the lift. Vanessa followed after them as they were taken up to the lorry and secured in their niches by the webbing cocoons. While Graham got into the cab, Des and Nina, who were riding with them in the back, sat Vanessa down in the spare swivel chair, clipped her wrists behind her, pushed a ball-gag into her mouth and strapped her into place.

The lorry set off.

It was not long before Vanessa began to smell the girls' excitement and frustration filling the close interior. Blushing, she realised she was also contributing to that intimate perfume. She had been so preoccupied with the looming decision that only now

229

did it dawn on her that she had gone without an orgasm even longer than the girls. She squeezed her thighs together and tried not to think about it, but the anticipation was becoming almost tangible. They wanted to get started, to serve, to be used. And, undeniably, so did she.

The journey took a little over an hour. When the lorry pulled up, Des and Nina climbed out presumably to meet the clients who had hired the girls. A few minutes later the engine started up again and the lorry was driven across some bumpy ground, then backed up and halted. The rear doors were flung back and the ramp extended. Vanessa saw they were opposite an arched gateway set in a high wall. A pair of green garden doors stood wide open and through them she glimpsed a rambling orchard of mature apple trees.

The sudden realisation of her helplessness struck her. She was strapped naked to a chair in full view of any stranger who might look into the back of the lorry. But instead of shame she found a thrill of excitement coursing through her at the thought.

Graham, Des and Nina took out the ladders, dragged the equipment cases down the ramp and shut up the lorry again, leaving the girls to their frustration. Vanessa wished she could talk to Kashika, but from where she sat she could not even see her. They would just have to stew in the juices of their mounting need. Her own juices, she could feel, were already making a stain on the chair seat.

A good half-hour passed before Des returned to the lorry and freed Vanessa. 'Might as well make use of you,' he said.

'May I bring my camera, Master?' Vanessa asked when he had removed her gag. 'I'd like some pictures of the girls on display for my article.'

'OK, but remember nothing identifying this place can show in any picture you publish.'

'Yes, Master.'

He clipped a leash to her collar and a hobble chain to her ankles and then gave her the remote camera case to carry. As he led her out of the back she flashed Kashika, still strapped into her niche, a look of sympathy in passing and she smiled ruefully back over her gag.

Vanessa found the orchard was completely enclosed by the high wall. There was another gate at the far end with the steeply pitched roofs of a large house rising beyond it. The branches of the trees were hung with paper lanterns and the stakes and coloured glass pots of garden flares had been stuck in the grass between the trees.

Nina and Graham were up the ladders hanging the last of twelve conical canopies the size of large garden parasols to the undersides of selected branches. On the grass beneath each parasol, rubberised quilts had been spread out. At the corners of each quilt four stakes had been driven into the ground. Vanessa followed Des about, handing him cameras from the case as he placed them unobtrusively about the orchard, nestling in the forks of branches and angled to cover every spot where a girl would be placed.

Only when all the preparations were complete did they let the girls out of the lorry. Still cuffed and gagged, they were allowed to roam freely about the enclosed orchard to stretch their legs and explore the setting in which they were to serve their purpose.

Vanessa saw such a look of wonder and excitement on Kashika's face as she inspected the parasol under which she would soon be staked out that it brought a lump to her throat. She was in love with an unashamedly submissive girl slave. She might claim a special place in her affections, but she could never possess her totally, as she yearned to do, while she belonged to Shiller. Could she learn to share Kashika, not just with her chain sisters but also with those strangers who would use her perfect body for their pleasure time after time? She had the power to prevent it ... but in choosing that path would she simultaneously destroy Kashika's love for her?

The girls' chastity belts were finally removed, much to their evident relief, and they were made to squat and pee in a corner of the orchard. Kashika beamed in utter unselfconscious delight at Vanessa as the stream gushed from her. Nina then used a portable douche machine to freshen them and give their rears a final greasing.

Des checked his watch. 'Right, let's get them staked out ...'

Eight of the girls were spread out on their backs and chained to the stakes with broad padded cuffs, while the remaining four were bound face down for variety. Kashika was one of them. The girls were then blindfolded with slim bands of black silk holding neat round pads over their eyes and fitted with ring bits.

These soft black rubber bars were held in place with elastic cords running round the back of their heads and hooking into the ends of the bars that protruded from the corners of their mouths. Inside, the rubber bar was wedged between their back teeth, giving them something to bite on during punishment while keeping their teeth parted. The section of bar between their teeth opened up into a ring which filled the insides of their mouths, going under their tongues. They prevented the girls from fully closing their jaws or biting even by reflex. Their mouths were thus kept invitingly part-open, permitting easy access for any user who wished to probe the depths of their gullets, while still allowing them to suck and lick if required.

Finally, a cat-o-nine-tails and a light chastising paddle were placed beside each girl. Both devices used soft light materials and were designed to make a satisfying swish and slap and deliver a stimulating sting while doing little real harm.

Des, Nina, Graham and Vanessa stood back to admire the girls, as they lay spread-eagled under the trees. Their nipple-crowned uptilted breasts and rounded buttocks gleamed golden in the fading evening light, the tongues of their hungry love-mouths pouting and glistening, tight puckered anuses shiny with grease. Their helpless bodies were sweet offerings, ripe and ready for the taking. Vanessa, who had been dutifully snapping pictures, found herself entranced, aching at the sight of them.

'May I wish them good luck?' she begged, as Nina began lighting the lanterns.

'All right,' said Nina, 'but be quick about it. The hosts'll be along in a minute to check the display.'

With a jingle of her hobble chain, Vanessa shuffled as quickly as she could from one girl to another, kneeling over them to kiss their parted lips, gently squeezing breasts and stroking bottoms almost un-consciously as she wished them good luck. To Kashika alone did she add a whispered 'I love you', and felt her heart leap at the delighted smile she forced past her ring bit.

Then Graham took her back to the lorry and secured her to the chair once more while he activated the monitor screens. One by one they came to life and he focused the pictures and checked the sound. Vanessa found Kashika's image and gazed at it longingly. How she wished she could be with her now, staked out beside her, sharing her pleasure and pain.

She saw the party hosts, a perfectly respectable-looking middle-aged couple briefly crossing in front of the hidden cameras as they inspected the girls. What sort of party was it where such people could tell their guests: 'Do try the lemon misticanza, it's really rather good, and there are a dozen naked slave-girls staked out in the orchard for you to screw later . . .'

Briefly she wondered what was going on in the house itself if this was merely a sideshow, but then her attention returned to Cherry Chain and Kashika. That was all she cared about.

A few minutes later Des and Nina climbed back into the lorry and shut the doors.

'The guests are arriving,' Nina said. 'Looks like they're going to have a nice night for it.'

'While we spend the next six hours stuck in here watching rich idiots screw our girls and themselves silly,' Des said gloomily. 'I never thought that could be boring but –'

'Turn it off Des, we've heard that one before!' Graham interrupted with good-humoured scorn.

'Well it's true.'

'Then read a book or something.'

'Or we could always have a bit of fun ourselves,' Nina said, stroking Vanessa's hair suggestively.

The two men turned to look at Vanessa, grins spreading across their faces.

'Nobody actually said we couldn't play with her,' Graham said slowly.

'Might help pass the time once they've settled down in there,' Des agreed.

'Where shall we put her for now?' Nina asked. 'She's in my chair.'

Vanessa didn't care what they did with her as long as she could see Kashika. 'Please, Mistress and

Masters,' she said quickly, 'do what you like as long as I can still watch Cherry Chain . . . for my article.'

'Better break out the spares box,' Des said.

They unlocked her slave chains, recuffed her hands and clipped them wide apart to rings set in the roof. A spreader bar cuffed to her ankles secured her feet. Nina popped her ball-gag back in, leaving her standing mutely splayed just behind the row of chairs, looking over their shoulders while they observed Cherry Chain's début.

It seemed an interminable wait until the first men and women in smart clothes, drinks in their hands, began to flit across the screens. They could hear them chatting and laughing as they inspected the girls. A man had bent down and was squeezing Amber's big breasts, lifting them by the nipples and letting them fall back with a bounce. A woman had thrust stiff fingers between Olive's glossy curls and was rolling her thumb curiously over her erect clit.

A couple had taken a liking to Kashika. The woman pulled up her dress, exposing a shaven pussy, and sat down in front of Kashika, her thighs straddling her head. Lifting Kashika's head by her hair, she shuffled forwards on her bottom until Kashika's face was pressed into her groin. Vanessa saw Kashika's head bob up and down as she eagerly began to lick the woman's pubes. Her partner meanwhile had picked up a lash and began swiping it across Kashika's bottom, making her buttocks clench. Kashika redoubled her oral efforts while the woman laughed.

After a minute the man threw aside the lash, unzipped his flies, dropped to the ground between Kashika's splayed thighs and rammed his cock into her sooty dark anus. He was up inside her beautiful hot bottom, Vanessa thought in horror. How she hated and envied him!

By now she was dripping on the floor. She wanted to be with Kashika, to show her love, to feel what she was feeling. But she was as helpless as any of the Cherry girls on the screens before her having their breasts lashed and bottoms paddled, cocks pumping into their gaping vaginas, women riding their faces and forcing their captive tongues to pleasure them. What she wanted did not matter. She was just a slave. Which meant . . .

Vanessa began to moan and jerk in her bonds, until Nina turned to her. 'What's the matter, girl? God, you're wet! Need the bucket?'

Vanessa desperately shook her head until Nina pulled her gag out.

'Please, Mistress, I think I should be punished!' she gasped.

'Why? You've behaved yourself like a good girl.'

'For . . . for using this lorry to sneak into Shillers that time. Didn't I get you into trouble?'

Graham turned from the screens looking puzzled. 'Nope. Actually we thought that was pretty damn smart of you.'

'And bloody brave,' Des added.

'Please, Master,' Vanessa begged. 'I deserve to be punished!'

Nina suddenly smiled. 'Oh, I see. Maybe it was bad of you to sneak in under our van like that.'

Des looked from Vanessa to the screens and back again. Understanding dawned. 'You want a taste of the action.'

'I think we can arrange that . . .' Graham added.

They forced a wooden rod in her mouth with a rubber sleeve grip for her teeth to bite on and elastic cords with spring clamps dangling from each end. These clipped to her nipples so that the tension stretched them into painfully taut cones, lifting her breasts to expose the tender pale curves of their undersides. She was holding her own breasts up so that they were more vulnerable to punishment, she thought with a shudder of utter bliss.

Taking turns from watching the monitors they caned her bottom and paddled her front. Her suspended breasts jumped and bounced as they were whacked upwards and she shrieked in wild abandon behind her gag rod as drool dribbled down her chin. She kept blinking back the tears so she could see every moment of Kashika's happy torment, sharing the pain and the ecstasy as each man abused and screwed her.

When she was thoroughly tenderised, Des and Graham fucked her front and rear at the same time, lifting her body off the floor with the strength of their thrusts, doubly impaling her on their shafts as she writhed between them. She orgasmed so intensely that she nearly passed out. Nina splashed her face with water to revive her.

'My turn now,' she said.

They unhooked Vanessa's wrist cuffs from the roof, pulled them behind her back and clipped them together. Attaching a length of chain to her cuffs they pulled them upwards, forcing her to bend forwards as her shoulder joints could not swivel any further. Taking the suspension rod from her mouth but leaving it clipped to her nipples, they tied a cord between it and the middle of her ankle spreader bar.

With another agonising jerk on her wrists they clipped the end of the chain to a roof hook, leaving Vanessa trembling in exquisite torment, torn between the upward strain on her arms and shoulders, and the terrible downward stretching of her breasts and nipples. Stripping off her jeans and panties, Nina swivelled her chair round and tilted it back, hooking her knees over the arms. Grasping Vanessa by the hair, she ground her face into her slippery cleft.

As Vanessa licked and sucked her sweet pussy flesh, Des and Graham took turns paddling her outthrust scarlet bottom and then ramming their cocks into rectum and vagina again and again . . .

An unknown interval later, Vanessa became aware that it was very dark and quiet outside the lorry. She was once more gagged and cuffed to one of the swivel chairs. Her arse burned, her breasts throbbed and her ravaged vagina and rectum pulsed and dribbled sperm.

What had she done?

Dimly she realised that Des, Nina and Graham were leading tottering and exhausted Cherry girls back into the lorry and strapping them into their niches. Through puffy, tear-sore eyes she saw them load the equipment trunks and close the doors. The engine started and the lorry set off for home, but Vanessa fell asleep before it reached the main road.

Vanessa dragged herself to her flat on Sunday morning, sore and aching and not knowing who or what she was or even if she could trust her own mind any more. She slept through the rest of the day and then spent half the night watching television until the monitor ordered her back to bed and made her masturbate herself into an exhausted sleep, which, Vanessa conceded wearily, was better than taking pills.

The next morning she went to work in a daze, only to find the Cherry Chain girls looking perfectly fresh and exuberantly happy. As soon as she entered the training yard she was smothered by an onslaught of bare scented bodies as they hugged and kissed her.

'Miss Kyle said we passed with honours!' Kashika said, her eyes sparkling with joy. 'They're holding our graduation ceremony tomorrow afternoon!'

That was the day Vanessa's agreement with Shiller ended.

Fifteen

It was Shiller's own voice that woke Vanessa on the morning of Cherry Chain's graduation and her release from bondage.

'Wake up, Vanessa . . .' A gentle jolt from her anal plug lock brought her to dim awareness. She still felt deathly tired.

Only half awake, she mechanically obeyed the instructions of the disembodied voice as she had done for the last month, pulling out her now deflated anal plug and wiping it clean, then going to the corner to unlock her handcuffs. It was only when she had done so that she realised she had not been told to put on her house collar first. It was still hanging by the bed. Her spywear was on the dressing table plugged into the charger. She was not controlled in any way. She was free!

A brief frisson of guilt assailed her, coupled with the feeling that she was not naked but in an odd way improperly dressed, as though missing something that had become an integral part of her life. With an effort she gathered her thoughts and the sensation passed.

'So, that's it,' she said, omitting the word 'Monitor' only with an effort.

'Yes, our agreement is ended, Vanessa,' Shiller confirmed. 'I thought you might as well enjoy a full day of freedom. Zara is not expecting you in the office today. Whether you come in tomorrow, or ever again, is up to you.'

'What do I do now?' she asked, realising the foolishness of her question even as she spoke. She was no longer a slave, she could think for herself.

'That's your choice. If you want my advice, I would suggest you contact your editor and arrange a meeting so you can report on your progress as an undercover spy. We have removed our taps on your computer and phone, so you may speak perfectly freely.'

'Don't you want to know what I've decided?'

'I think if you were sure you would tell me now,' Shiller said. 'Goodbye, Vanessa . . .' And the speaker went dead.

As Vanessa exercised, washed and breakfasted she kept expecting the voice of Monitor to chide her for being slow or careless. She had flushed out and greased her anus before the fact that it was now unnecessary occurred to her, so strong had the routine become. Her own underwear felt incredibly light and flimsy. There was no cable hugging her spine, no controlling choker round her neck, no micro cameras in her earrings. She felt light-headed. This was freedom. What had she been doing acting like a slave?

She phoned Enwright and told him she had a day off work from Shillers, so she was able to give a full report of her activities. Enwright said she should come straight in and that he was sure Sir Harvey would like to hear what she had to say as well.

The thought of deceiving the man who had entrusted her with such an important assignment convinced her. It would not be easy but she had to do what was right. She would say she was close to uncovering some dark secret but needed a little more time. She would use that as a lever to force Shiller to give up the girlflesh trade.

Vanessa literally felt empty driving to the *Globe* offices, perversely missing the pressure of the seat pushing her twin control phalluses a little further up inside her. For the first time in a month she was absolutely alone and isolated, with no invisible monitor to watch over her.

She suffered a brief attack of doubt. What else would Kashika do? For better or worse she was a natural slave, like the other Cherry girls. Perhaps she could take care of her, even be her mistress? The thought of Kashika as her personal slave sent a thrill through her. But how was that better than slavery on a commercial scale? Slavery was slavery. Because it was consensual, of course, and it would make Kashika happy. But all the Shiller slaves had consented and were happy. No. She had to stick to her decision.

The conference room appeared just as it had done all those weeks before when Sir Harvey had given her the task of uncovering Shillers' secret. Once again Sir Harvey's face loomed large in the conference screen, puffing at his cigar, while Enwright looked at Vanessa expectantly.

Vanessa took a deep breath. 'Over the past month I've explored most of the Shiller building, talked to as many other members of staff as possible and checked all the files I could get access to. It's hard to tell for sure, with normal company security and the legitimate confidential work they do, but I think they may be hiding something . . .'

'You only think they're hiding something?' Sir Harvey cut in with a scowl. 'Aren't you sure?'

'No, Sir Harvey. Perhaps with a little more time
. . .'

'Yes or no, damn it?' Sir Harvey demanded,
jabbing at her with his cigar. 'You should be able to
tell by now, girl, with something as big as this!'

Vanessa began to wonder just how much Sir
Harvey actually knew about Shillers' secret. Could he
possibly suspect the whole incredible truth? But if so,
why not go to the police? And why keep her
investigation secret even from other *Globe* staff?

'As big as what, Sir Harvey?' she asked innocently.
'Can you give me some clue as to what I'm looking
for?'

'If you were any good, you'd have found it by
now!' he snapped impatiently. 'I was told you had the
right stuff in you. It seems I was misinformed.'

Enwright said: 'I'm sure Vanessa's done her best,
Sir Harvey.'

'I didn't ask for your opinion, Enwright!' Sir
Harvey barked.

As she saw Enwright shrink back in his chair under
the baleful gaze from the screen, Vanessa suddenly
realised she did not like Harvey Rochester. She had
admired his self-made success, but now she saw
underneath that famously gruff, no-nonsense exterior
there lurked a thug and a bully.

'I'm sorry to have disappointed you, Sir Harvey,'
Vanessa said coldly. 'Perhaps you'd better get somebody else to investigate Shillers. Maybe you'll give
them more to work with than you gave me.' She
made to rise.

'Sit down, Buckingham!' Sir Harvey bellowed. 'I'll
say when you can leave.'

'You don't own me, Sir Harvey.' Vanessa said.

'You do what I tell you, girl or you'll never work
in this city again!'

Enwright had his head bowed, but Vanessa looked at Rochester's glowering, livid features unflinchingly. She had survived a month that would have broken ten men like him and she knew it. How long would he have lasted as a sex toy in chains? Now she understood that when she had begged for a beating for the love of another it meant she was not weak but strong. She could do anything she wanted.

With all the contempt she could muster she said simply: 'Screw you and this job.'

Before the conference-room door closed behind her, she heard Rochester shouting: 'You're fired! Enwright, throw that bitch out, do you hear me?'

This mood of defiant elation lasted until Vanessa got back to her flat with her cardboard carton of personal effects from her desk at the *Globe*.

The camera mirrors had been removed from the walls. The hose and douche gun no longer hung in her shower. Her control bra and thong, her house collar and charger were gone from her bedroom. Her bed was just a bed again, with only a few innocent screw holes where cuffs and anal locks had once been mounted. Swiftly and efficiently, Shiller had withdrawn from her life. Only her Press fedora was left to show for all she had been through.

She sat on the side of her bed turning the hat round in her hands and feeling horribly alone. There was no one to look out for her, no one to care. No, that was not quite true. There was always Kashika, and many others behind her who, in their strange way, did care about her. She had made one choice, now she could make another. If she was strong enough . . .

By the time she had parked her car in level B2 Sandra was waiting in front of the lift, bare and unashamed amid the concrete pillars. She was holding up Vanessa's slave chains in one hand and had a questioning look on her face. Vanessa nodded, smiling foolishly. Sandra beamed, came forwards and kissed her passionately.

'Welcome home,' she said.

Vanessa stripped off her clothes as the lift ascended and let Sandra snap the cuffs about her wrists and the silver collar about her neck. She hadn't realised how comforting their weight and solidity was until now. It meant she belonged.

'What did you tell the Director about me that first day?' she asked.

'That you were a natural submissive and quite a pain slut,' Sandra said with a grin, 'but that you'd need a kick up the behind to dump your inhibitions and accept it.'

'I'm frightened,' Vanessa admitted.

'Of course you are. We all are at first. But don't worry, you're not alone . . .'

Vanessa sat back on her heels on the green-leather top of the Director's desk, her thighs wide, hiding nothing from Shiller's penetrating gaze. She felt a stirring in her loins under the scrutiny of those bright-blue eyes. For the first time she appreciated the difference between the Director's personality and that of Sir Harvey. Shiller carried the same aura of power, but had none of his barely subdued cruelty and anger. She cherished what she controlled instead of abusing it.

'So, you've made your decision, Vanessa,' Shiller said.

'It didn't quite come out as I planned, Director,' Vanessa admitted, finding it delightfully easy to speak the simple truth. 'I was going to say I was close to uncovering something here but would need more time, and use that threat to make you give up your girlflesh business.'

'And what happened?'

'Sir Harvey got angry before I could finish, Director. Then I knew I didn't trust or like him. I told him . . . to screw himself.'

Shiller smiled. 'Rochester always was his own worst enemy. Apart from myself, perhaps.'

'You know him, Director?'

'You might say we're business rivals in the girlflesh trade.'

Vanessa blinked. 'I . . . beg your pardon, Director?'

'Harvey Rochester runs his own, less principled, girl-slave business. We've been competitors for years, and I'm afraid you got caught up in our rivalry. I doubt if he would ever have published any incriminating evidence you uncovered. He was using you to gain enough evidence to blackmail me into handing him this business. It would be financially far more rewarding than simply destroying me in some sensational newspaper exposure and then trying to pick up the pieces of my operation afterwards. He does not just want the competition eliminated, he wants to assimilate it. A greedy man, Rochester, but I'll never let him get his hands on my girls!'

Vanessa was still trying to come to terms with this revelation. 'Then . . . that's why you were so suspicious when I first said who I worked for, Director? And why Zara seemed to distrust me?'

'Yes. Zara despises Rochester even more than I do. She may have let it colour her attitude towards you, even after it became apparent you were simply Rochester's innocent pawn. But I think she has mellowed now.'

'Why didn't you tell me about Rochester from the beginning, Director?'

'Would you have believed me? Besides, I wanted you to judge my operation on its own merits, not as an alternative to Rochester's crude business.'

'But Director, if he's as bad as you say, why don't you expose him?'

'Because I have no evidence that would stand up in court. Rochester's very careful to hide any personal connection with his slave business.' Shiller mused. 'But perhaps one day he'll get careless, then we'll see . . . However, that's for the future. What shall I do with you right now?'

Vanessa hung her head meekly. 'Whatever you want, Director. I . . . I want to be a Shiller slave. I think that's what I am. I won't fight it any more.'

'You know what will be expected of you? Obedience, acceptance of discipline, unquestioning service, the pain and the pleasure?'

Vanessa felt her nipples rising at the thought and a warm slickness seeping between her labia. 'I think the last month has given me a good idea, Director.'

'This is not just because of Kashika? Don't deny your feelings for her must have some influence.'

'I don't, Director. It's what I want to be, though of course I want to see her as much as possible as well.'

'You know that Kashika's service as part of Cherry Chain must come before any personal considerations? Chains are being rotated to our regional centres all the time. We would not deliberately keep you apart, but there will be periods of separation.'

'Can't I join Cherry Chain, Director?'

'Twelve girls only to a chain is the rule. Besides, I would not risk upsetting the bond they have formed.'

'Then may I beg to join a new chain, Director? I'll go to the Institute and take all the tests. I could start tomorrow . . .'

Shiller smiled. 'There's no need, Vanessa. You've already passed the most important test. Dr Gold's analysis of your responses the day you visited the Institute confirmed my own and Miss Kyle's original assessment of your nature. You'd make an excellent chain girl, but you also have a certain independence of mind I want to preserve. For the moment I wish you to continue as slave reporter for the *Girlflesh News*. I've read your articles with great interest.'

Vanessa felt a thrill of pride and hope. 'I still have the job, Director?'

'On the same terms as before ... though I assume we will no longer have to worry about you trying to liberate any of our girls in front of police stations?'

Vanessa blushed. 'No, Director. When can I move into the slave dorms, Director?'

'For the moment it would be best if you stay in your flat and continue with your routine. It's possible Rochester is suspicious of you, in which case maintaining an outwardly normal lifestyle will confuse him.'

'I understand, Director.'

With a twinkle in her eye, Shiller added: 'Of course, your position will still allow you frequent opportunities to follow the activities of our newest chain girls ...'

'Oh, thank you, Director!'

'Then report to Zara. You've got a graduation ceremony to cover this afternoon.'

The training yard was once again packed with an eager throng of naked slave-girl onlookers.

As before, the trainers stood on the low podium with Cherry Chain kneeling on mats before them, their hands cuffed loosely behind their backs. They wore special graduation dress of black mortarboards with red tassels, which somehow enhanced their nakedness. One addition behind the podium was a row of black-painted wooden boards set in ornate gold picture frames, which stood on hinged stands tilted back at a slight angle. Each board was hung about with restraint straps.

Vanessa happily snapped away and made notes, in between gazing longingly at Kashika. She felt ridiculously pleased for her.

Unexpectedly, Zara had accompanied her to the ceremony. 'This brings back memories of my graduation,' she said wistfully. 'Believe me, it's something you never forget.'

'I do believe you, Mistress Editor,' Vanessa said with a smile.

Shiller appeared and took her place on the podium. The yard fell silent and she gazed round at the assembly with a smile.

'We are gathered here today to celebrate the graduation of the girls of Cherry Chain into the status of full slaves. To mark this happy occasion, each girl will shortly be fitted with a ring to mark her achievement, and also awarded a diploma . . .'

She gestured to a side table on which lay a row of scrolls bound with red ribbons and seals, then down at the Cherry girls.

'Though these awards have no meaning outside the Shiller organisation, believe me when I say that we, your masters and trainers and most importantly your fellow slaves, take them very seriously. They are a mark of your special talent and achievement, the basis on which you will live for the next ten or fifteen years, and will forever shape the rest of your lives.'

She picked up a scroll and unrolled the sheet of laminated paper set between two wooden rods with bulbous ends.

'Each diploma bears your name and chain number, followed by this statement:

' "The above has been tested with whip, strap and rod and has proven herself to be a natural, willing and consensual submissive, ready to offer her body without reservation for whatever purpose that is required of her, be it pleasure or pain.

' "We award her the status of full slave, worthy to become a chattel of the Shiller company and fit to be traded as a sample of its merchandise, proudly representing its principles of reliability, quality and service." '

Shiller rolled up the scroll, retied the ribbon and smiled down at the girls. 'Never doubt that you are special and that we prize you for being so. Cherish the love of your chain sisters and remember this: from now on you will never be alone, because from this day you are company girls!'

There was cheering and applause from the watching slave-girls. Miss Kyle stepped forward and called out: 'Amber 1 Cherry.'

Amber got to her feet and climbed on to the podium. Shiller kissed her and then she turned round and bent over, presenting her bottom, pulling her fleshy cheeks apart with her cuffed hands to expose her greased anus. Shiller slid the tightly rolled scroll up into her rectum until half the scroll was left jutting out from between her buttocks, together with the dangling ribbon and seal.

What better way for a submissive to receive an award, Vanessa thought, as the watching girls applauded loudly.

Mr McGarry and Miss Scott escorted Amber over to the first of the row of stands. Mr Winston and Mr Tyler undid her cuffs, lifted her up on to the angled board and strapped her into place. In a few moments she was perfectly secured within the golden frame, with her arms bent and pulled flat to the board and hips and knees drawn hard up and then turned outwards so that her knees and elbows almost touched. The strain showed on her inner thighs, exposing the soft mound of her vulva and the deep cleft that clove through it. The upturning of her hips caused the end of her scroll to jut out provocatively at an angle from her bulging anus.

Mr Hirsch, holding a device like a small metallic staple gun in his hand, bent down between Amber's spread thighs. She gave a small gasp of pain. Hirsch stepped back and a fine gold ring glinted where it pierced Amber's left inner labia.

The watching girls cheered. Vanessa saw a few of them beginning to rub themselves off. It no longer shocked her. What more natural way to show and share pleasure where shame had no meaning?

'Charlotte 2 Cherry,' Miss Kyle called out.

By the time Kashika was called up to receive her diploma, the yard was filled by the scent of slavish arousal. Glorying in her new freedom, Vanessa was rubbing herself along with the rest, winning a knowing smile from Zara. Vanessa's stomach fluttered at the tiny yelp Kashika gave when she was ringed, but not out of distress, knowing what the prick of pain would feel like to her. She saw tears of joy in Kashika's eyes as she beamed across at her.

Finally, all the girls had been plugged with diplomas, ringed and mounted in their golden frames like living pictures, their clefts glistening with barely contained excitement. But there was one frame left unfilled and one diploma still on the table.

'Vanessa Buckingham!' Miss Kyle called out.

For a few seconds Vanessa could only gape about her stupidly. Zara took the camera from her numbed hands and clipped her wrists behind her back. 'Go on!' she said, giving her a shove. Vanessa stumbled forwards and knelt on a mat in front of Shiller, who smiled down at her.

'As a few of you know, Vanessa came to us under unusual circumstances. You might say that she was sent here to judge us, to test the principles of our girlflesh trade to see if they were still fair and ethical according to those standards I first set down many years ago. If she was a provisional slave, then we were provisional slave-keepers. I am pleased to announce today that, even at some personal cost to herself, she has chosen in our favour. Furthermore, she has paid us the ultimate compliment in begging to be allowed to join our company as a full slave – a request I am happy to grant!'

A great cheer went up and Vanessa felt a wave of welcome enfold her.

'But first,' Shiller continued, when the cheers had subsided, 'we must put her in a proper collar . . .'

Miss Kyle stepped forward with the new collar in her hands. Vanessa felt the breath catch in her throat. It was a white collar!

As Miss Kyle removed her old metallic utility collar and locked the new one about her neck, Shiller said: 'Though she will still be your Slave Reporter, I have decided to make her a member of my own personal chain. She will now be known as Vanessa 19 White!'

There was another cheer. Vanessa glanced round to see Kashika looking at her in wonder and delight.

'Vanessa 19 White, prepare to receive your diploma!' Miss Kyle said.

In a daze, Vanessa stepped up and was kissed by Shiller. Then, heart thumping, she turned round and presented her bottom, pulling her anal sphincter wide with her fingers, silently thankful that she was properly cleaned and greased like a good slave should be. The scroll slipped easily into her, its hard, comforting presence filling the void her control phallus had left. How wonderful it was to be plugged once again, to let control of her body slip away into the hands of those who would use it for a greater purpose.

She was taken to the frames, lifted up and strapped into place. She revelled in the tight constraint of the broad bands of rubber as they closed over her wrists, neck, waist and ankles. The final pair of straps went across her knees, pulling them flat against the board, stretching her inner thighs as she was opened for all to see, making her pubic mound stand out, squeezing her rectum tighter about her precious diploma.

Now she was totally restrained, as helpless as a pinned butterfly. Her nipples were hard red pulsing cones, while the blossoming flower of love-mouth ran with dewdrop juices, its depths begging to be probed.

Mr Hirsch bent down between her splayed thighs, pinching her left labia minora between his thumb and finger and stretching it wide. She felt a stab of sharp joyous pain as the gold ring was threaded through her flesh. Now she was a true company slave!

The cheers of the watching slave-girls rang in her ears as they masturbated with even greater vigour, filling the air with their sweet perfume and showing their own labia rings. They were all her sisters now.

The trainers formed themselves into a line in front of the thirteen stands, each with its gold-framed captive. They all held lashes in their hands, the long leather thongs trailing across the ground.

At a sign from Shiller they began to swipe them across the girls' defenceless breasts, bellies and groins, the crisp crack of leather and flesh echoing back from the walls of the yard. This was a proper slave beating, to confirm who served and who must be obeyed. It seared into their flesh once and for all the certain knowledge of what they had become.

In between her yelps and sobs of pain, Vanessa was calling out: 'Yes . . . more please . . . thank you!' Miss Kyle had been right all along. She was a slut for pain and it felt wonderful, as though each hot stroke merely stoked the fires of lust and love inside her. She saw Kashika rolling back her eyes in ecstasy, arching her back against her straps as she tried to thrust her brown breasts closer to the tongues of the lash.

By the time the ceremonial punishment ceased, their bodies bore criss-cross lattices of scarlet stripes from trembling breasts to weeping groins. As one they ached with a desperate thirst that could only be quenched in one way.

Shiller waved the watching slave-girls forwards. 'Now it's your turn!' she shouted.

A wave of bare flesh descended upon them, four or five girls clustering about each stand, turning them into thirteen little orgies of lustful female bodies. Vanessa was half-smothered by urgent lips kissing hers, teeth nipping at her tormented India rubber teats, thrusting hot tongues lapping and sliding up her yawning cunt. Then one at a time they straddled her outthrust scroll, rubbing their salivating pussies along its length until their labia kissed against her own pouting pubes. Love-mouth sucked on love-mouth and hard erect clit rubbed against its twin. It was girlflesh on girlflesh, an uninhibited joy such as she had never known before.

Vanessa cried out as she was caught up in the throes of her first orgasm as a true slave. The first of so many more . . .

nexus

The leading publisher of fetish and adult fiction

TELL US WHAT YOU THINK!

Readers' ideas and opinions matter to us so please take a few minutes to fill in the questionnaire below.

1. Sex: Are you male ☐   female ☐   a couple ☐?

2. Age: Under 21 ☐   21–30 ☐   31–40 ☐   41–50 ☐   51–60 ☐   over 60 ☐

3. Where do you buy your Nexus books from?
☐ A chain book shop. If so, which one(s)?
_____
☐ An independent book shop. If so, which one(s)?
_____
☐ A used book shop/charity shop
☐ Online book store. If so, which one(s)?
_____

4. How did you find out about Nexus books?
☐ Browsing in a book shop
☐ A review in a magazine
☐ Online
☐ Recommendation
☐ Other _____

5. In terms of settings, which do you prefer? (Tick as many as you like.)
☐ Down to earth and as realistic as possible
☐ Historical settings. If so, which period do you prefer?
_____
☐ Fantasy settings – barbarian worlds
☐ Completely escapist/surreal fantasy
☐ Institutional or secret academy

☐ Futuristic/sci fi
☐ Escapist but still believable
☐ Any settings you dislike?

_____

☐ Where would you like to see an adult novel set?

_____

6. In terms of storylines, would you prefer:
☐ Simple stories that concentrate on adult interests?
☐ More plot and character-driven stories with less explicit adult activity?
☐ We value your ideas, so give us your opinion of this book:

_____

_____

_____

7. In terms of your adult interests, what do you like to read about? (Tick as many as you like.)
☐ Traditional corporal punishment (CP)
☐ Modern corporal punishment
☐ Spanking
☐ Restraint/bondage
☐ Rope bondage
☐ Latex/rubber
☐ Leather
☐ Female domination and male submission
☐ Female domination and female submission
☐ Male domination and female submission
☐ Willing captivity
☐ Uniforms
☐ Lingerie/underwear/hosiery/footwear (boots and high heels)
☐ Sex rituals
☐ Vanilla sex
☐ Swinging
☐ Cross-dressing/TV
☐ Enforced feminisation

☐ Others – tell us what you don't see enough of in adult fiction:

_____

_____

_____

8. Would you prefer books with a more specialised approach to your interests, i.e. a novel specifically about uniforms? If so, which subject(s) would you like to read a Nexus novel about?

_____

_____

_____

9. Would you like to read true stories in Nexus books? For instance, the true story of a submissive woman, or a male slave? Tell us which true revelations you would most like to read about:

_____

_____

_____

10. What do you like best about Nexus books?

_____

_____

11. What do you like least about Nexus books?

_____

_____

12. Which are your favourite titles?

_____

_____

13. Who are your favourite authors?

_____

_____

14. Which covers do you prefer? Those featuring:
(Tick as many as you like.)

- ☐ Fetish outfits
- ☐ More nudity
- ☐ Two models
- ☐ Unusual models or settings
- ☐ Classic erotic photography
- ☐ More contemporary images and poses
- ☐ A blank/non-erotic cover
- ☐ What would your ideal cover look like?

_____

15. **Describe your ideal Nexus novel in the space provided:**

_____

_____

_____

_____

16. **Which celebrity would feature in one of your Nexus-style fantasies? We'll post the best suggestions on our website – anonymously!**

_____

THANKS FOR YOUR TIME

Now simply write the title of this book in the space below and cut out the questionnaire pages. Post to: Nexus, Marketing Dept., Thames Wharf Studios, Rainville Rd, London W6 9HA

Book title: _____

NEXUS NEW BOOKS

To be published in May 2007

LOVE SONG OF A DOMINATRIX
Cat Scarlett

Dinah is a tough-talking bisexual dominatrix with a weakness for
redheads. So when she meets Grace, a beautiful hotel receptionist
looking for excitement, she can't resist converting her to a life of
lesbian submission. But Grace is forced to overcome her timidity
and take up the whip herself when ex-boyfriend Aidan finds out
about their relationship and decides to teach Mistress Dinah a
lesson.

£6.99   ISBN 978 0 352 34106 8

BLUSHING AT BOTH ENDS
Philip Kemp

Funny, full of surprises and always arousing, this is a brilliant
collection of stories about innocent young women who find
themselves faced with the delicious, scary, sensual prospect of a
sound bare-bottom spanking. Half against her will, each of them
is inexorably drawn towards the moment when, bent over lap,
desk or chair, she tremblingly awaits that punishment for which
her rearward curves were so perfectly designed.

£6.99   ISBN 978 0 352 34107 5

ENTHRALLED
Lance Porter

Matthew Crawley has always dreamed of sleeping with a beautiful woman and when the stunning Jasmine Del Ray suddenly walks into his life he believes his prayers have finally been answered. But Ms Del Ray proves to be no ordinary girlfriend. Rich, successful and supremely confident, she expects complete obedience from her men and knows exactly how to get her way. An expert in teasing and denial, she soon has the hopelessly infatuated Matthew Crawley jumping to her every command and begging on his knees for her slightest indulgence. Skilfully brought to heel, he is ready to commence the next stage of his training in which liberal applications of the cane and a variety of cruel and unusual punishments will play an essential part. But how much suffering and humiliation can a man endure to win the favour of a superior young woman – and what will be his reward?

£6.99   ISBN 978 0 352 34108 2

If you would like more information about Nexus titles, please visit our website at www.nexus-books.co.uk, or send a large stamped addressed envelope to:
  Nexus, Thames Wharf Studios,
  Rainville Road, London W6 9HA

NEXUS BOOKLIST

Information is correct at time of printing. To avoid disappointment, check availability before ordering. Go to www.nexus-books.co.uk.

All books are priced at £6.99 unless another price is given.

NEXUS

☐ ABANDONED ALICE	Adriana Arden	ISBN 978 0 352 33969 0
☐ ALICE IN CHAINS	Adriana Arden	ISBN 978 0 352 33908 9
☐ AQUA DOMINATION	William Doughty	ISBN 978 0 352 34020 7
☐ THE ART OF CORRECTION	Tara Black	ISBN 978 0 352 33895 2
☐ THE ART OF SURRENDER	Madeline Bastinado	ISBN 978 0 352 34013 9
☐ BEASTLY BEHAVIOUR	Aishling Morgan	ISBN 978 0 352 34095 5
☐ BELINDA BARES UP	Yolanda Celbridge	ISBN 978 0 352 33926 3
☐ BENCH-MARKS	Tara Black	ISBN 978 0 352 33797 9
☐ BIDDING TO SIN	Rosita Varón	ISBN 978 0 352 34063 4
☐ BINDING PROMISES	G.C. Scott	ISBN 978 0 352 34014 6
☐ THE BOOK OF PUNISHMENT	Cat Scarlett	ISBN 978 0 352 33975 1
☐ BRUSH STROKES	Penny Birch	ISBN 978 0 352 34072 6
☐ CALLED TO THE WILD	Angel Blake	ISBN 978 0 352 34067 2
☐ CAPTIVES OF CHEYNER CLOSE	Adriana·Arden	ISBN 978 0 352 34028 3
☐ CARNAL POSSESSION	Yvonne Strickland	ISBN 978 0 352 34062 7
☐ CITY MAID	Amelia Evangeline	ISBN 978 0 352 34096 2
☐ COLLEGE GIRLS	Cat Scarlett	ISBN 978 0 352 33942 3
☐ COMPANY OF SLAVES	Christina Shelly	ISBN 978 0 352 33887 7
☐ CONCEIT AND CONSEQUENCE	Aishling Morgan	ISBN 978 0 352 33965 2

☐ TOKYO BOUND	Sachi	ISBN 978 0 352 34019 1
☐ TORMENT, INCORPORATED	Murilee Martin	ISBN 978 0 352 33943 0
☐ UNEARTHLY DESIRES	Ray Gordon	ISBN 978 0 352 34036 8
☐ UNIFORM DOLL	Penny Birch	ISBN 978 0 352 33698 9
☐ WHALEBONE STRICT	Lady Alice McCloud	ISBN 978 0 352 34082 5
☐ WHAT HAPPENS TO BAD GIRLS	Penny Birch	ISBN 978 0 352 34031 3
☐ WHAT SUKI WANTS	Cat Scarlett	ISBN 978 0 352 34027 6
☐ WHEN SHE WAS BAD	Penny Birch	ISBN 978 0 352 33859 4
☐ WHIP HAND	G.C. Scott	ISBN 978 0 352 33694 1
☐ WHIPPING GIRL	Aishling Morgan	ISBN 978 0 352 33789 4
☐ WHIPPING TRIANGLE	G.C. Scott	ISBN 978 0 352 34086 3

NEXUS CLASSIC

☐ AMAZON SLAVE	Lisette Ashton	ISBN 978 0 352 33916 4
☐ ANGEL	Lindsay Gordon	ISBN 978 0 352 34009 2
☐ THE BLACK GARTER	Lisette Ashton	ISBN 978 0 352 33919 5
☐ THE BLACK MASQUE	Lisette Ashton	ISBN 978 0 352 33977 5
☐ THE BLACK ROOM	Lisette Ashton	ISBN 978 0 352 33914 0
☐ THE BLACK WIDOW	Lisette Ashton	ISBN 978 0 352 33973 7
☐ THE BOND	Lindsay Gordon	ISBN 978 0 352 33996 6
☐ THE DOMINO ENIGMA	Cyrian Amberlake	ISBN 978 0 352 34064 1
☐ THE DOMINO QUEEN	Cyrian Amberlake	ISBN 978 0 352 34074 0
☐ THE DOMINO TATTOO	Cyrian Amberlake	ISBN 978 0 352 34037 5
☐ EMMA ENSLAVED	Hilary James	ISBN 978 0 352 33883 9
☐ EMMA'S HUMILIATION	Hilary James	ISBN 978 0 352 33910 2
☐ EMMA'S SECRET DOMINATION	Hilary James	ISBN 978 0 352 34000 9
☐ EMMA'S SUBMISSION	Hilary James	ISBN 978 0 352 33906 5
☐ FAIRGROUND ATTRACTION	Lisette Ashton	ISBN 978 0 352 33927 0
☐ IN FOR A PENNY	Penny Birch	ISBN 978 0 352 34083 2
☐ THE INSTITUTE	Maria Del Rey	ISBN 978 0 352 33352 0

- - - - - - ✂ -

Please send me the books I have ticked above.

Name   ....

Address   ....

                        ....

                        ....

                        .... Post code ....

Send to: **Virgin Books Cash Sales, Thames Wharf Studios, Rainville Road, London W6 9HA**

US customers: for prices and details of how to order books for delivery by mail, call 888-330-8477.

Please enclose a cheque or postal order, made payable to **Nexus Books Ltd**, to the value of the books you have ordered plus postage and packing costs as follows:

UK and BFPO – £1.00 for the first book, 50p for each subsequent book.

Overseas (including Republic of Ireland) – £2.00 for the first book, £1.00 for each subsequent book.

If you would prefer to pay by VISA, ACCESS/MASTERCARD, AMEX, DINERS CLUB or SWITCH, please write your card number and expiry date here:

....

Please allow up to 28 days for delivery.

Signature ....

Our privacy policy

We will not disclose information you supply us to any other parties. We will not disclose any information which identifies you personally to any person without your express consent.

From time to time we may send out information about Nexus books and special offers. Please tick here if you do *not* wish to receive Nexus information.   ☐

- - - - - - ✂ -